WHITE BONDS

WOUNDED WINDS

SARAH URQUHART

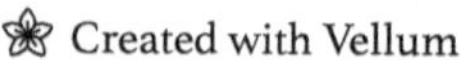 Created with Vellum

To my family.

ACKNOWLEDGMENTS

Writing a book isn't easy. Making that book the best you can isn't easy either. It comes with struggles, but a support system helps to make those struggles a little better. My husband is one amazing guy who supports my passion. He might not understand it, but he gives me all the time in the world to do what I need to do. I wouldn't be able to do this without the support he provides for the whole family.

I have one friend in particular, Veronica, who always asks how my writing is going. She always asks the right questions to make me think or get my butt in gear when I'm second guessing myself. Thank you.

A huge thanks to my beta readers. You generously provided your time when I needed help.

And to the ladies of Level Up and all my friends in the sprint room. I have learned so much from all of you. You are the best kind of support.

PROLOGUE

The sound of rattling glass woke Asher, pulling him out of a deep sleep. Asher gasped, sitting up in bed. He searched his room, looking over his bin of cars and trucks, his table of Lego, all sitting exactly how he left them, trying to find the source of the noise that woke him. He tried not to be scared. He didn't want to wake his parents, even knowing they'd check his room for him, scaring off the imaginary monsters, and tuck him back in bed.

The glass in his window shook from another rush of wind. Asher sighed, the pounding against the inside of his chest fading away. He got up on his knees and rested his arms on the window sill. He expected to see a storm, but he didn't. The full moon was as bright as he'd ever seen it. He'd gone camping with his family after his seventh birthday last summer and spent almost every night looking at the moon and the stars. And never had the sky been as bright. Asher looked at the trees that made up the stretch of woods behind his house. They were calm. He didn't understand. How were the trees calm when it was windy enough to shake his window?

Just as he was about to tuck himself back into his red checkered comforter, the trees moved with the wind before they settled again. But it wasn't only the moving trees he saw. He saw the wind. It swirled through the air like in pictures of story books or paintings. He waited, tapping his fingers on his window sill, hoping to see it again. Everything stayed calm, illuminated by the moon.

Asher straightened when the swirling wind appeared again. He watched it move from his backyard to the trees, moving them one by one like it was playing a game.

This was so strange. Wind couldn't be seen. He remembered asking his parents when he was five why he couldn't see the wind. It had to be the extra bright moon. Asher wanted to get a better look. He winced, knowing he'd be in big trouble if he left the house in the middle of the night without his parents. He thought about waking them so they could see the wind too, but he knew they'd only put him back to bed. Grown-ups always wanted more sleep and didn't listen well when they were tired.

He decided he wouldn't go far or stay long. Just off the back deck and only until the next swirl of wind appeared. Then he would come straight back to bed and tell his mom and dad about it in the morning. He didn't want to keep something like this a secret. He hoped they wouldn't be too mad with something so cool.

Asher hurriedly tiptoed out of his room and down the hall. He grabbed his thick winter jacket and slid on his boots. Looking behind him to check for his parents or his younger sister, he slowly reached for the back door. Maybe he should wake Madi to come see it. No, she would get in trouble too, and that wasn't fair. Biting the inside of his cheek, he gently opened the door and slid out. He paused on the deck, turning his ear toward the house then sighed when he didn't hear anything from inside the house.

He looked around the yard and toward the trees. Everything looked clear even though it should be pitch black. The moon was huge and so bright. He couldn't believe it. He could see all the different craters a lot more clearly. Asher stared up at it for a moment in awe. As interesting as it was, he was probably one of the few kids in his class that didn't want to go to the moon. But it wouldn't stop him from looking at it when it looked like this.

Shaking himself, he took the two steps down off the deck and looked around waiting for the wind to show itself again. There it was, a clear swirl weaving in and out of the trees. And straight toward him. He braced himself, uncertainty kept him still. White air raced toward him and quickly swerved around to push him in the back propelling him forward. Asher stumbled a few steps, but didn't fall over. The wind was warm. It wasn't quite winter. The weather was definitely getting colder, but not this white wind that he could see. It was a warm breeze at his back. It stopped pushing him and swirled around the yard until it disappeared. But not for long.

Only a moment later, it came at him again and pushed at his back. Asher looked over his shoulder. He was halfway across the yard now. He shouldn't be this far away from the house. But the wind clearly wanted to take him somewhere. He found it odd, but believed the idea that the wind was pushing him toward the woods on purpose.

"Okay, white wind. But I'm totally telling my mom and dad that this was your idea." As if that would get him out of trouble. Asher spoke to the air around him and then slowly started taking his own steps into the woods, the white wind following him with its own whooshing pattern through the air, ahead of him, behind him, above him, but it didn't disappear. Not until Asher made his way through to a clearing. He frowned. There was no clearing in the woods behind his house. Well, there wasn't before tonight.

A light dusting, as he'd heard his mom call it, of snow covered the ground around the almost circular space where there hadn't been any in his back yard. The moon seemed to be directly above him. The air was fresh. Asher wasn't sure what was different about it, but it felt good to breathe in. The entire circle held still and quiet.

Too quiet. The moment stretched and so did the silence. The circle began to look eerie rather than beautiful. Unease crept along his back.

"Hello? White wind?" He felt silly calling to the wind and expecting it to answer. Nothing happened. Asher knew he shouldn't be here, never should have gotten out of bed. He turned to walk back to his house when a rustle in the bushes froze him in place. The sound of his heart beating against his chest thrummed in his ears. Asher turned back around slowly. A white puppy emerged from the trees. Relief relaxed his body and he looked closer. It looked like his friend's husky.

"Hi there, puppy." Asher slowly walked closer with his hand out to meet the puppy in the centre of the circle. The bundle of white fur carefully met Asher and sniffed his fingers. Asher still moved slow so he didn't scare him while he ran his hand over his head and down his neck. So soft. And no collar. A small sliver of excitement ran through him. Maybe his parents would let him keep him. "Do you have a home, little guy?"

A growl emerged from the silence around them. Asher lifted wide eyes to the edge of the circle. A much larger version of the white puppy in front of him stalked forward, sharp teeth baring beneath curled lips. Asher knew what it was even though he'd never seen a real one before. He'd seen a few coyotes roaming neighbouring farmer's fields. Coyotes were small. But this was the moment Asher understood the difference between a dog, a coyote, and a wolf. There was a white wolf growling at him for petting her pup.

"Shit." He was in so much trouble and it wasn't for swearing. "Easy." The wolf was about to take another step closer, her front foot lifting, but the white wind came back. It swirled in front of her and around, blocking her from moving forward. The wolf stopped growling and her eyes followed the wind as it left her and circled Asher and the puppy. She tilted her head. With her teeth covered, Asher thought she no longer looked mad that he touched her baby. Instead, she sat and waited.

Asher waited too, not taking his eyes off the mother wolf until he was sure she was no longer angry.

The puppy must have realized he wasn't in trouble anymore either and decided to play. He crouched down, his front end on the ground and his bum and tail wiggling in the air. Asher giggled and tried to copy the puppy. He got on all fours and moved his chest closer to the ground. The puppy's paw came out and knocked him in the head. "Hey!" But Asher laughed and swatted him back.

With his tongue hanging out, the puppy lunged. Asher yelped gleefully and rolled out of the way then stood. He and the puppy chased each other around the circle, often swatting and trying to wrestle. Asher tried to keep an eye on the mother to make sure she didn't get mad again, but she only laid down and continued to watch, so Asher kept playing.

After a bit, both Asher and the puppy sat beside each other, smiling.

"You're really cool. Can I call you Kai?" Even though he wasn't a puppy he could take home, Asher wanted to give him a name. The puppy laid his paw on Asher's thigh and let out a high bark. "Kai it is then."

But Asher needed to get back home before his parents found out he left. He couldn't wait to tell them he played with a wolf and that the mother wasn't mad. He wasn't going to tell them she growled at him first, though.

Asher sighed, getting ready to leave, but then the white wind came back. It ambled between the trees then around the circle. He felt the warmth it created and saw the fur on the wolves move. He set his hand on Kai and scratched behind his ear while they watched the wind together. The wind sped up and came closer to him and Kai. It circled the two of them, moving faster and faster. Asher suddenly felt like something wasn't right, like the wind was moving through him. Shivers and tingles raced along his body. He felt an ache as parts of him moved. He didn't understand. He was scared and wanted to go home. It was a big mistake coming outside in the middle of the night.

The ache grew and more tingles followed. His body shook. Kai stood beside him and watched, and his mother did the same but from outside the circle of wind. His eyes found the mother wolf through the white air, silently begging her to help him, but he wasn't sure how. Maybe she could alert his parents. They would come find him.

The wind slowed and lifted away, moving back to swirl through the trees. Asher breathed deep and looked around, but everything looked a little different now, sharper, clearer. And the smells. He could smell the puppy beside him and his mother a few feet away. He didn't realize they smelled before. Something still didn't feel right, but at least he wasn't hurting anymore. His shoulders shook with a shiver and he felt it continue down his back like a wave, shaking something off his back. He turned to see what it was and he saw his pajamas and coat, but they were baggy and falling off something white, white fur and a white tail.

Asher looked beside him. Kai was still there. The white fur and tail weren't his. Asher quickly looked at his hands, but instead saw white paws. He swatted each paw with the other, then at his face and head, feeling the pads of his feet fold down his ears. Tears pooled in his eyes, but couldn't escape. He heard himself whimper instead. He was a wolf, a wolf puppy like the one he'd been playing with. He whimpered louder and yelped as he flailed around, not sure what to do. He tripped over his own feet, unsteady and unsure how to move on four legs, real legs, not just his hands and knees.

The mother wolf slowly walked over and gently grabbed him by the scruff of his neck and set him next to Kai. She licked him, over his head and neck.

You're safe. He didn't hear the words, but he felt them, a smooth current. He understood and knew exactly where they came from. He tried to answer by thinking what he wanted to say.

But I'm a wolf. I'm supposed to be a boy.

You won't always be a wolf, little pup. She soothed him by licking over his nose.

I want to go home. Fear that he wouldn't get to see his parents again was an ache in his belly.

As soon as you change back, you can go home. Asher continued to whimper as he shook beneath the wolf mother. Kai sidled up beside him and laid with him, their sides touching. *You two are very special.* She smiled, the way a wolf might, but Asher felt it more so, and laid down with them. As soon as Asher relaxed, the warm, white wind brushed their fur and Asher felt the ache across his body. He whim-pered and shivered while he felt his body return to normal.

When it was over and the ache disappeared, he hunched on the ground, his fingers digging into the grass and debris, and tried to catch his breath. It hurt for a moment and he took his time to search the circle, wanting to know what happened, but he was too scared of it all. He hugged the wolves and gathered his clothes. Asher dressed and ran toward his house, but before he left the circle, he turned back to Kai and his mother watching him. He lifted his hand to wave and saw the puppy wag his tail. Asher would never forget the puppy.

Once he reached his house, he entered just as quietly as when he left. He just wanted to sleep and to see his mom and dad. Instead of going back to his own bed, he went to his parent's room. He didn't wake them and ask if he could sleep with them like he normally would. He crawled in between them and wrapped his arms around his mom. She stirred.

"Asher?" He burrowed his face in her neck. "Baby, you're freezing." She hugged him back and held on. It was only a few minutes and Asher was sound asleep.

CHAPTER 1

"Hey, Dr. Ash!" Asher was already smiling at the door when Jeremiah and his German Shepherd barrelled into his office. He heard them the moment they walked into the clinic. He listened as Laura put them in the exam room to wait and then he counted the seconds before the boy came to find Asher himself, using the back door into his office. His receptionist made it in through the front door in time to catch him with a look of admonishment on her face. It was a familiar dance for everyone.

"Jeremiah. Dr. Morestead isn't ready for you and Bruce. You need to wait in the exam room," said Laura. Asher could hear Jeremiah's mother muttering in the hall outside his office, embarrassment radiated from her.

"It's all right, Laura. I'm ready. I'll take them back to the exam room."

Laura sighed and left, but Asher caught the tilt to her lips before she closed the door.

"How are you, Jeremiah?" His mother stood in the doorway Jeremiah came through.

"I'm great!" His 'g' hit like a gong that echoed in Asher's office. The boy was the most enthusiastic child he knew. It was rare Asher saw any emotion other than joy and he looked forward to seeing him and his dog.

"And how is Bruce?" Asher eyed the German Shepherd who politely sat beside Jeremiah. The dog kept a close eye on Asher, but he was no longer nervous around him. Asher wasn't sure if he'd be able to be a veterinarian. Most animals were spooked by him, but he'd learned to use the wolf inside to his advantage and the dominance in him to calm and soothe rather than scare. Of course, he could scare when needed.

"He's great, too." Jeremiah wrapped an arm around the dog's neck and squeezed.

"And Amy," he looked to Jeremiah's mother, "I hope you're just as great?" he asked, putting the same childlike emphasis into the word as her son.

She laughed. "I am. Thank you. How can I not be?" Her gaze drifted to Jeremiah.

Asher stood. "Shall we?" He scratched Bruce's head and held his hand out toward the back office door. Jeremiah and his mother turned and walked back to the exam room Laura first put them in. A routine check and Bruce's annual shots didn't take long, but there was an extra ten minutes of tales to be told by Jeremiah. Amy flushed. Her hands patted his shoulders any moment he paused and tried to turn his little body toward the door. Asher only smiled patiently and listened. He never rushed patients, especially when accompanied by passionate little children.

Deciding to be a vet had taken Asher by surprise. It hadn't been something he'd considered growing up. But having rescued several of Kai's pack when he was eighteen sealed his fate. A few broken bones, several gashes and scrapes, and one from the river. All from a fight with a bear for food.

Asher's pair, Kai, had howled from inside the woods by his house, calling for him. Asher had raced out of the house, scaring his mother and Madi who were sitting at the table, and ran into the woods. He'd shucked his clothes, ditching them in a bush and shifted, letting his wolf free, mid sprint. By the time Kai led him to the fight, thankfully far away from his home, the bear had left, a trail of blood leading away from the other side of the river. The first thing Asher had seen, and heard, was the dark grey wolf fighting to keep his head above water. Seeing the crash of the water against the banks, Asher had decided to shift back to rescue the wolf. It was easier to help him with hands rather than paws. The water had been cold, but Asher hadn't dwelled on it. He'd tried to wrap his arms around the wolf from behind. The wolf hadn't liked it. They'd never met before. With a struggle, he'd swam backwards and heaved him onto the bank. Asher had collapsed beside him then taken his first look around. Injured wolves with glassy eyes had stared back at him.

He hadn't been worried about a fight with the wolves he didn't know, his wolf was strong, an alpha, but he hadn't known what to do. It hurt to see his kind, his other kind, like this. But he'd still been just a kid.

He'd looked at the dark wolf beside him and knew that if he could save this massive beast, he could save them all. He'd gotten to work and done the best he could with his own common sense and first aid training from school, often shifting back and forth from man to wolf to help calm the pack.

Asher had been missing from home for two days. The smell of his family's fear and heartache had torn through him long before he emerged from the trees. He'd returned, exhausted and ragged in the same clothes he'd stashed in the bush that were damp from the previous day's rain. Police officers had filled his house. His mother and sister had been crying and his father had looked worn.

That had been the only time his family was suspicious of his whereabouts, despite disappearing in the woods with Kai and his mother often through his childhood. At the time, he regretted not finding a way to call them, but he'd been far from people and with no clothes. He also wished he could have been quicker to think of an excuse to disappear the way he did. The cops had questioned him for half an hour and the only answer he could give was he had something urgent to do.

Asher still felt guilty for putting his family through that, but he wouldn't have done anything different. He wouldn't have left Kai or his pack without help.

Eleven years later, he was Dr. Morestead DVM, owner of Morestead Veterinary Clinic. He set up in Alder Ridge and built a house near his family's. Asher had a powerful connection to those woods and to Kai. He wouldn't leave them. His roots were buried deep in these woods. But he may never find others like him staying close to home. If it could happen to him, it could happen to someone else. Whatever *it* was.

Asher pulled up outside of his house and smirked. He caught Kai's scent before he got out of his truck. A huge, white wolf stepped out from the side of his house when Asher approached his deck. The same white wolf he played with at seven years old, his pair. They were each half of a matching set.

"Hey. I need to eat first," he said.

Kai's tail swished happily.

"Not that kind of eat."

His tail dropped.

It had taken years for Asher to hunt with his pair and the pack. The wolves had teased him, but it hadn't helped him get over it any faster. It wasn't so difficult once he reached maturity and the animal's instinct could take over. Full moons and new moons had a contagious sense, an excitement, to which even Asher wasn't immune. He hunted with Kai and the pack during the days surrounding those moons.

Asher heated leftovers and ate while the white wolf stared at him from inside his door. A patient beast. When he finished eating, Asher grinned with a slow build of anticipation. He sniffed the air and listened carefully to make sure no one was around while he took his clothes off. The coast was clear. He rolled his shoulders and began to shift.

As a kid, the shift had been a dull ache through his body, but when he hit adolescence, shifting turned difficult. For a time, it had been very painful, but the stronger he grew, the calmer it became, receding back to an ache, although no longer dull as it'd been when he was just a kid.

Asher shook, his fur moving over his body. *Let's run.*

Kai pushed open the screen door and they ran to the woods, two flashes of white, two equal beasts. All the wolves Asher had grown up with or known as a child were gone, but not Kai. The night they were paired, he changed too. His aging slowed and strength increased to match Asher's. They were larger than an average wolf. His pair was alpha of the pack, staying in control as the generations changed.

They chased each other down, wrestled, and ran some more. One never able to beat the other. Slowly, they circled back to his house. The wolves panted and lay inside the tree line, taking in everything around them, the sounds, the smells. Asher could smell dinner being cooked at his parents' house. He heard small animals scurrying further away from them. He noted the direction of the wind and the scents that travelled in on it. These moments were a key to his soul. This was who he was.

Nudging Kai to say goodbye, he stood and sauntered to his home, pleasurable exhaustion from the run weighing him down. His life was his best kept secret. No one knew he could shift to a wolf. It took a long time after his first shift to tell his parents. As amazing as that night was, it also scared him. But his parents had only placated him with a smile and brushed it off as a dream.

If it weren't for Kai, he would be alone with this part of his life. There had to be more, but without knowing how to find them, Asher chose to live his life to suit himself. There could be more to learn, if he could find another. The monotony of his life was beginning to wear on him. He knew deep down it was time to explore his past. The how, the why. His purpose.

GWEN TAYLOR finally found another job. She breathed in, letting the coolness of the air off the lake fill her body and banish her nerves. Gwen needed the walk after her interview with Walker Woods. He was a bit gruff and she found him hard to read, but felt he would be kind and fair when needed. She was taking a chance on herself and trying something new. Gwen knew she'd never be able to discover who she was without doing things for herself. Not having a life plan meant she worked at a few of her father's businesses. He had a collection of them throughout Alder Ridge and the surrounding areas. Owned franchises, restaurants, small realtor companies, accounting offices, whatever a person could think of, he dabbled in it.

Telling her dad she quit hadn't been as hard as she expected. But his initial reaction had stung. His face had slackened turning the sides of his mouth downward and his eyes widened. Guilt still niggled over not giving him two weeks notice, but he could replace her in a day.

"Why, Gwen?"

"I want to do something for myself." It wasn't the best explanation, but it was the best way to summarize how she felt. "I rely too much on you."

"Gwen, you're treated like any other employee. You aren't relying on me. You're doing the work properly and all my managers you've worked for value you."

"Dad, I like working for you, but I don't enjoy it."

"You're not making any sense, hun." Her mother had set her utensils down and held her wine glass while she followed their conversation. Gwen sighed through her nose and looked down at her half-eaten plate of chicken and veggies.

"I want to enjoy what I do for a living. I want it to be mine. I'm sorry." She shook her head, knowing that she still wasn't making any sense. She looked up at her father again expecting the same frown her mother now had, but his face softened.

"I understand."

"You do?" Gwen asked, her voice squeaked.

Her father nodded and finished eating. Her mother watched her a little longer, but soon Gwen saw understanding dawn and she continued to eat. They hadn't asked any more questions and hadn't brought it up since.

The warmth of gratitude filled Gwen. She was beyond lucky to have the parents she did.

Back at her apartment, she sent Julian a text letting him know she had a new job. Julian was the son of one of her father's business partners and a close friend of Gwen's. She wouldn't call him a best friend, but they spent a lot of time together.

Most of her father's earlier businesses were partnered with Julian's father giving them the chance to grow up together with their mother's also building a strong friendship. Being a year older than her, they got along well.

Now, he was following the path from which she just pulled herself away. He happily worked in one of his dad's office companies in the hopes to take over one or two of them as his own when his father retired. A built-in career and life waiting for him to grow up. Something he still hadn't done.

Gwen's phone rang in her hand.

"Hello?"

"What do you mean you quit?" Julian's snarky tone hit her ear abruptly through the speaker. One of the job's she'd worked was under his supervision. He had been upset to see her leave that one, but was appeased when she said she was still working for her father. That was six months ago.

"I quit. I'm working at *Woods Bistro* starting tomorrow."

"This is a joke," he said.

"Sorry, no joke."

"Why?" He dragged out the word. The image of him closing his eyes and his always clean-shaven face scrunching up in disgust was clear in her mind.

"Because, it's what I want. You knew I didn't want to work for my dad forever."

"Yeah, I thought you'd grow out of that."

Gwen pinched her lips together and shook her head. She had to laugh, at least inwardly, at the fact he didn't take her seriously. If she didn't laugh, she might strangle him. And despite his flaws, he was her friend. "Goodnight, Julian. I have a new job to start tomorrow."

"Night, Gwen," Julian said with a petulant tone to match his immaturity. Although, she wasn't sure why he would care so much. After so many years and so many businesses, the likelihood of them both following their father's footsteps and working together were slim. She couldn't imagine having Julian as a business partner. Gwen cringed at the thought. A friend, he was. A partner, definitely not.

ASHER STRETCHED as he got out of his truck, rolling his shoulders. The smells coming from inside *Woods Bistro* assaulted his nose and made his tongue swell, eager to host the flavours. The smell of coffee, espresso, tea, and pastries beckoned him in. There were several chain coffee shops in town, but they were often overcrowded for his preference. He didn't like being in large groups when he could help it. They overwhelmed him, sending sparks through his senses. He preferred the friendly atmosphere of the smaller, locally owned shops. It gave him a sense of companionship when he forced distance in all of his friendships and relationships.

Inside there were two people ahead of him and a handful of tables occupied. Unintentionally, he noted everyone in the room, his instincts always forcing him to be watchful. A couple RCMP officers sat near the window. A young couple had their heads together in the corner, Asher's lips twitched as he listened to their conversation. The rest of the tables had single occupants. He recognized most people in the room by their scents, unable to remember names.

He moved ahead in line, thinking of his usual coffee and cream puff. Someone else entered the bistro, a potent scent ran through his senses. His nostrils flared and his eyes widened, the wolf inside waking up, as he searched the room. He couldn't see anyone new. The person didn't enter from the door behind him. The powerful scent, floral and coconut, went straight to his head. Dizziness swamped him and his knees began to buckle. Sucking in deep breaths to steady himself didn't help. It only drew more of the heavy aura into his body. He caught himself on the counter, trying to control his reactions. A quick glance around showed everyone still engrossed in their own conversations or their food and drink in front of them.

The scent grew stronger, closer. He looked across the counter and found the source. A new employee, his wolf narrowed in on her.

"I'm so sorry I'm late." A sweet sing-song voice started a ringing in his ears.

"Gwen, this is only your second day." Walker, the owner, looked down his nose.

"I know. I'm sorry. It won't happen again."

Walker nodded once and passed her an apron. Gwen took over at the cash and turned wide, welcoming eyes on Asher that would have melted him to the floor had he not held onto the counter.

"Good morning." Asher wasn't recovered enough to speak. He politely waved the next person in line ahead of him while he pretended to peruse the menu on the wall. No one's scent had ever affected him like this before. He didn't understand what was happening. Just as dizziness continued to swamp him and his limbs grew weak, he craved to move closer to the cause.

The cause being a short brunette with freckles dotting her pale skin with warm, brown eyes. He guessed her hair would reach her waist if it wasn't tied into a messy bun on top of her head.

Asher tensed, forcing himself past the effects of her scent. She was smiling at him, having already waited on the people behind him.

"What can I get for you today?"

"Large coffee, please. Black." His voice came out deeper than usual, a low growl weaved through it. The brown orbs of her eyes grew, but as she swallowed she seemed to recover from her surprise.

"Sure." She rang it up and gave him his total. As soon as he paid, she got his coffee and passed it to him. His fingers wrapped around hers when he took the cup. He froze. The feel of her skin sent a wave of sensations through him, increased sensitivity to her, her touch, sound, smell. All of it sending pinprick sensations through his system. Steeling himself, he released her.

"Thank you. Gwen." Her small gasp gave him some satisfaction to know he wasn't the only one affected. With a final nod, Asher made his way out of the bistro still on two legs and walking steady. But he froze in place with what he saw. Moving in a figure eight around the parking lot was the white wind he saw for the first time as a child. He'd only seen it one other time since then. When Kai's mother, his wolf mother, had passed away. The wind had called to him with a cry of its own early in the morning. Today, the wind looked like it was dancing. Asher discreetly looked around the parking lot. He was the only one who could see the white swirls. Customers and pedestrians walked right through it. Asher didn't have the energy in him to figure out what the wind was trying to tell him.

In his truck, he breathed deep to dispel the dizziness and waited for it to pass.

What the fuck was that? The weakness that assailed his body confused him and not knowing what any of it meant pissed him off. But it seemed the white wind knew. Growing up as a wolf had given him a lot of new puzzles to figure out and he'd had to do them on his own or with Kai. Not everything that affected him did the same to his pair or other wolves. Adolescence had been a tough few years. He'd had to learn a lot of control. But he'd always gotten through and figured it out, despite the many close calls. But this was different. Never had anything involved someone else. The scent of someone triggering a reaction within him and with his wolf.

Cursing, he took his first drink of coffee, the heat sliding over his tongue, and started his truck. As soon as he walked into his clinic, there were already patients waiting to be seen. His agitated state set off all the nerves of the animals. The day turned out difficult, trying to calm the animals when he couldn't calm himself with Gwen's scent still lingering inside him.

He had messages from his mother and Madi waiting for him on his phone by the time he got home, but he couldn't deal with them. He rarely ignored them. Tonight he had to. Asher didn't even go inside after leaving his truck. He walked straight to the woods and stripped. His wolf needed out. He needed some freedom and a chance to run off the odd weakness and turmoil that stuck with him since the morning.

Asher didn't set out to find his pair, but Kai must have sensed him because it wasn't long into his run Kai appeared and matched his pace. Asher didn't stop. Long after his legs were tired and sore and with his tongue lolling out, he settled with Kai and his pack, remaining as a wolf for the night to leave the animal in charge. It was the calmest he'd felt all day, allowing him the ability to sleep when he knew if he was in his own home, he wouldn't.

CHAPTER 2

Gwen sighed as she entered her apartment after work. Plopping herself on her couch, she lifted her feet and rolled her ankles to give them some relief. She wanted this job, so she happily stayed and worked a double shift after someone called in sick. It grated her that she was late on her second day. Julian had caught her outside her apartment. It surprised her he had been up that early. He didn't go into work until he absolutely had to. It wasn't the first time Gwen got the impression he was interested in her, but he was always easy to ward off. He was a nice guy, but she couldn't bring herself to reciprocate the feelings. They'd been friends since childhood and knew too much about each other. She would never be able to see him in a romantic light.

This morning was a little odd. He was more attentive than usual. No, that wasn't the right word. He was forceful. She'd had to push him away, not giving him a chance to finish.

"What's the rush, Gwen?" His hand had wrapped around her elbow, gentle except for the sharp, stabbing points of his fingertips on the underside of her arm.

"I need to go to work. We'll have to talk later."

"Work? You don't need that job. You know a job with any of your dad's companies is better." He wasn't wrong.

"That isn't what I want." Her father's companies held no interest for her. She wanted to live on her own and find her own future. Her family would always be there to help her when needed. Gwen was grateful for the financial freedom to make these decisions and have a family to fall back on if something went wrong. The need for this job was for herself.

"Why does that matter?"

"I need to go." She'd had to pry her arm out of his grasp. Gwen had caught the frown on his face as she jogged to her car. Those minutes talking to Julian put her behind enough to get caught in traffic. If he came by again, she'd be more assertive in explaining herself. She might not truly need the job, but she wanted it.

Gwen dragged herself to the kitchen to make something to eat and poured a glass of wine. She settled in for a quiet night, knowing she'd be back at the bistro bright and early tomorrow.

Even with only two days into the job, she felt she would enjoy it. During her interview, Walker had looked rather confused. It was well known her father owned several companies in town that held plenty of job options for her, from restaurants to office work and with opportunities to excel in each. He built all that himself. She wanted to do the same. She didn't intend to build her own miniature empire, but Gwen wanted to build the life she would lead on her own. Thankfully, her parents understood that need.

So far, she enjoyed working for Walker and hated disappointing the gruff father figure type man so quickly. She wouldn't let it happen again. Did she intend to work in the bistro for a long time? No. Nor did she intend to stay in that industry. But proving her dedication and worth was her goal. She didn't need to prove it to Walker, to Julian, or even her parents. Gwen needed and wanted to prove it to herself.

ASHER STEADIED himself before walking into the bistro the next day, but it didn't work. Gwen's essence instantly assailed him. His limbs didn't fall weak, but his head still swamped with overloaded senses. His wolf homed in on her, determined to get closer. Without a line, he went straight to her. Involuntarily, he inhaled.

"Good morning. It sure smells great in here, doesn't it?" she asked, her bubbly tone that of a morning person.

He smiled, deciding it best not to correct her mistake. "It does." His voice was once again a low growl despite forcing politeness. "Large coffee and I'll have a cream puff as well, please. Gwen." He added her name to watch her reaction, not because he enjoyed saying it.

A cherry pink flush filled her cheeks and she looked downward while she got to work on his order.

Asher took the time to take in the rest of his surroundings. It wasn't easy with his nose so full of Gwen. He didn't like not being aware of the people around him. He hoped to clear his head running through the woods with Kai the previous night. But all he did was agitate his pair, despite feeling calmer with his wolf free. The only thing he could think to do was continue to come into contact with Gwen until the feeling passed or he could figure out why she had this affect on him.

"Here you go." She held out the cup and a small paper bag.

"Thank you, Gwen." Asher let his eyes take in her appearance as he discreetly pulled in her scent. Her apron cinched a slim waist and hid short legs. Her high breasts lifted the top. Light tendrils of hair escaped around her face. Florals and coconut filled him further as he watched her eyes widen with his perusal. It was rude of him to stare the way he was, but he couldn't help himself. And from the faint smell of arousal, she didn't seem to mind.

Well, damn. Asher might have just figured it out, but he still felt too dizzy to analyze.

"Have a good day."

"You too." She paused and her brow arched in question. He smirked, letting his amusement reach his eyes.

"Asher."

"You too, Asher."

GWEN RELEASED the air that stuck in her lungs. Damn, he was a beautiful man. She'd seen him twice for five minutes each and she was crushing on him. He seemed to growl at her when he talked, his attention focused on her rather than his order or the others in the room. Tall and broad. Clear muscles showing through his button-up shirt. Ruffled, sandy hair gave him an almost boyish look, but the piercing depth of his eyes and the way he growled at her when he spoke took that away.

Seeing the next customer approach, Gwen shook her head. She was being silly, but that didn't stop her from smiling a little brighter throughout her day.

She didn't date often. It was more a waste of time than anything else. Gwen discovered too many guys were condescending. She wished she knew what about her made it difficult to take her seriously. Taking the time to weed through all the bad to find the few good did more harm to her self-esteem than it did good. It wasn't worth it. It would happen for her when it did. She focused on seeing a connection with someone before she ever agreed to go on a date.

"You're doing well, Gwen." She knew she was, but the brusque praise from Walker validated her own feelings. In only three days, she noticed who the regulars were, the daily regulars. There would be more as time went on.

"Thank you, Walker." Pride forced a smile on her face from his acceptance. Gwen was good with people, but only once she warmed up to them. She was actually shy, but could make conversation and be polite so that most never noticed. A sort of *fake it til you make it*. No one but her knew her insides twisted with nerves when meeting unfamiliar people.

It was the reason she applied to the bistro, to have more interaction with strangers. No matter what career path she chose, she would need exceptional social skills and she would prefer if those weren't a pain for her to manage.

It was difficult for her to describe the stage of her life at the moment. She carried an eagerness to move forward, but didn't know where she was going. So, she saw this as her opportunity to learn, to stroll down a few paths and see where she found herself. The important thing she wanted was to learn something new with each step she took. There was a lot she could take away from working at the bistro and she would carry those forward to her next job. But that was far enough in the future that she needed to push it from her mind. It was too soon to allow herself to become restless. She wasn't ready.

It was becoming problematic to work while dizzy and weak. He started each day at the bistro seeing Gwen. Laura, and Annie, his part-time assistant, wouldn't stop looking at him, concern etched in their eyes. They'd never seen him ill in any form. As a shifter he didn't get sick, or if he did, his immune system fought off the virus or illness before symptoms began. Just another detail about himself of which he wasn't sure.

Part of him gave up trying to answer questions. He couldn't bring himself to leave Alder Ridge, his family, Kai, or the wilderness he grew up with, in search of those answers. He did what he could and stayed home.

But it had also been a long time since he stumbled on a new obstacle, a new learning curve, in the life of a shifter. His problems he had growing up were usually with his control and his emotions. Those were personal issues that he had to learn to cope with himself before he could regain his control. For everything else he went to Kai. It was all about learning the life of a wolf.

Something told him this was altogether different. His own emotions and control couldn't help, and neither could Kai.

Without a clear direction to go, he stayed as he was, working his clinic, running through his woods, and managing his own life. He would continue this journey exactly how he started it, alone.

And with that lonely feeling, he found he craved his family. He walked into his parents' house on his way home from work.

"Knock knock," he yelled as he opened the door that was

never locked. Asher had adopted the same habit. It was rare for him to lock his own door.

"Hi, Asher." His mom walked out of the kitchen. She stretched up so he could kiss her cheek.

"Hi, Mom." He paused. Something was different in the house. "You guys got a dog?"

"How did you know that? Did your father already tell you?"

"I did not." His dad walked in carrying a tiny ball of long black and white fur. Asher begged for a puppy until he was seven. They always told him and his sister they'd think about it. They must have figured he gave up when he stopped asking. In reality, why would Asher ask for a puppy when his best friend was a wolf pup?

The baby Collie looked at Asher. He trembled and then climbed his way out of his dad's arms.

"You're scaring the puppy, son."

"That's all right. Let him go." Asher crouched to the floor the same time his dad set the puppy down. Asher breathed deep and let one hand rest in front of him on the floor. He didn't take his eyes off the puppy. His muscles relaxed and he felt warmth spread through him. The puppy took one slow step toward Asher.

That's it. You're safe, he thought. He projected the same calm authority he felt from Kai's mother the night he changed. It was how he calmed nervous animals in the clinic. He'd learned a lot from her in his early years. Just as much as he had from his own parents.

The puppy came over and sniffed his hand.

"What did you name him?"

"And how do you know it's a him?" His mother crossed her arms, annoyance flowed off her at having her surprise ruined.

"Lucky guess." Asher picked up the puppy and he nestled into his arms.

"I'm not sure how you do that. He was terrified of you only seconds ago." His father murmured.

"We named him Cody." His mother took the sleeping puppy from Asher. "You'll stay for dinner, right?" She pinned him to the floor with a glare and waited for his answer.

"Of course, Mom."

"Good. Call Madigan and tell her to get her butt here too." She turned on her heel back to the kitchen with the puppy cradled in her arms like a babe.

Asher laughed. Just as much as he needed to ground himself as a wolf with Kai, he needed to ground himself with his family too.

GWEN CURSED the flush in her skin every morning. Barely a week had passed since she started working at Woods and she knew Asher was there simply because her skin heated. As soon as she felt warmth spread through her, saw even her arms or chest flush, she turned around and Asher would be waiting in line. Even if she wasn't working the cash that day, he would always stop on the opposite side of the counter to talk to her. He didn't say much. Always something sweet or charming, but with a growl.

He touched her any chance he had. A brush of his fingers, laying his hand over hers. Each small gesture like a static shock. But it was all she needed to send her into overdrive. Her body reacted to him instinctively. She knew nothing about him other than his first name and how he liked his coffee. But she felt that any more information wouldn't matter. There was something there. Some days she felt it was a physical something that connected them. Thoughts and images of him always stuck with her until the next time she saw him.

Unless it was a day that Julian showed up at her door.

He was a friend, so she tried to be patient with him. Often inviting him in for coffee or accepting the takeout he brought. Any time they spent together never crossed the line of friendship, despite his hints for more. But showing up a week before her cousin's wedding, he upped his game.

She opened her door and found Julian there holding up a bottle of wine.

"Gwen, I'd love it if you'd allow me to escort you to the wedding next weekend." He smiled gallantly, knowing precisely how it showed off his dimples. She knew he was attempting a romantic gesture. She'd seen him do it before, seen the same fake expression he used to gather women, but Gwen pushed that aside.

"You know you don't need to do that, Julian. I appreciate it, but I'm perfectly happy to attend alone."

"And if I'm not offering out of consideration?" His voice dropped and he stepped closer. His hand touched her shoulder and slid down her arm to her wrist. Never had his touch sent sickly shivers under her skin.

"Julian, we've talked about this. I'm just not interested in you that way. You've always been a friend to me." She softened her expression and dislodged his hand by using hers to squeeze his arm then pat it with an affection she didn't have. "I was about to watch a bit of T.V. Want to join me?" Gwen didn't want to invite him in, but she insisted on being polite and breaking up the awkwardness that had settled between them lately.

"No." His jaw clenched and he looked to the floor for a

moment before he looked back at her, his face opposite what it had been. The instant change unsettled her. "That's okay. You enjoy. See you next week." He turned and left before she could say goodbye. She walked back to her door and closed it. Her hand hovered over the lock before she decided she would feel safer if she locked it earlier than normal.

Gwen sighed and hoped Julian would soon understand so he would stop trying to get her to date him. Some of his actions were making her wary around him when before she only saw him as harmless. Just the boy she knew growing up.

◢

"HAVE YOU *FOUND* YOURSELF YET?" Asher heard the harsh snicker that followed the question through the phone.

"Stop calling me here, Julian. I'm working. I'll talk to you later." Gwen's irritated answer narrowed Asher's eyes. She hung up the restaurant landline and rushed over to the counter. Her jaw was clenched, probably to hide her quivering bottom lip. She didn't look up until she reached the counter. She gasped when she saw him. "Asher. Hi."

"Are you all right, Gwen?" He spoke low.

"Of course." Gwen's smile was insincere, but even when upset, her eyes brightened like a light behind a window, letting him see inside. "How are you today?"

"I'd be better if I knew you were all right." He was lucky there wasn't anyone in line behind him, because he intended to push the issue.

"I'm okay," she whispered.

He leaned forward across the counter. "Was it the phone call that upset you?" He spoke low as to not gather the attention of other customers or her coworkers. She nodded her head and looked down at her hands resting next to his on the counter. "Who was it?"

"Just a friend." One of her shoulders lifted halfway to her ear. Asher raised his brow, expecting more information, hoping she would volunteer it without him asking. "He doesn't agree with my recent job choice."

"Here at the bistro?"

"I used to work for my father, but I wanted to start something of my own. Find what I'm good at for myself."

"There's nothing wrong with that." Asher leaned down to rest on his elbows and allowed one of his hands to move and cover hers.

"I know there isn't," she said proudly. "But there's only a few people that take me seriously. I've never been able to figure out why."

"Everyone deserves the chance to be heard, to explore, to make their own choices. You're doing that despite how people see you, how your friend sees you."

"Thank you. I didn't realize how much he was bothering me." When Gwen's face lifted with a gracious tilt, his chest hurt from the lack of air.

"You're welcome." And because he needed more contact, he lifted her hand intending to kiss the inside of her wrist, but he hesitated. He didn't want to scare her away when he felt the need for her growing. He turned her hand over and circled her palm with his thumb twice. She looked as if she was starving for contact as much as Asher. He felt a spark created by his thumb. It travelled through his system and settled throughout his body. He had to wonder if she felt the same thing ignite within her. Her wide eyes and sharp breath left him thinking she did. He set her hand back down on the counter, regretting the loss.

He wanted to talk more, ask more, but customers lined up behind him. He ordered his coffee and paid.

"See you tomorrow, Gwen."

"Bye, Asher." He left feeling a stronger pull toward her than he had when he walked in there.

CHAPTER 3

Asher did indeed figure out why Gwen swamped his senses. The obvious answer was attraction. As time went on and he continued to see her in the bistro, the dizziness faded leaving deep seated arousal behind. But the decision to act on it wasn't easy to make. This differed from attraction to a female. There was still something he was missing. He wasn't just human, he was an animal, and he had to look at it through an animal's, his wolf's, point of view. A mate. His wolf recognized his mate. As soon as he realized that, it was difficult for Asher to control himself, but he managed. He refused to get closer than they did at the bistro, but each time he stayed a little longer and talked with her a little more.

"Good morning, Gwen." He reached across the counter and ran the back of his knuckle down her cheek, allowing himself that contact to soothe his wolf. Hell, to soothe himself.

"Hi, Asher. Your usual?" He enjoyed the instant blush in her skin when he touched her. Fuck, it was getting more difficult with each day.

"Mmm, please," he hummed, and he saw her tongue trace her bottom lip.

She passed him his order. "You know, I've never asked what you do? You always come in here on your way to work."

"I'm a veterinarian. I own Morestead Veterinary Clinic."

"Seriously?"

He chuckled. "Yes."

"Wow. Maybe I need to get a pet. So I'll have an excuse to come visit you."

"You don't need an excuse."

The next customer moved forward to the counter, not caring about interrupting their conversation. Asher let the moment go and left. He had parked his truck at the end of the lot. Halfway there, he froze, sensing something odd for the middle of town. He was sure he could smell a bear. It was faint, but it was there. Cautiously, he scanned the parking lot and out into the street toward the pedestrians. No bear, but the scent led to a man standing just as still as Asher across the street, his head cocked to the side. Asher's heart pounded. Was he another shifter?

Asher couldn't believe what he saw above him. Swirling white air. It was so rare for him to see until lately. It circled above the man's head. He looked up, then looked above Asher. Asher followed his gaze and saw a translucent auburn wind circling above him. The two men locked eyes for a moment. Asher took a step closer, but that seemed to break the spell. The wind shifted and the man started walking again.

"Damn it," Asher cursed.

It soured his cheerful mood at seeing his mate. If he was a shifter, he wasn't interested in Asher being one too, let alone he smelled of bear. Wolves and bears merely tolerated each other, unless the situation involved food. That fact wouldn't bother Asher if it meant finding more shifters.

Asher spent years searching, looking through legends, folklore, news reports, and even fiction trying to find exactly what he was and if there were others out there. He used that information and lessons he had learned growing up with his own best explanations, but never was he able to find anything concrete or anything that pointed to other shifters, past or present. He certainly found no reference to coloured winds. Asher only believed it was the white wind out there that he followed as a child. But it seemed the possible bear shifter followed an auburn one.

Dispelling his frustration, he continued toward his truck. Next time, he wouldn't hesitate to follow.

GWEN SAT with her parents at her cousin's wedding. The ceremony had been simple and short and now the reception was in full swing. Although she'd intended to attend the wedding alone, she ended up partnered with Julian, who clung to her with his arm around the back of her chair. His inability to take a hint was getting on her nerves. No matter how much she insisted they remain friends, he felt she was only playing hard to get, so he just tried harder. In all the years she knew him, he never acted so forceful.

"I'm going to get a drink."

"Let me get that for you." Julian rested a hand on her shoulder to keep her in place.

"No." She spoke loud enough the rest of the table turned her way. She attempted a graceful look and calmed her tone. "No, thank you. I need to stretch my legs." She moved before he could stop her again.

"Then I'll come with you."

Gwen sighed, not even trying to hide her irritation. The line at the bar had them standing too close and she couldn't stay still, trying to put distance between them while his hand rested on her lower back.

For over a week, he mocked her for working at *Wood's Bistro.* He refused to listen to her reasons, believing she was acting childish, and he refused to believe her when she pushed him away.

"Is something wrong, Gwen?"

She'd already answered that question several times tonight. She would not answer it again.

"Why don't you wait over there and I'll get the drinks." He pointed away from the bar.

"Sure." It got her out from underneath his hands. Gwen rolled her shoulders to disguise the shiver that ran along her skin. It was the most space she had since entering the reception hall. But her space didn't last long as she felt heat cover her back.

"Hi." She turned excitedly at the sound of the rumbling voice and landed in Asher's arms, his hands resting on her elbows.

"Asher. Hi. What are you doing here?"

"The groom is a friend of mine from high school."

"And the bride is my cousin."

"Small world." His sexy one-sided smirk was all it took for her to lean closer.

"I guess so." He was even bigger up close. She only saw him from across the counter taking his coffee order. But this close, she felt engulfed by his size and drowning in his eyes.

"Who's your date?" His smile looked just as sharp as the edge she heard in his voice. It gave her relief to know she hadn't imagined his attraction to her.

"Just a friend. No date." Asher looked above her head toward the bar, raising a disbelieving brow. "Although, he's trying," she added under her breath.

Asher turned his piercing blue eyes back down to her. "Then dance with me?"

She felt her face light up and she nodded with too much excitement, like a child who'd been offered a chocolate bar. He led her to the dance floor and pulled her close, his hand hot on her lower back and her right hand tucked inside his left and held against his chest. She was flush against him, feeling the move of his muscles along her body. He didn't waste time easing them into the dance. Gwen swallowed when she felt his erection along her stomach.

"Your friend. Is it the same friend that didn't like your career decisions?"

"Yeah." She pursed her lips.

"You said he's trying. Trying what?"

"Oh." It surprised her he'd heard her say that. "He's trying to be more than friends. But he's not taking the hint very well tonight." She said it lightly, but she felt Asher's grip tighten and he would have pulled her closer if there were any space left between them.

Luckily the song faded into another slow one and they continued to move together.

"You look beautiful tonight."

"Thank you. You're looking pretty good yourself." Gwen cringed and looked to the side. She wished she could have said something more eloquent, but her speech still wasn't always working properly around him. She opened her mouth to say more, or to say anything, but nothing came out. His gaze and his touch trapped her. Heat sizzled along her skin. Her breathing was shallow, and she felt herself dampen between her legs. And he noticed all of it. He discreetly moved against her.

"I'm glad you feel it too." His low tone swept over her face. He bent his head and captured her parted lips. She let him claim her. It was good that he seemed to have some control because she didn't want to stop him or go slow. She could feel the power in him, could feel him holding himself back. Her body hummed for more. But all too soon, he lifted his head. He didn't look at her. His gaze landed directly behind her. Did she do something wrong?

"Gwen, darling. I have your drink at the table." Her head snapped around at Julian, her body still held tightly against Asher. She stared, shocked that he would interrupt someone in that position. Asher's hand tightened at her back for a moment before letting her go. He brought her hand to his lips and pressed a kiss to her pulse on her wrist. She barely knew this man, but she felt herself pulling toward him. She would much rather spend more time with him than return to her table with Julian.

Gwen saddened with the loss of Asher's touch, but it soon turned to anger as Julian took her arm to steer her back to the table.

"How inappropriate. That must have been embarrassing for you, Gwen." The admonishment in his voice infuriated her. She threw her head back to look at the ceiling, keeping herself from snapping at him. "If I had known you wanted to dance, I would have gladly danced with you." The man just wouldn't shut up.

"Excuse me, Julian." He looked startled by her sudden outburst. "I need some air."

"I'll take you out."

"No. Don't follow me." She spoke clearly, punctuating each word, barely keeping herself from grinding the words through her teeth. She'd been polite enough to him all night. She couldn't take it anymore. Escaping through the side door, Gwen stepped to the side of the building. The night was chilly, so crowds didn't stay outside for long. She sighed as the few stragglers went back inside. Leaning against the building, she wrapped her arms around herself. Too eager to escape Julian, she didn't grab her coat on the way out.

He thought Asher embarrassed her. An idiot wouldn't have looked at the two of them and seen embarrassment. She never knew Julian to be so determined or obtuse. She'd already spelled it out for him. What more did she have to do?

"Gwen. You're going to freeze out here."

She closed her eyes and locked her jaw, but it wasn't enough to block him out. "Julian. I told you not to follow me."

"I didn't think you meant it."

"I meant it," she said slowly, attempting to imitate a growl of her own.

Something changed in his face. His mouth flattened straighter than his slicked down hair and his eyes narrowed. Finally, maybe he was starting to understand. "You've been pushing me away all night."

"Yeah. I intended to come to this wedding alone, not with a date. And Julian, I am not interested in you that way, which I've already told you before."

"You didn't seem to hold him to the same standard." Really? He was acting jealous. He already took all her energy tonight. She didn't have enough to deal with this.

"I'm sorry, Julian." She tried to sound nicer, a tad sympathetic. "We can still be friends, but please, give me some space."

"I don't think I'm going to do that." Something changed in his voice and each word was carefully punctuated.

Bells rang in her head, alarm tightening her muscles, sensing danger. "Julian?" He moved, closing the distance quicker than she thought him capable. She tried to pull away, but he had her hands pinned against the brick. His weight against her, he tried to kiss her. She moved her head from side to side, evading him, feeling her hair being pulled out of the twisted knot from the rough surface.

"Stop fighting me," he snarled and adjusted so one hand held both of hers and his other could move down her body.

"No!" She fought and struggled free, but he was still on her. Julian pulled back and slapped her. She was shocked, motionless from the sharp pain, and he took advantage, grabbing the front of her dress and ripping.

With her hands momentarily free, she tried to pull her dress up, and she steeled herself for a fight. Anger filled her at this insecure man and his attempts to ruin her.

She screamed when he lunged at her, pushing her back against the brick wall. Silence followed. There was no one outside to hear her and help.

ASHER TRACKED GWEN, and her conversation with her *friend*, as they walked away. "No. Don't follow me." He saw her walk outside and sighed to help dispel some frustration. His instincts wanted to rip that guy apart. His wolf's teeth were out and ready. Unbelievably, Asher kept from outwardly showing his true mood and he walked to the bar. Gwen was his. He was being patient in claiming her, but it didn't change the end result. Her taste was better than he'd imagined. His control clawed at the inside of his skin. It was a struggle to keep it contained. The guy was lucky Asher didn't bite him when he interrupted their kiss. The bitter scent of jealousy had curled Asher's nose, forcing him to look up and pull away from the purest taste of ecstasy that only began to satiate his core.

Before he could order his beer, his ears picked up a scream. A quick look around the room told him he was the only one who heard it. As calmly as he could, he left, following Gwen outside. As soon as he hit the cooler air, he smelled her fear and anger. He heard them at the side of the building. His wolf went into a rage, threatening to force Asher out of control. Before he shifted, Asher turned and went to the opposite side of the building and climbed up the fire escape. He stripped on the roof and gave into the wolf, shifting to appease his animalistic instincts so they didn't take over and he killed the guy, her *friend*. He recognized the terrible smell.

He peered down the side of the building, his wolf eyes sharp and clear in the dark alley. Gwen's dress was ripped open in the front, her breasts exposed, and the guy had a hand on her throat while he groped under her dress and tried to suck her nipples. Gwen was trying to struggle, to kick, to pull his hand off her throat so she could breathe. Rage engulfed Asher. With a snarl, he leapt from the roof and landed on the dumpster, the cover denting under his weight.

"What the fuck?" Julian jumped back, his eyes widening. Asher bared his teeth and didn't disguise his growl. He leapt off the dumpster and stalked toward Julian, separating him from Gwen. Gwen was shaking against the side of the building, scared and hurting. Julian's fear filled him with satisfaction. He attempted bravery by stomping forward to scare

Asher away. Asher snapped, forcing Julian back again with a squeal.

Asher lunged, hitting Julian in the chest with his front paws and knocking him back against the dumpster. He hit his head with a satisfying thunk and passed out. Good enough. Asher turned to check on Gwen, eyes wide and holding the torn red silk over her chest.

"Easy there, big boy." Asher was no longer growling or snarling, his teeth hidden. He wanted to move closer, but he gave her some time. Instead, he sat and watched her. Her breathing slowed down. "You're magnificent. You're big." A nervous giggle escaped her throat. She sucked in a breath to stop herself from what Asher hoped didn't turn into hysterics. "But beautiful."

Asher stood and slowly walked to her.

"Oh. Oh. Um, easy. Okay." She froze and closed her eyes as Asher ran his nose and head along her hip. This was the first time he made contact with a person in his wolf form. He only realized that now as he took in the comfort of his mate. Slowly, her eyes opened. Adjusting her hold on her dress, she lowered one of her hands and tentatively set it on his head. Asher closed his eyes and leaned into her touch, feeling warmth spread under his fur. His tail wagged. "You saved me. My white knight." He looked up at her. "Thank you."

Gwen calmed despite her body still shaking. She took more liberties, running her fingers through his fur. And he didn't feel the least bit shameful for enjoying her touch.

"Your eyes. They're so bright, but almost navy. I've never seen a blue like them." She started shaking her head. "That's not true. There's another pair I know that are very close."

A groan from Julian broke the spell surrounding them. Asher turned in front of Gwen and bared his teeth. When

Julian didn't move, Asher turned back around and nudged Gwen, pushing her to go back inside, but she wouldn't go. If he wasn't afraid of scaring her, he would have snapped to get her moving. But luckily Julian settled back down.

Nudging Gwen one last time, running his nose along her stomach, Asher left, leaping onto the dumpster first. Bending his haunches, he leapt against the wall and used his momentum to jump to the opposite building and back again, then onto the roof. Crouching, he waited. Neither of them moved. *Damn it, Gwen. Get out of there before he wakes up.*

Silently, Asher shifted and dressed. He climbed back down the fire escape on the other side of the building. A few people were milling in and out as he passed the front of the building to get to Gwen.

"Gwen?" He reached the corner. Eyes that still held shock turned to him. That's why she never moved. "Gwen." He went to her and folded her in his arms.

"Asher." She tried to pull away and stand tall. He wouldn't have it. He already saw her at her worst. It didn't matter that she didn't know that.

"Shh. I've got you." She shook at his words and allowed herself to be held.

People turned curious and started finding their way over to the alley, just in time for Julian to wake. Too many people for Asher's liking filled the opening to the alley. Some he knew, some he didn't.

"Where is it?" Julian jumped to his feet, then grabbed his head in both hands. He tried to look around, his squinted eyes circling the area with panic. "Where did it go?"

"What, Julian? What was it?" asked a man from the crowd, about the same age as Julian. Asher didn't know him, but recognized him from inside the reception. He and many others were frowning at all three of them, unsure of what really happened.

"A beast! That dog, wolf, something. It was huge." He looked around frantically. "Gwen!" He charged toward her and Asher tightened his hold. Not that Julian noticed him. "Where did it go?"

A sliver of uncertainty made its way through Asher's gut. He hadn't thought it all through, what being spotted by humans would mean for him. There were reasons he kept that part of himself a secret, even from those closest to him. But when Gwen spoke, his uncertainty vanished.

"I don't know what you're talking about, Julian. I didn't realize you hit your head that hard."

"What are you talking about?" The muscles around Julian's eyes tightened.

"What happened here, Gwen?" A woman from the gathered crowd stepped forward, staring at Gwen's torn dress.

"Julian followed me out here. He..." she took in a shaky breath, but didn't stop despite the growing crowd, "he assaulted me. I got free enough to push him. He fell back and hit his head against the dumpster. Asher found us shortly after that." Her shaken state made it impossible for other to detect her lie. But his ears caught her increased pulse and he smelled the excess perspiration. And he already knew the truth.

A couple guys took a hold of Julian and offered to call the cops for Gwen. Asher wanted to protest when she turned them down, but it was her decision to make. Julian continued to go on about a white beast as they ushered him into the passenger side of his own car and drove him away.

Asher refused to let go of Gwen. He ran his hands up and down her arms and back, continuing to comfort her.

"Are you all right?"

"Yes. Thank you." She tilted her head back and he saw pure trust emanate from her eyes. Then she frowned and Asher realized her gaze was locked on his eyes. "Your eyes."

"What about them?"

She shook her head. "They're a very special colour."

CHAPTER 4

Gwen winced when she looked in the mirror the next morning. Gingerly, she caressed the bruise that surrounded her swollen bottom lip then moved down to the ones on her neck. She'd received a lecture from several people, including Asher, that she should have filed a report with the police. And now that she saw the damage, she wished she had.

It wasn't too late, but she didn't want to hurt his parents. Something obviously got into him last night. He wasn't acting like himself. They'd known each other for years. She wanted to give him the benefit of the doubt. For now. Gwen rolled her eyes at herself in the mirror. She was too generous.

Then there was her other problem. Julian was insisting to anyone who listened that he saw a wolf, although he was claiming it was a beast. He looked at her like she had two heads when she said she saw nothing and that he must have imagined it when he hit his head.

She couldn't get the wolf out of her mind. It haunted her dreams through the night. The bright blue eyes watching her from the shadows. Then Asher showed up and the wolf disappeared. There was something she wasn't seeing.

Why was a wolf in town, let alone on the roof of a building? And why would a wolf save her? Save anyone? He easily put himself between her and Julian, forcing Julian away. She didn't want to tell anyone about the wolf, to do anything that could bring him harm. He saved her.

Then she had Asher, who refused to leave her side until she was home and tucked in bed. He had literally tucked her into bed. She smiled remembering him standing almost awkwardly in her bedroom waiting for her to shower and change in her bathroom. She didn't think he could be awkward. He was too graceful when he moved, too confident. He had helped her in bed and pulled the covers over her before sitting beside her.

"I'm glad you're okay." He had braced his hands on either side of her and he had scowled at her mouth and neck. "Would you like me to spend the night?"

Gwen had searched his eyes, wanting to know why he offered, but he had given nothing away. She had considered saying yes. "No, that's okay."

"Are you sure you don't want to go to the police?"

"I've known him for years, and his parents. This isn't like him. I'm sure it was just a bad night." It was difficult to believe that.

"All right. Do you want to talk about it?"

What would Asher have said if she'd told him about the wolf? She had shaken her head, not willing to risk it. Still wasn't, not yet anyway.

"Okay. I've left my number on your nightstand. Call me if you need anything."

"Thank you, Asher." Gwen's voice had dropped. His hand had come up and he'd traced her cheek before he cupped her jaw. Leaning down, he'd placed a kiss on the uninjured side of her mouth. The gesture had been enough to have her insides quivering.

Even now, the morning after when the entire night settled in her mind, the thought of Asher set her stomach fluttering and her core heating.

A knock on her door made her jump as if she should be ashamed at her thoughts of Asher. She wasn't expecting anyone, having already talked to her parents to ensure them she was fine. She froze on her way to the door with the sudden thought it could be Julian. Despite giving him the benefit of the doubt and letting it go, she didn't want to see him again. Not this soon. Fear started her shaking.

"Gwen?" Asher's deep rumble sounded from the other side. She sighed, relief rushing through her and deflating her body, and continued to open the door.

"Hi, Asher." She held the door open for him.

"How are you feeling?"

"I'm good."

"Good." They stood just inside her apartment, Asher's eyes raked over her, taking in every detail. Gwen tried not to fidget under his scrutiny. Before she gave in to the urge, she turned toward her kitchen.

"Do you want coffee or anything?"

"If you're making some, yes. Thank you." He followed her in and sat at her table while she poured coffee she already had made.

"Thank you again for bringing me home last night." She put cream and sugar on the table with a couple spoons and sat down beside him.

"You don't need to thank me." He paused. "Gwen, are you sure you don't want to talk about it?"

"I'm sure." She wasn't. She hadn't thought much about

what Julian did to her. Her mind was solely on the wolf. Her scare from Asher's knock on her door forced her to realize the bigger issue. Bigger than being saved by a wolf. Asher was about to say more, but another knock interrupted him. The same sliver of fear spiked through her. Asher set his hand on her.

"I can get it if you want." How did he know she was scared?

"That's okay." She stood and made her way to the door, trying to hide her fear. She felt Asher follow closely behind. Opening the door, she held her breath. Julian stood on the other side, looking no worse for wear.

"Gwen." At least he sounded remorseful. "May I come in?"

"No." Her voice squeaked. Clearing her throat, she tried again, holding herself high. "No."

"Please. I'd rather not say this in the hall for others to hear."

"Too bad." She was proud of her even tone this time. Julian still hadn't seen Asher. He stood out of sight behind the door, but close enough that Gwen could feel him.

"Gwen, I'm sorry about last night. I'm not sure what came over me."

"Okay." She wouldn't forgive him, not now.

He sighed. "I really am. But I want to talk to you about something else from last night. Please, let me in."

"No." She didn't care that she was coming off rude with clipped answers.

"I need your help. I'm going to Fish and Wildlife to report that beast. I need you to come with me to tell them what you saw after it knocked me out." He took a step closer. Gwen tensed and tightened her grip on the door, ready to shut it if he tried to come into her apartment.

"There was no beast. I'm not coming with you to report something that wasn't there."

Another step put him inside the door frame. "Why are you lying?" His eyes narrowed and she saw the corrupt monster he let out last night.

"I'm not lying and if I go with you I will tell the Fish and Wildlife officers exactly everything that happened, none of which includes any sort of beast other than the one that came out of you."

"I know what I saw. I'm reporting it and I will find it." He turned abruptly and left. Gwen quickly shut her door and felt her knees weaken. Asher was there to catch her. He held her elbow and wrapped an arm around her middle from behind. His heat sinking into her skin gave her strength. That poor wolf. She needed to stop Julian, but she didn't know how without admitting the wolf was there and putting him in more danger.

"I have to stop him." Her broken whisper hurt her throat.

"Why, Gwen?" Asher still held onto her, pulling her a little closer so his chest covered her back.

She turned her head and looked up, ready to tell him everything, but his eyes stopped her. The colour was so similar to the wolf's. They were such a unique blue.

"It's okay. He isn't going to find anything." Asher sounded so sure, but he didn't know what she knew.

"What if their search puts an innocent animal in danger?"

"I won't let that happen. I'll personally monitor their search myself. I happen to be one of the vets they often consult."

"Really?" Gwen wasn't sure if that worried her more or helped her. If they found the wolf, he would discover she was lying. What would he do if she told him about a giant, beautiful white wolf that saved her?

ASHER LEFT GWEN'S, hating letting her go. Chucking his clothes behind a bush outside his house, he took a deep breath and shifted, the ache flowing through him as his body changed. The pack's territory wasn't far from his home. Nose to the ground, he caught the most recent scent of Kai and tracked him. His pair was leader of an ever-changing and ever-growing pack. They travelled further into the woods away from his house to hunt. They never went close to town or near people. That didn't stop Asher from worrying. He cursed himself for letting Julian see him. As a wolf, he was identical to Kai, therefore putting Kai in danger too, not just himself.

He caught the scent of the pack as he entered their territory, some of their hackles raised at the presence of a new wolf. He saw his pair emerge on a hill and Asher picked up his pace.

I let myself be seen as a wolf. There could be people searching for me. This is far away from where I was spotted, but you should move further into the woods. It was only a precaution. The odds of them searching over here for him were slim. This was far enough away from where the wedding had been and they wouldn't search so far away from civilization for whatever Julian claimed he saw.

You're the only one that ever ventures this far into the woods. If we scent another, we'll move. Asher nodded. Kai was smart, he wouldn't let himself, or any of his pack, get caught.

Because he had made the trip out, Asher stayed with the pack, meeting the new members and playing with the pups.

Feeling the need to hold on to this side of himself a little longer, he even stayed to hunt with Kai and a few of the other wolves into the evening. Peace settled over him. They were just as much family as his parents and sister.

Reluctantly, he left, starting his trek back through the woods. If he didn't have to work tomorrow, he would have camped with Kai and the pack. Asher turned his thoughts to Gwen while he watched the moon rise during his hike. Gwen was his mate. He didn't get dizzy or weak around her anymore, but her scent still invaded and affected him more than he thought possible. Deep arousal and a possessive instinct consumed him when he was near her.

He was thankful she denied seeing a wolf last night, and he appreciated her worry for him. But how was this going to work out? A human as a mate. Not that he really had other choices. He doubted it was even a choice at all based on her scent. This was Fate's doing. She was meant to be his whether either of them agreed with it. Thankfully, Gwen was just as aroused by him as he was of her. Smelling her arousal every time he got close threatened his control. Last night could have gone very differently if Julian hadn't interrupted them and then attacked her.

The urge to take her was getting stronger. If he didn't tell her about his wolf, then eventually his wolf would do it for him. She saw him and already she held some sort of loyalty and a need to protect.

Shaking himself before shifting, he tried to push her from his mind. But he couldn't. After having tasted her last night, it was too late to back away, too late to hold off and wait for things to progress naturally between them.

Dressing, he made his way back to his truck. He should stop and pick something up on his way there. It was the polite thing to do. It was too late for dinner, but he could take a dessert, a bottle of wine, anything. But the longer she stayed on his mind, the less patience he had. Pulling to a sudden stop in front of her apartment building, he slammed his truck door and jogged to her apartment. His knock was louder than he intended.

He heard her gasp and smelled her fear just as he had this morning, but this time he didn't call out her name to let her know it was him.

"Asher?" Confusion furrowed her brow as she gripped the door.

"May I come in?" He cursed the sound of his voice, gruff and impatient.

"Of course." She stepped back. Asher took the door from her and shut it behind him. "Is there something you wanted?"

"Yeah. You." Asher stood rigid a few feet away. He kept himself from grabbing her and pulling her closer so he could wait for her answer. But he didn't need to hear one when he could smell it on her. Her skin flushed in the dim light and her tongue pulled her upper lip down to pinch between her teeth.

"Me?" she squeaked. Asher tried to smile, but it wouldn't work. He stepped closer and took her hand. He lifted it and pressed a kiss to her wrist, enjoying the jump in her pulse.

"I'll leave if you want me to." How he would force himself to do that, he wasn't sure. He would make it out of here, one way or another. But only if that was what Gwen truly wanted.

Relief swamped him when she shook her head. "No. I don't want you to go."

Asher pulled her against him with a groan and kissed her, cautious of her injured lip. Sliding his hands down her back, he cupped her ass and lifted, surprising a yelp out of her. He allowed the kiss to end and stalked to her bedroom. Asher could feel his control wavering, could feel his wolf at the edge, ready to pounce.

"I can't guarantee I can be gentle, Gwen." Thank God she wasn't seriously hurt. He'd never lost control in the bedroom before. In fact, he revelled in holding onto control. But with Gwen, nothing felt normal. He didn't know what to expect out of himself.

"I'm okay with that." She was panting, seemingly having her own control issues.

Letting her slide down his body, he grabbed the hem of her t-shirt and lifted. She wasn't wearing a bra and he inwardly howled with joy. He dropped to his knees and allowed his instincts to take over. He nuzzled her stomach while he pulled her sweats down over her hips, taking her panties with them. Asher wasn't interested in what she was wearing, only what was underneath it all.

She stepped from her clothes, pushing them away with her foot, while his hands roamed over her skin. Smooth, soft, and slowly heating under his touch. He kissed, nipped, and licked around her torso and over her ribs, grinning when she giggled and squirmed. He tightened his hold so she couldn't move away. Finally, he reached her breasts, bigger than average with rosy nipples that poked out, begging for him. He nipped and kissed around the swell until he reached the peak. When he sucked it into his mouth, Gwen gasped and placed her hands on his shoulders.

His hands continued to move over her body while he licked his way to her other breast. He needed to get as close to her as possible, take in as much of her scent and taste as he could. He moved lower, tracing down to her centre. Gripping her thighs, he pulled her legs apart. Her arousal filled his nose as he rubbed it over her mound. He felt his eyes gloss and his senses, his wolf's senses, take over.

My mate.

GWEN COULDN'T BREATHE. Overwhelmed by Asher's hands and mouth, by the control that came over him and the spell that was happening between them. Gwen decided to let go and let it happen. To give herself over to this man and release everything that happened in the alley. Thoughts of Julian, the wolf, the consequences of Julian's determination, all of it melted away so that all she could feel was Asher.

She gasped as he nuzzled and nipped his way to her core and finally allowed his tongue to slide out and over her clit. Gwen's knees buckled when he sucked strongly on the bundle. Instead of helping her stay standing, Asher grabbed her knees and pulled, tumbling her back onto the bed. He barely lost contact with her. He followed the motion and latched back on.

Even if she wanted to, Gwen wouldn't have had any control with this. Asher wasn't letting up. Her own sensations built and held her to the bed. She fisted her pillow above her head and her knees fell further apart. Her body held so much instinctive trust for this man. It freed her to enjoy something more than she ever thought possible. And he'd only just begun. His teeth, lips, tongue. She felt it all. With her legs open for him, his fingers roughly traced up her leg to circle her entrance before thrusting in with no mercy.

He wasn't lying when he said he couldn't be gentle. She was boiling with enough heat that her body took whatever he gave her. Gwen cried out on a gasp when he curled his fingers. Her orgasm peaked almost instantly. She froze on the edge, as high as she could go, before she looked down. Asher's blue eyes pierced her and she plummeted over, her hips bucking gently, her legs shaking, and torrid pleasure shooting through her blood.

He didn't withdraw, his mouth, fingers, or his eyes, until the last quiver flowed through her body. She felt trapped, and if it weren't for Asher looking at her, maybe that feeling would bother her.

He didn't say a word, and neither did she, as he finally released her and stood. He took off his clothes. Gwen tried to see every inch of him, muscle definition she'd never seen on another man. His strength was part of who he was, not just something he built and added to himself. But he moved quickly, tossing his clothes to the side and coming back to cover her body.

He kissed her, with the same expertise he used between her legs, pulling her under the same spell that trapped her with heat scoring through her veins. He didn't release her as one hand moved down her side and angled her hip. She felt his cock push at her entrance as if it knew exactly where it wanted to be.

He stretched her impossibly wide, stealing her breath, as he pushed in until his groin came in contact with her clit. After grinding against her, he pulled out and repeated, not giving her any time to adjust to his size. She couldn't adjust to any of it. He was her source of air, her source of pleasure, her only source of release.

Gwen gripped his shoulders, trying to pull herself out of the spell, trying to find the end to the rising bliss. There was so much, so overwhelming, she didn't know if she wanted it to end or keep going.

His pace picked up and he slammed into her with each

thrust. Gwen had a vague thought she might be sore tomorrow, but it was soon wiped away with her orgasm. It hit her suddenly with no time to prepare. She screamed through the kiss. Moments after, Asher growled, and she felt the spurts of his release deep inside her.

Gwen shook. She shook through the aftermath of their orgasms and she continued to shake when he pulled out and wrapped her in his arms.

"Shh. I've got you." He turned her on her side and tucked her head under his chin. "You're absolutely beautiful, Gwen. Rest now."

Gwen inhaled and rested against him, his chest hair tickling her nose. He smelled like the woods, fresh, earthy. Gentle shivers continued over her skin while Asher pulled the blankets over them and pulled her closer still. Gwen closed her eyes, letting the warmth he gave her pull her into a deep sleep.

⁂

ASHER HELD Gwen's quaking body until she settled and slept, holding in his own shaking. He was someone different when he was inside her. He had no more control over his actions than he allowed her. All he knew at the time was he needed to consume her, devour her. He was too rough, too intense, he knew, but it was the closest thing he'd had to an out of body experience. He felt something else between them grow. A bond that was so small before, but now, it was almost unbreakable. Almost. He knew something else was missing, was needed. Asher kept their kiss sealed so he didn't do exactly what his body was telling him to do. Bite her.

The words had flowed through his body, urging him to

pull back and allow his canines to extend. *Mark her. Mate her. She's mine.* It had surprised him, so he'd forced himself to remain connected to her to ensure he didn't do something he knew nothing about.

Sleep didn't come easy for him, but he dosed while Gwen slept peacefully in his arms. Asher's mind raced with the possible repercussions biting Gwen would have. It wouldn't be a playful bite in the heat of the moment. That much was clear to him. This was a mark. As his mate, he needed to mark her as his.

He couldn't do it. Not yet. Not without her knowing what he was or who she was to him. Was he ready to hand his secret over to another?

With enough rest, her scent roused him again, his cock lengthening. His control worried him, but there was no stopping him when he woke her by rolling her onto her stomach and lifting her hips into the air.

"Asher?" Her sleepy question echoed over her shoulder. There was no hesitation or fear about where she was or who had her. Her trust in him was plainly visible for him to see, and sense.

"I need to take you again, Gwen." They weren't the most romantic words, but they were the truth. And he wasn't capable of lying to her in this moment.

Her breath shortened and she nodded while reaching her hands up to grip the pillows. Asher lined himself up and thrust in quickly.

"Your body is mine." It was another truth he couldn't keep in. He didn't need to worry about scaring her. Her walls clamped around his cock and she pushed her hips back to meet him. Asher threw his head back and let his body take over.

Her slickness increased, giving him more ease, more

power. His entire focus centred on where they connected. He felt his canines lengthen. Asher kept his head back and kept himself upright to avoid the temptation. He increased his pace and force to get himself closer to the end and over the urge. As soon as she tightened with her climax, he let go, feeling deep satisfaction as his seed spilled inside her heat.

He held himself there until his cock softened and his teeth retracted. Then he pulled out and flattened on top of her before rolling to the side so he could roll her over too and kiss her. He drank in her taste while his body calmed and sleep finally took him under.

Gwen almost cried at the loss of Asher's arms and her warm bed early Monday morning, not that he let the absence last long. He followed her out of bed and into the shower. She stopped him when his hands slid between her legs.

"I refuse to be late for work and I'm already late getting out of bed. Please, don't do this to me," Gwen whined. Asher laughed, then nipped her neck.

"All right. But I'll need to get out of the shower if I'm going to leave you alone." After pulling her in for a deep kiss, he stepped back and quickly washed. Gwen held in her own whimper. She loved how he couldn't keep his hands off her.

She met him in the kitchen, her dressed for work in jeans and a tank top and Asher dressed in the clothes he showed up in, a long sleeve shirt and jeans.

"Still running late?" he asked, his lips lifting and heat flaring in his eyes.

Gwen sighed. "Yes."

He held out one of her travel mugs and she could smell the coffee it already contained.

"You're a saint." She stretched to kiss him, and he hesitated.

"If I kiss you again, neither of us will make it into work today."

"Oh." Images of the previous night flooded her mind and she had to agree with him. If they got started again, they'd take all day.

Despite the heat inside the bistro, Gwen's skin chilled without Asher. The night with him was intense. She was able to work and not dwell, but he was always in the back of her mind.

She sighed as she looked at the clock and saw her lunch break was approaching. But that relief was short lived when Julian walked in the front door. Panic chased her fear as she saw two others walk in behind him wearing Fish and Wildlife uniforms.

"This is Gwen Taylor." Julian threw her name out with his nose in the air as they approached the counter.

"Miss Taylor. We're sorry to bother you at work. I'm officer Tony Green and this is officer Morton Field. We're trying to track down a dangerous animal and Julian says you might be able to help. We fear for public safety."

A quick look at Julian and she knew that if she refused to speak to them, he would create a scene. A couple customers started lining up behind them.

"My break is in five minutes. If you can wait, please have a seat." Julian's smug face curled her gut. He clearly thought she was going to agree with what he said. But she planned to stick to her story. There was no wolf, or beast as Julian was claiming.

After waiting on her customers, she told Walker she was taking her break and joined the three of them at their table.

"What can I do for you?"

"Julian says you also saw the animal the other night outside the wedding hall. Can you describe it for us? He said you got a much clearer look." Officer green leaned forward on the table.

"I can't help you because there was no animal that night."

"I'm sorry? Are you sure? Any wild animal of any kind? Julian gave the image of a dog. Maybe a large stray dog?" asked officer Field, tilting his head. Suspicion lined his tone. And why wouldn't it? He'd already heard Julian's story with no reason not to trust him.

"No dog. No wild animals. I'm sorry. I'm not sure why Julian thinks he saw something." Julian was sitting beside her and she felt him vibrate. Being this close to him made her nervous. She had to stand to say this next part, but she lowered her voice so it didn't carry across the restaurant. "Julian attacked me in the alley. I freed myself enough to shove him back. He stumbled and fell, hitting his head and knocking himself unconscious." She watched Julian's eyes widen and the two officers looked at the bruise on her lip and lower to the ones on her neck that her scarf couldn't hide. She was thankful that they were still there and that Julian hit her. It was visible proof of her version of the story. It destroyed Julian's credibility. The officers exchanged a look, then glanced over at Julian with a moment of hatred before pulling professional masks back over their features.

"We understand. We're sorry to waste your time." Officer Green offered a look of sympathy despite the roll of thunder she heard behind his words.

"She's lying." Gwen expected an outburst, but instead,

Julian spoke low through his teeth, pure anger radiating from him. She was glad she stood when she did. "Something attacked me and knocked me over. Not her. It jumped down from the roof."

"Of course. Why don't we head over that way now and see if we can track anything down?" Officer Field gestured to the door and stood and the rest followed suit. "Have a good day Miss Taylor." They both waited for Julian to walk to the door before nodding again at her with apologies settling on their features then following Julian from the bistro.

Despite him beginning to sound a little nuts, panic rose in Gwen's chest and stifled her breathing. What if they found something in the alley that pointed to a wolf and pointed to her lie? Sucking in air through her nose, she tried to calm down. She still had the rest of her shift to get through and she couldn't follow them even if she wanted to.

She had to convince Walker that she was fine a few times through the rest of her shift. She pushed through, but didn't waste time getting out of there when it was over. Needing air, she drove with her window down and cranked the heat in her car to keep from freezing.

Gwen itched to call Asher, but she refrained. He already told her he'd be back tonight and would bring dinner with him. She needed to wait. Entering her apartment, she turned to shut the door and lock it. Someone pushed hard against it, pushing her back before she closed it. Julian slammed the door behind him and stood in front of it, blocking her from getting out or anyone from getting in.

"Why did you lie again, Gwen?" He was visibly vibrating. His words were low and spoken through his teeth, just as he had earlier at the bistro. She'd never seen this kind of anger in him before.

"Please leave, Julian." It was still too early for Asher to show up.

"No, I won't do that. We're going to talk. You will tell the truth about what happened starting from when that thing jumped down from the roof. I'm not crazy and was in my right mind before hitting my head."

"You sure about that, or did you forget what you were doing to me?" Her smart response came quick on her tongue.

"Shut up!" he yelled.

"I thought we were going to talk?" Gwen cursed herself. Why the hell was she antagonizing him?

"Quit being a smartass, Gwen. What did you see?" He narrowed his eyes and started walking toward her.

"Nothing." She looked him directly in the eye and spoke as coherent as she could manage.

"Bullshit! Tell me what you saw."

"I already told you. Why don't you tell me what you saw?" This way she could figure out what description he gave to Fish and Wildlife and who knows who else.

"It looked just like a white wolf. But wolves rarely travel without a pack and don't come into the city, and they definitely don't hang around on the roofs of buildings."

"You're not wrong about wolf habits," she agreed, trying to sound noncommittal.

"Why didn't it attack you?"

She shook her head. "Because it wasn't really there."

Julian took a menacing step forward, but suddenly his limbs and head folded forward with the force of being yanked back. Asher threw Julian behind him and stood between them, looking down on Julian with his arms crossed. Gwen finally released the breath that had knotted in her chest. Tears threatened at the corners of her eyes. She never heard him come in and she knew he didn't knock. She didn't care how he knew she was in trouble, only that he was there and she was safe.

ASHER HAD KNOWN something was wrong before he entered Gwen's building. He was suddenly thankful for the cancellation of his last appointment. Silent feet had taken him to her door and into her apartment. Neither one of them had heard him. Looking down at Julian on the floor, Asher wanted to hurt him, but he refused to do anything to make things worse for Gwen. If he'd laid a hand on his mate, Asher wouldn't be so lenient. Aside from his night with Gwen, Asher hadn't lost control of his emotions since he'd been a teenager, and even then, he'd never hurt anyone. His control was being tested now. He needed to move things along quicker with Gwen. He wanted to protect her, not hide behind social acceptances. Beating on the man on the ground wouldn't be considered acceptable, no matter what his intentions had been.

"I suggest you leave. Now." His voice was as tight as his body and resonated with the lowest note of a bass. Asher readied himself and clenched his fists, hoping the bastard didn't listen. He kept them hidden with crossed arms.

"This isn't over, Gwen." With his final threat, Julian scrambled out the door. Asher shut it behind him and locked it before turning to Gwen. Silent tears were running down her cheeks and she threw herself into his arms.

"Shh. It's okay. I'm here." He stroked a hand over her hair and down her back, repeating the gesture until she calmed against his chest. As she calmed, so did Asher, his wolf receding.

"I'm so happy you're early." She pulled back, but didn't go far, staying within the circle of his arms.

"What did he want?" Although, Asher already knew, having heard them talking on his way up the stairs. Shifter hearing was a blessing.

"He wanted me to tell him what I saw Saturday night." She wrung her hands between them.

"Come sit, Gwen." He pulled her to her couch and settled her on his lap. "Are you sure you don't want to go to the police?"

"Maybe I should." She nodded and looked up at him. "I didn't expect him to come after me again. I'm worried about what he'll do." He heard her fear.

"Would you like to stay at my place for a while?" Asher wasn't planning on bringing her that close to home so soon, but it was what would keep her safe.

"It's not just that. He's convinced he saw something. I'm worried what he will try to do about it. I'm not sure if anyone believes him. He brought Fish and Wildlife officers to the bistro today to talk to me." She turned jittery on his lap and her words flowed fast the more she said. The knowledge that he went to her earlier, and while at work, stirred Asher's control and possessiveness.

"What did you tell them?" She seemed so adamant about protecting the wolf, he didn't think she told them the truth.

"The same thing I told everyone on Saturday. I didn't see anything."

"And?" Asher prompted her to confide in him. The sooner she told him, the sooner he'd be able to tell her it was him.

"They went to inspect the alley behind the hall. Asher, what if they found something?"

"What could they find?" He already knew the answer. The only thing they could have found was a dented dumpster. Asher was sure to check for any sign himself after taking her home that night. Gwen tensed on his lap and she became increasingly agitated. Asher took her hand, drawing circles on the back to help ground her. "Talk to me," he coaxed.

"Not yet. Will you come with me to file a report with the police?" she asked quietly to change the subject.

"Of course." Asher hid his disappointment. He held her in silence a few moments longer, then helped her pack a bag and drove her to file the report. He stood over her while she recounted everything that happened that night and Julian's attempts to come at her since. He listened carefully as she relayed what Julian was saying about a beast and that there was no such thing there that night. Julian was continually being discredited. Asher could relax. But he still had to tell Gwen what he was. She was his mate and he refused to hide from her. Refused to hide his true self or the importance of her role in his life. Despite not fully knowing that himself.

After leaving the police station, he drove them straight to his place. Opening the front door for her, he paused. Kai was approaching. Asher inhaled. He wasn't alone.

"Go on in and get settled. I just have to check on something and I'll be right in." He waited, listening to her movements through the house, ensuring she wasn't near the windows to watch for him. Asher quickly strode to the woods. Kai emerged from behind a wide tree. Asher searched for the other scent. His pair reached back and pulled a pup from behind the tree. The pup was badly hurt.

"Oh, damn. What happened?" Of course, Kai wasn't able to tell him while Asher wasn't a wolf himself. He didn't have time to shift and find out. The pup might not make it as it was. "I have company in the house." Kai needed to know. "But I'll take her back and do what I can." Kai's head bobbed up and down once and he laid down behind the tree to wait. This would be a long night.

Asher took his shirt off and wrapped the pup to carry her back to the house. Maneuvering to get himself inside, he called for Gwen on his way to his kitchen table. She wasn't far into the house.

"Oh my God! What happened?"

"In the closet by the door there are sheets and a small black bag. Bring me the bag and one sheet, please." Asher spoke low and calm, but his voice sharpened to ensure she did as he said. Gwen looked shaken by the sight of his bloody shirt, but she nodded, listening carefully, and ran to the closet. She returned clutching the sheet to her chest and her knuckles were white from her tight grip on his bag. "Good. Set the bag down by the table and spread out the sheet." Shaky breaths escaped her lungs while she did as he asked.

"What happened? Are you hurt?"

"I'm not hurt and I'm not sure what happened." When she finished straightening the sheet on the table, Asher set the pup down. "How well do you handle the sight of blood?"

"I honestly have no idea." Her eyes were glued to the pup. Asher nodded, more to himself.

"Make sure the pup doesn't fall off the table." He waited for her to move closer. He didn't have to worry. The pup wasn't moving and was barely breathing. Asher washed his hands and up past his wrists. Reaching into the bag, he pulled out a pair of gloves and put them on. He set a second pair on the table for Gwen in case he needed her help more than he planned. "Go wash your hands. I'm going to need your help."

"Okay." She spoke absently as she was already walking away.

Asher inspected the pup to see where she was injured and tried to gain an understanding of what happened. She wasn't very old, he thought maybe ten weeks. Her left ear was torn horizontally across the centre. Her front right foot was injured, possibly broken. And she was covered in claw marks and puncture wounds, all deep and still bleeding. He needed to stop the bleeding.

"That's not a dog, is it?" Gwen stood at the end of the table close to his bag.

"She's a wolf pup."

"How did you find her? You were only outside a minute."

"I heard something whimpering in the bushes. I went to see what it was." The lie felt odd, a little difficult to say. Gwen might not know what she was to him, but he did.

"You must have great hearing. I didn't hear anything."

Asher kept his eyes on his patient. He concentrated on the bleeding, asking Gwen to pass him what he needed out of his bag. He hoped to avoid having to take the pup into his clinic, but he wasn't sure if that was possible. He hadn't yet brought in a wild animal, despite having treated many. He kept as much as he could in his own home for these situations. But he'd never had one struggling so hard for life as this little pup.

With the bleeding stopped and the worse bandaged and stitched, including her ear, Asher turned his attention to her foot. There were more puncture wounds and swelling. He felt the bones carefully. He couldn't feel any breaks, but it was possible there was a fracture or crack. He asked Gwen to get the splint from his bag.

Gwen hadn't said a word while he worked. She only watched the pup and quickly retrieved everything he described. While he was wrapping the splint to the pup's leg, Asher took his first real glance at Gwen. Although her face was pale and her eyes a little wide, she was steady.

"Are you all right?"

"Um... sure... yeah." She looked away from the pup and up at Asher. "Is she going to be all right?"

"I don't know. I hope so."

"Why would there be a wolf pup so close to your home?"

"An adult wolf must have left her there." Not exactly a lie.

"That doesn't make sense, does it?" Asher realized she was searching for answers to explain her own recent experience.

"No, it doesn't," he admitted. Unless the adult wolf had an unusual bond with that person, and that person could also change into a wolf. He finished by tying off the wrap. "All done. All that's left to do is watch her carefully. I may have to take her to the clinic, but the antibiotics and pain medication should work while she rests. Think you could get more sheets and blankets from that closet and make a bed for her?"

"Of course." Gwen bounced and quickly turned away toward her new task. He started the cleanup until she finished. "All done. I've set it up next to your fireplace if that's okay."

"That's perfect. Thank you." He lifted the pup and settled her in the bed. "Watch over her for me while I finish cleaning up."

"What should I watch for?" Her voice hitched with panic.

"Just make sure she keeps breathing. Holler if you need me." He crouched in front of her. Asher leaned forward and kissed her, moving his lips over hers for as long as he could hold the position. After nipping her bottom lip, he stood. He could almost hear the questions in her head. Why was she suddenly seeing wolves?

GWEN SAT on the floor next to the pup. She hadn't moved, but finally stirred a little in her sleep. Asher said that was encouraging. After cleaning up and looking in on her and the pup, he left. He didn't say where he went, just that he needed to check on something. Gwen grabbed two more blankets. She laid one over the pup and wrapped the other around her shoulders. Slowly, she used her finger to stroke the pup's nose and suddenly realized it was only Monday.

She laughed, an awkward and odd bubble that rose and pitched. A wedding, an annoying date, an amazing kiss, getting attacked, saved by a wolf, confronted twice by her attacker, a night with Asher, and helped to save a wolf pup. And it was only Monday. It couldn't really be a coincidence that this was the second time she saw a wolf in as many days. It wasn't common to see a wolf to begin with, let alone in town, or have one come to her rescue, then to help save a pup. The odds were against any one of those. Asher didn't bat an eye at the fact he found a wolf near his home, and he didn't hesitate to save her.

Didn't that just make Gwen's heart skip. He'd concentrated solely on the pup, doing everything he could. She still didn't know enough about him to have the trust in him she did. She was in his home after only seeing him in the coffee shop and spending an evening and a night with him. But she felt safe. She'd seen glimpses into the type of man he was. Any man who would save a wild animal without hesitation was a good man, selfless and honourable.

There was something else about him Gwen couldn't put her finger on. An intense attraction to him from the moment they met. A pull, a physical line connected them where she felt him, heard his heart beat. She knew she wasn't alone. He felt it too, not that he said as much. Although, they hadn't had time to talk in the past couple days.

Gwen startled as the pup pulled in a sharp breath and held it. Sitting up straighter, she waited. "Come on, baby. Breathe." Her breath finally let out with a shaky whimper. The panic in Gwen's chest settled and she sighed. She looked to the door, hoping Asher would walk in soon. The pup's breathing became normal again, normal for her current state, but she would feel better if Asher checked on her. Gwen hesitated before standing up and leaving to find him. She kept an ear on the pup as she walked to the door.

Opening the inside door, she left the screen door shut. Darkness engulfed the outdoors, and the chilly breeze blew through the screen. She tried to search the yard, but she saw nothing with the lights on inside the house.

"Asher?" Nothing. No sound or movement. "Asher?" She tried again, waiting another moment. She opened her mouth to call again when she heard something rustle in the bushes. Gwen narrowed her eyes, hoping it would help her see into the night. Asher started jogging toward her from the woods. Relief she didn't know she needed coursed down to her core.

"Is everything okay?"

"Yes. I think so. She held her breath for a little while. I thought you should check on her." He laid his hand on her back and turned back inside the house and closed the door behind him. "What were you doing in the woods?"

"Trying to find answers to how the pup was hurt." He knelt next to the pup and placed his hand on her chest for a moment and then held the back of his hand in front of her nose. "She's okay. Not out of the woods, but stable for now. We can only wait."

"Poor girl. Did you find anything out there?"

"Not exactly." He stood, his eyes lingering on the pup. "I'd say another wolf attacked her. One much older, if not a grown adult."

"That's so sad. Why would it attack a pup?" Asher pursed his lips and shook his head. She wasn't sure if that meant he didn't know, or if he didn't want to say.

Asher reached out and ran his knuckles down her cheek. Her skin heated with the contact and it didn't stop when he pulled his hand back. The line continued down her body. That same line that connected her to him. She felt her own heart thunder, but she could hear his. "Asher?" His name filtered through her gasp, quiet and filled with longing.

"You should get some sleep." Gwen saw how difficult it was for him to suggest that. "I'll watch the pup."

"Yeah." Tilting her head, she smirked and stood from the floor. "Okay."

"First door on the right. It's my room."

"Thank you." She felt his eyes on her as she walked away, still clutching the blanket around her shoulders. Her head spun. There was something she wasn't seeing. This wasn't a coincidence. She even believed waiting on Asher, on only her second day at the bistro, was meant to be.

Gwen sighed after she entered his bedroom. Sleep wouldn't come easy, but Asher was right. She needed it. At least here, she felt safe from Julian and anything he might do.

CHAPTER 6

Asher stretched on the couch after stoking the fire. The pup was finally stirring in her sleep, trying to get more comfortable. When he'd left Gwen with her, he'd gone to find Kai to ask what happened. Asher'd had an idea. A strange wolf's scent was all over her, and the teeth and claw marks were unmistakable. But a pup being attacked by another wolf made little sense.

He had entered the woods and shifted. Kai had climbed down over the hill. Asher's senses were always strong, but even more so as a wolf. He had smelled the strange wolf on him too. They'd fought. A lone wolf had come in to challenge the alpha and the pup had run in the way. Aggression made the lone wolf attack. It would only take seconds to cause that kind of damage to a tiny pup. The wolf ran off while the pack had been distracted with the hurt pup. His pair was tense, on alert. And now, so was Asher.

But he was tense for more than one reason. It wasn't only the concern of the lone wolf crouching on territory. It was Gwen. She would start asking questions soon and Asher wanted to give her the answers.

He didn't sleep well. Thoughts of the pack, Gwen, and watching the pup kept him tossing and turning. The sun would rise soon. Asher sighed and settled back down, hoping to at least rest. A piercing howl echoed down through the trees. Asher sprang from the couch. He doubted Gwen heard it. He didn't want to wake her and have her worried, but he needed to go.

He grabbed the pen and paper from the end table and scribbled a note. He left it next to the pup to be sure she'd find it. He stripped from his shirt and ran out the door. His pants went next as soon as he hit the tree line. After shifting, he ran, his paws digging into the dirt, following the scent and sounds.

The pack circled Kai and the lone wolf. He was dark grey and as large as Asher and Kai. At Asher's growl, the pack let him through the circle. He lunged at the grey wolf, hitting him in his side and knocking him over, but he was quick to recover. Twisting his head, he sank his teeth into Asher's shoulder. He grunted through the pain while Kai knocked him off. He got a hold of Kai's neck and Asher did the same to him, dislodging his grip. They continued back and forth, he was strong, until Asher and Kai finally had him pinned to the ground.

The grey wolf's eyes, a deep grey to match his fur, brightened and focused on Asher.

You're different. The two white wolves growled in unison. *I'm like him.* His eyes darted to Kai. The implication suddenly hit Asher. He flew into a panic, pushing the grey wolf further into the ground.

Where's the other like me?

Gone. Asher could smell the despair and anger on him.

His name? Asher snapped his jaws.

Zachary. From Hull Creek.

You don't touch another member of this pack. It's up to him what's to be done with you. Asher released him, but Kai still kept him pinned to the ground. The grey wolf didn't attempt to get up. Asher paced, his shoulders sore from the bites.

He knew there had to be more. But he was gone. He looked back at the grey wolf. *Gone how?*

I don't know.

Asher looked at his pair, not needing to ask. Kai nodded. He would keep the wolf close, allow him into the pack temporarily until Asher could find Zachary. Hull Creek was a few hours north of here.

Asher continued to pace, trying to calm himself before heading home to Gwen. It was morning, and he needed to get back. He searched the pack and did a check on Kai for any injuries. He also gave an update on the pup.

Starting back to his house, he couldn't run as fast as he had when leaving. His shoulders hurt. They would heal soon. Injuries didn't last long for a shifter. But Gwen would still see them in the meantime. Shifting was painful with the wounds that also had to shift to conform to his human body. He found his pants, which he left in plain sight, and put them on. Barefoot and bleeding, he walked to his house, knowing he would have to tell Gwen something.

I NEED TO LEAVE. I'll be back.

I don't know when and you won't be able to reach me.

Stay in the house and stay with the pup.

I'm sorry.

Gwen read the note again, the paper starting to wrinkle from moving it between her fingers for the past few hours. She woke from the bang of the door and made it to the living room in time to see a shirtless and barefoot Asher race into the trees. She wanted to follow him and if it weren't for the pup, she would have.

Although confused at first, she remained calm while tending the pup who was waking for a few minutes at a time, had a shower, and made breakfast. But now, Gwen was worrying. Why would he need to race into the woods, only leaving a vague note behind? She wondered how often he did something like this.

She called the bistro and told Walker there was an emergency and she wasn't sure what time she would get in today. He sounded fine with it, but guilt still settled in Gwen. She didn't understand what kind of emergency it was or how it affected her. She would offer time off to whoever Walker got to cover her shift.

She rubbed her hands over her face in frustration, she stood abruptly, startling the pup.

"Oh, I'm sorry girl." She crouched down and petted her nose until she settled again. Gwen moved to the window and watched the spot where she saw Asher disappear. Just as she itched to leave and find him, he emerged, his gait slow and his shoulders and chest covered in red. Her hand raised to cover her gasp. She bolted from the house and met him halfway across his yard.

"What the hell happened to you?" She took his arm, thinking he needed help, but he was still standing straight and walking fine except for his speed.

"Would you believe a fight with a wolf?"

"Yes. I would. As long as it wasn't a white one," she snapped, unable to let go of her frustration. She was certain everything that happened and everything she'd seen was some sort of Fate.

"A white one, huh?" His lips twitched. He knew something. Did he know she lied about Julian's story? "How's the pup?"

"She's fine," Gwen snapped again. "Waking up for short periods of time." She couldn't keep the sharpness from her voice.

"She did that through the night too. It's a good sign." His smooth tone was that of a normal morning at the bistro. They got into the house and she pushed him to the kitchen. He turned his head over his shoulder to look at her, but allowed himself to be moved.

"Where are you hurt?"

"Bites on both shoulders. I'll be fine."

"Seriously? You'll be fine? You're a vet. You should know better. They need to be looked at." She couldn't believe he was smiling at her, laughter in his eyes, while she continued to yell at him. He took her hand, guiding her down into a chair while he took the one beside her and faced her.

"Gwen, what did you mean outside when you mentioned a white wolf?" The way he asked so calmly and held her eyes, she was certain he knew something.

"What do you think I meant?" She threw the immature question back at him. It would be easier for him to put the puzzle together himself, and all she would have to do was nod along.

"Tell me." His demand was calm. She held onto her frustration when his solid face and deep eyes could easily calm her down.

"No! We still don't know each other very well."

He laughed. "You're right." Gwen pulled her hand away and crossed her arms with a huff. "I grew up not far from here. I have one younger sister. I opened my veterinary clinic here in town as soon as I graduated and got back from school."

"And did you always want to be a vet?"

"No, I didn't. I figured that out when I was eighteen, but that's a story for another time."

"Well, okay then." She huffed again.

"Now, what about you?" He mimicked her tone with a mock frown. Laughter burst from Gwen, hearing how silly she sounded scolding him with questions when he was sitting in front of her bleeding.

"My dad owns like five or more businesses in town, I've lost count. He has a partner for some of them, Julian's father." She paused a moment to allow the connection to sink in. "Not really a Jack of all trades himself, but his businesses are. My mom was a stay-at-home mom to an only child who is twenty-three years old and is unsure what she will do with her life, but enjoys her job at the bistro."

"Speaking of your job. Are you comfortable going to work where Julian can find you?"

"I already called and said there was an emergency and that I'd be in as soon as I could. I won't be alone. I'll be fine. As long as you can come pick me up." Her voice dropped and colour flooded her cheeks. It was a little embarrassing to feel she couldn't take care of herself, to be afraid of someone like Julian.

Asher cupped her jaw and ran his thumb along her lips. "Of course, I'll pick you up."

Gwen drew her attention to Asher's bloody shoulders to keep the heat from his touch from spreading through her body.

"I won't be long and we'll leave."

"What about the pup?" Asher paused behind her. "And what about your shoulders?"

"I'll have someone look in on her throughout the day if I can't come back and forth. And my shoulders will be fine."

He left, heading toward his bedroom. Gwen sat next to the pup on the floor while she waited. She lifted her head and looked trustingly up at Gwen.

"I think it's time you have a name, don't you? How does Cinder sound?" The pup nudged her hand with her wet nose and settled back down to sleep. She had to agree. Sleep sounded like a great option. All of her unanswered questions left Gwen feeling drained.

"GOOD MORNING, Laura. Can you do me a favour?" Asher walked into his clinic, thankfully before any patients arrived. "Something has come up that I need to take care of soon. Can you look through my appointments for the next couple days and reschedule anything that isn't urgent and create a couple large blocks of time?"

"Sure thing. I hope everything is okay?" She started opening up his calendar on her computer.

"It is. Just something I need to do sooner rather than later."

Laura got him most of the afternoon off and tomorrow morning. He worked through lunch and finished up. He sent Laura and the rest of his staff home. Luckily, they didn't have any animals spending the night in the clinic. Asher sat at his computer and started a search for Zachary from Hull Creek. Hull Creek wasn't much larger than Alder Ridge or this list of possibilities would become too large too fast. As it was, he had five to look through, and that was after narrowing down by age based on the age of the grey wolf, and by structure. The last was an assumption. Asher assumed his own body structure and strength was due to being a shifter. The grey wolf was a similar size and strength to Asher and Kai, so he searched for his own age plus or minus five years.

Two of the five had died and the other three, as far as Asher could tell, were fine and living in Hull Creek at the moment. If Zachary had kept the other half of himself as secret as Asher, then there would be no way for Asher to figure out who he was by searching on the computer.

But there was one way.

He found head shots of each of the five and arranged them into one image and printed it off. Folding and tucking the paper into his pocket, he left and drove for home.

Asher checked on the pup, making sure she was hydrated and offered her a little food to see if she would eat. Then he headed straight for the woods.

Halfway to their territory, he allowed himself a partial internal shift to change his voice. He howled, letting them know he was coming. Kai and the grey wolf met him on the outskirts. Kai wasn't letting the grey wolf out of his sight.

Asher pulled out the paper and laid it on the ground in front of the wolf. "Which one is your Zachary?"

The wolf only stared. Asher sighed. He straightened and stripped so he could shift. As soon as the ache from the change left and he shook himself off, Asher asked again.

Which one is your Zachary?

None.

Is there anything else you can tell me about how to find him?

No. The wolf's head hung low. There wasn't a human scent on him. They must have been separated for too long. Asher couldn't sense any tension between him and Kai. The grey wolf seemed to accept his temporary home, no longer carrying uncontrolled anger at Zachary's disappearance. It was all replaced with worry and fear. Asher understood.

The bond between himself and Kai was strong. He had to assume it was the same for all of them.

Asher shifted back and dressed. "I'll keep looking." He ran his hand over each of the large animals, an animal that held so much of his soul, and left, feeling discouraged himself.

He was unsettled. He had confirmation that he wasn't the only one, not just an assumption or a scent he couldn't pinpoint. Asher needed to see Gwen. To ensure she was all right, to ensure he was all right.

He arrived at the bistro just in time to see Julian enter from the side entrance, but he didn't approach the counter. He sat and pulled his hood lower, his eyes darting out to search for Gwen. Asher hung back. Instead of going to Gwen himself, he stepped outside the doors and called the bistro. Gwen answered.

"Gwen, it's Asher."

"Hi." Her voice softened.

"I don't want to scare you, but it looks like you'll have a follower. I think it's safer if he doesn't know you're with me. He doesn't need to know where to find you when you don't show up at home." He could hear her swallow through the receiver. "It's okay, Gwen. I won't let him get near you. But we need to get you out of there and in my truck without him seeing you or me."

"Okay. Pull around to the street behind the bistro. I can cut through the lots to get to you. I'll send Walker over to distract Julian."

"You sure?"

"Yes. I'll be there in about five minutes." She hung up and went back to the customers as if nothing was wrong. Asher watched Julian to see if he showed any sign of leaving. Gwen's shift wouldn't end for another hour. If Asher were in his shoes, he'd leave shortly before her and wait in the parking lot.

He saw Walker talking with Gwen, and moments later Walker went to Julian's table, attempting to take an order. Asher dashed to his truck and drove around the block. His breath stuck in his chest while he waited for Gwen to show. He left her to get herself out of there alone. He should be with her. Asher had the windows rolled down so he would be sure to hear her and catch her scent, or any others that might come along behind her.

There, floral and coconut sifted through his truck with the breeze. The same scent that nearly brought him to his knees the first time he smelled it. She got in the truck and Asher quickly drove off, taking turns at random, bringing himself to a long way around town to get to his house. He wasn't taking any chances that Walker couldn't distract him.

"You probably didn't have to do all that. I asked Walker to call me if he left the bistro within half an hour of me leaving."

"Good."

"You know, he might think to look for me with you. You're the one I left with after the wedding. And the one who interrupted him at my apartment."

"True. But better he suspects than has confirmation. And I have places we can go if he comes around."

"Where? In the woods?" She tried to be funny, but Asher only glanced sideways at her.

So much was weighing on Asher's mind, but finally having his mate beside him brought him some peace.

GWEN CHANGED into pajamas after having a shower. It felt good to wash the day off, especially when that day started and ended with panic. She reached the living room as Asher was coming in from outside carrying a couple bottles of wine.

"You're a smart man."

"So I've been told." Laughter crinkled the corners of his eyes.

"How are your shoulders?" She reached up to touch one, her hand barely hovering above the bloody marks she'd seen that morning.

"They're fine." Not an ounce of pain showed in his features, but they must hurt.

"Did you get them taken care of?" She had wanted to take care of them herself.

"They're taken care of." He kissed her forehead and stepped back. Disappointment tickled her chest at how he brushed off her concern.

"How's Cinder?" she called to him while she went in the other direction to check on the pup for herself.

"Cinder?" He appeared behind her. "Ah, you named her. She's doing better. Still a ways to go, but I'm pleased with her progress."

"What will happen to her when she's healed? Will she have to go to a wildlife sanctuary?"

"No. She'll go back to her pack. Actually, she'll go back fairly soon."

"Soon? How can she do that while her leg is still healing?"

"I'll explain later. Want a glass of wine?" He was changing the subject, but at least he didn't lie. He said he would explain, and she believed him. She had a little explaining of her own to do.

"Absolutely," she said, closing her eyes and tilting her head back. Gwen stood from the floor. Asher already had two glasses poured when she got to the kitchen. "Dinner smells amazing."

"It's nothing special, but I can cook a decent meal."

"I'm the same. For years I've tried to duplicate my mother's recipes and no matter what I do, I never get them quite right. But the basics to cook something edible, even tasty, I can do that."

"So, why so unsure of what you want to do for a living? Did you have a dream growing up?"

"No, I didn't. Nothing that stuck anyway. I figured the only way to know would be to put myself out there on my own. I'm thankful my parents supported that." Gwen suddenly felt silly realizing that she was twenty-three, just beginning life on her own. And he was a vet with his own clinic. "How old are you?"

He flashed a smile over his shoulder as he stirred something on the stove. "I'm twenty-nine." From the look in his eyes, he knew what just crossed her mind. "Does that bother you?"

"I don't think so."

"You don't think so?" Even his deep voiced elevated as he tried not to laugh.

"I hadn't really thought about it. Until now." Their attraction, the mystical line that attached them, was too strong for the age gap to bother her.

An awkward silence engulfed the kitchen while Asher cooked and they sipped their wine. Gwen offered to help, but he wouldn't take it. Eventually she wandered back to Cinder, happy to see her more awake.

"Here." It was only a few moments and Asher was handing her a plate.

"I can come back to the kitchen."

"In here is more comfortable, and it's good to give... Cinder... some company."

"Thank you." Gwen settled herself on the couch and held the plate against her chest. They ate while they watched Cinder. The company and the smell of food seemed to rouse her. Asher finished first and took his plate out to the kitchen. He came back with a couple small dishes. He sat on the floor next to her and held the dishes for her one at a time. One held water, the other looked like raw meat. Gwen wrinkled her nose. Cinder slowly picked at the meat and drank down half the water. When she tried to move to adjust herself, she whimpered, but she settled herself into a new position.

"It's good to see her eat a little." Gwen's heart melted for the pup. She was so strong to recover from that kind of attack.

"It is. I think she will be just fine. Only time will tell at this point." With Cinder asleep, Asher moved himself to the couch. He reached over, lifting Gwen and maneuvered her so she straddled his lap. "It's been a crazy few days, hasn't it?"

"Very."

"Then I think we could both use this." His hand traced around the back of her neck and he pulled her down. She might be above him, but in no way did she feel in control. His lips layered over hers and moved, commanding, demanding, forcing her to let go and submit to him. Her hands flattened on his chest and she sank closer to him to feel the taut muscles under his shirt. She craved to feel his skin.

Part of her mind told her to pull back, to stop, so they could talk. There was so much left unsaid this morning. But her body wouldn't listen. Not with his lips on hers or his hands beginning to wander. He wasn't as frantic as the first time, but she could feel that changing, feel his heart, feel his heat. Her body changed its rhythm to match his.

She could feel the same spell that seemed to control both of them last time building now. Gwen wanted the opportunity to look and feel for herself before it took control this time. Gripping his shirt, she pulled it from his waist and started undoing the buttons. Asher leaned them forward when she finished and Gwen pushed his shirt open and down his shoulders, mindful of the bites. He released her so he could finish taking it off and Gwen had a moment with an unimpeded view. But it wasn't the view she expected.

The bites on his shoulders were barely scars, almost fully healed.

"Your shoulders. How?" She pushed back on his chest and stared open mouthed at the healing skin, his tribal tattoo below his left shoulder returning to its normal shape. He didn't answer right away. Instead, he sighed and started lifting her shirt.

"I told you my shoulders would be okay." He pulled up, lifting her arms and taking her shirt off.

"I don't understand."

"I know." Asher reached around and undid her bra. As soon as the garment was free, he pulled her back down and reclaimed her mouth. Gwen's questions about his shoulders vanished. Her hands skated up his abdomen and chest, her fingers flexing along the way. It should irritate her that she couldn't control her thoughts.

Her arousal and heat skyrocketed. Instinctively, she knew no other man could give her what Asher could. Sex and connection with someone else would never measure up.

It was something about him, or him and her together, that created this bond, this almost physical line between them. If there came a time that she needed to let him go, she wasn't sure if she'd be capable of it.

GWEN'S QUESTIONS about his shoulders almost brought Asher out of the moment. But restlessness inside kept him on his goal. He knew they needed to talk, and too much had happened for him to put off telling her what he was any longer, but he needed her. It took all his energy to act as sensibly as he did at the bistro when emotions screamed at him to go to her and carry her into the woods where she'll be safe, surrounded by a pack of wolves. They both needed to get this out of their systems. He only hoped he could fight the urge to mark her. Marking her before telling her what he was wasn't fair. She didn't deserve that.

Asher moved his hands down to her ass. With a firm grip, he lifted her and stood. She broke the kiss and gasped.

"What about Cinder?" She looked over his shoulder to the pup curled up by the fire.

"Would you rather she watched?" Asher's lips twitched.

"No! Of course not." She laughed through her indignation. "Besides, she's asleep."

"Then she'll be okay." He sauntered to his bedroom and threw Gwen onto the bed. He chuckled when she bounced and yelped. He grabbed her ankles and pulled her toward him so he could rid her of her pants. She sighed and her eyes looked their fill down his torso and paused at the button on his jeans. "Is there something you're looking for?"

"Definitely," she said with husky confidence, not moving her sight away from his groin.

Asher released the button and zipper and pulled his pants and boxers down over his hips. Gwen moved herself into a sitting position on the bed.

"I want to do something this time." Her confidence went as quickly as it showed and she seemed to be asking him permission, but Asher didn't answer her. He only waited to see what she would do on her own.

Gwen moved to the edge of the bed so her face was level with his cock. Asher's breath caught in his chest and every inch of him tensed. Her tongue peaked out and she raised her hand to wrap around the base. He had to clench his jaw to keep from protesting. Not that he wasn't about to enjoy every second, but his control was still so fragile, he didn't want to scare her. He was sure his face must look angry with how rigid he was. But she didn't falter when her eyes darted upward before she leaned in with her mouth slowly opening.

The first touch of her lips sent a jolt into his body where it spread throughout his limbs. He wished he could have held in his growl. It was low and more wolf-like than he wanted, but after only a second of hesitation she continued, moving her head forward to engulf half his cock. He squeezed his eyes shut, knowing the erotic sight of her brown hair and full lips moving back and forth on him would erase his control. His air was sharp through his nose, panting through the ecstasy she gave him. Her movements were slow. He itched to sink his hands into her hair and speed her up, allowing himself to spill down her throat. Asher couldn't take this away from her. So he kept his eyes closed, fists clenched, and breathing sharp so he wouldn't touch her and ruin her plans.

But it only took moments for his canines to lengthen and his body to hum with the urge to mark her. Running his tongue over his teeth to gauge their length, he growled and fisted her hair. He thrust into her mouth a couple times before pulling her off. But her face nearly broke his heart.

"It's not you, Gwen. My control is slipping." Her face turned down. She didn't understand what he meant, but she would.

Asher pushed her back on the bed and ran his hands up her legs. He pressed his thumb over her nub and set his mouth to her entrance to drink in the juices caused by her own ministrations to him. Her sounds, her moans and cries, and especially her taste spurred him on, and he fucked her with his tongue while his thumb drew circles and applied pressure.

As soon as her hips thrust toward him, he switched. He covered her clit and suckled as his two fingers thrust quickly into her pussy. Asher had to hold her still with his other hand clamped onto her hip, using a little more strength than he normally would on another person, especially with a woman in his bed. He expected to see bruises in the morning.

Curling his fingers, he worked hard to bring her to a quick orgasm. His canines lengthened again at her cries through the spasms of her climax. But he couldn't stop himself. He didn't let up until he pushed her immediately into another peak and fall. He slowed and matched the rhythm of her pussy walls.

Gwen whimpered on a sigh and Asher released her to move up her body, aligning himself along the way. He angled her hips and thrust in, her lips swollen but slick. His control almost vanished as he pounded into her, grinding against her with each thrust. He wanted to stop himself, but Gwen's next words sealed their fate.

"Asher. I don't know what's going on." She panted. "There's something missing. This can't be real. I need more."

"What do you need, Gwen?" His gravely baritone staggered from his chest with fear of what he knew he was about to do. He didn't let up his pace with their conversation. Her pussy tightened and his orgasm swelled at the base of his spine.

"I don't know. I don't understand. I should be fine after what you just did to me. I need more." He understood all too well what she needed, but it shocked him she felt the same urge running through her.

With all control gone, his teeth lengthened and there was no holding back. Asher roared as he came then quickly leaned down and buried his face. His teeth sank into her unmarred skin where her shoulder met her neck. Relief coursed through his body at the same time Gwen's climax coursed through hers.

There was no return now. Of that, Asher was sure. He licked and sucked on the wound on her shoulder, then watched it miraculously heal over into a light crescent mark.

Their breaths deepened and their bodies slowed. They matched each other's rhythms until they wrapped around each other and fell asleep. Asher hadn't wanted to do that to her, but he didn't regret it. Her body wanted it as much as his. This was out of both of their control.

CHAPTER 7

Lying with Asher, Gwen felt the first sense of contentment since she started her job at the bistro and Julian hung around more. She sighed while her fingers drew random designs over Asher's chest. He just settled back into bed after getting Cinder and bringing her to the bedroom. Gwen had thought it might be difficult to convince him, but with a smile he tried to hide, he'd conceded and came back carrying her and her bed of blankets wrapped around her.

Asher captured her hand, stopping her fingers. He pulled it up to his lips and kissed her palm, then pulled her up and sat up with her. She watched him arrange the pillows and settle himself against them. Even being as massive as he was, he moved with grace.

"Gwen. I need to ask you something?"

"Okay." She drew the word out and pulled the sheet up to cover herself. She wasn't trying to hide from him, but his tone made it sound like it wouldn't be a light-hearted question that fit their current mood.

"Why did you say as long as it wasn't a white wolf this morning?"

"You really want to finish that conversation now?" Her voice spiked with surprise. That hadn't been what she was expecting. Gwen wanted to talk about it, but not now, not in the vivid serenity that overcame them.

"Yes." His firm answer made it hard to deny him.

"Okay, but you have to promise not to think I'm crazy." She hunched into her cross-legged position and peaked up at him to watch his face carefully for any changes.

"I promise."

"How can you promise not to think I'm crazy when you don't know what I'm going to say?"

"Trust me. I promise." He took her free hand and gently nipped her fingertips. Every time he used any part of his mouth, a small piece of her melted. She was sure there were parts of her that would never re-solidify. She had to pull her hand back to allow herself to speak.

"Julian isn't wrong, except when he says there was a beast. It wasn't a beast. It was a big, beautiful, white wolf with eyes the same colour as yours. And he saved me. He jumped down from the roof, yes he really came from the roof, and he forced Julian to move away from me. He lunged at Julian and pushed him over. That's when Julian hit his head and knocked himself out."

"Then the wolf turned to you and sat down until you calmed. Then he walked over to you so you could touch him."

"Yes." Gwen lifted her head. "How did you know?"

Instead of answering, Asher's eyes flashed. They brightened and changed to the shape of the wolf's. She gasped and flinched, gripping the sheet, but didn't pull away from him. It was still Asher in front of her.

"It was you," she whispered. "But how? I don't understand." A form of shock numbed her body. She really didn't understand how that was possible. She should be scared. Gwen acknowledged the thought, but she wasn't scared. That wolf had saved her and so had Asher. Asher also saved a wolf pup. He wouldn't hurt her. "I don't understand." She unknowingly echoed herself, her body and voice reacting on their own without direction from her mind.

"It was me. I'm a shifter. I can change into a wolf." He spoke carefully, pausing between each sentence.

"So, we've both gone crazy. Because that probably makes more sense." Her tone was that of talking more to herself than to Asher. She sounded distant when she didn't mean to be.

"You're right. That's definitely a more sensible explanation. But it isn't true."

"No, it isn't." She didn't need to see his eyes flash like they had to know the truth. "How?"

"It's a bit of a story."

Gwen spread her hand out, gesturing to the empty and dim bedroom. "We aren't busy now."

Asher smiled, nodded, and told his tale.

"I was seven and the sound of the wind woke me in the middle of the night. When I looked out my window, I could see the wind, not just the trees moving because of it, but I could see the physical wind moving through the air. I went outside to look closer. The wind came at me and urged me into the woods. The woods behind my parents' place connects to the ones behind mine and they're mildly thick, not even small clearings. You'll always find trees, rocks, bushes taking up space. Except that night. Not far in, there was a perfect circle. The moon was huge and bright and shone directly above it. A white wolf pup with sharp blue eyes came out. Being seven, I thought it was a dog, until his mother showed up and growled. The wind stopped her. Somehow, she understood what was going on, and she stayed back and let me play with her pup. When we were done and tired, the wind started circling us, creating a wall. When it left, I was a wolf pup identical to the one I'd been playing with. After a while, I changed back to myself and left."

Gwen had so many questions, but Asher wasn't fully with her. His eyes had focused across the room. His mind had settled on that night.

"Sometimes, I felt I grew up with two lives. One as a wolf and the other human. I've never found another like me, so everything I know of being a shifter, what we are, what we're capable of, physiology, psychology, I've had to learn only from other wolves, my own reactions and experiences coupled with research that has widely varied depending on the origins." He paused, seeming to come back to himself. His eyes landed on her. Eyes that she now saw differently, her perspective forever changed. "I thought I learned all I could on my own until I met you."

"What do you mean?"

"Your scent almost brought me to my knees. Once I got past that, it stirred protective, and possessive, emotions mixed with heavy arousal. It took me longer than I'd like to admit to realize what all of that meant."

"And what did all of that mean?" Her voice squeaked as her belly turned.

"That you're my mate." He was still relaxed against the wall, but he wouldn't let go of her hand.

"Your mate? What does all that entail?" Gwen asked carefully, narrowing her eyes. Asher's expression turned thoughtful, and he hesitated before answering.

"I'm not sure about all the details. Only way to find out is to go through it. I do know that as each day passes, it's harder and harder to keep my hands off you. And now that I bit you, your taste is so far in my system it's both calming and is driving me crazy."

"Why did you bite me?" She knew what he'd done in that moment and she wouldn't have changed it. Something was missing and she begged him to fix it. He did, and the feeling was indescribable.

"From the first time in your apartment, I wanted to. I didn't know why. The urge was there, something calling me to mark you. I couldn't resist tonight. I just wish we had talked this through before I did it. I don't know the consequences."

The blue in Asher's eyes deepened and the muscles surrounding them softened, content radiating from him, while he talked about consequences. And rising panic was taking over Gwen's breathing.

"Gwen?" Asher straightened and gently pushed on her back to lean her forward while she tried to catch her breath.

"Consequences?" she asked between gasps.

"I'm sorry. I worded that wrong."

"You think?" Gwen concentrated on her breathing until it was even. She straightened and looked at Asher. She saw so much more of him now, understood so much more. And her feelings toward him were making sense. But were they hers, his, or Fate's?

WATCHING GWEN PANIC, Asher cursed himself for his word choice. He didn't expect negative consequences, but what or if this would do anything to her, he didn't know. Asher also had the sense this sealed their bond. She was inside him. He felt every part of her without touching her. Her panic increased his own heart rate.

He ran his hand slowly from her head and down her back, stopping at the very base of her spine before repeating the motion.

"I'm sorry, Gwen." She calmed with his motions.

"I'm not mad at you, or mad at all really. It's just so unreal and I'm still reeling about what you are that my role in this pushed me over the edge to overwhelmed." She looked up, eyes wide with worry, and let out a heavy sigh. "You really don't know anything?"

"I'm sorry, no. I've had to learn as I go. I've had no one to confide in and no one to exchange notes and experiences with."

"So, the wind did this to you?" Gwen sat straight, her spine lengthening. She placed a hand on her chest and continued to take controlled breaths.

"I don't believe that's what happened, not exactly anyway. The wind played an important role, but I don't think it was solely responsible. Do I have any evidence to support that? No. That's just my opinion." Asher had many theories over the years, and he did what he could to prove each of them with no luck. But he somehow knew there was more to it than the white wind.

"Mate." Her nose scrunched. "It sounds so..."

"Barbaric?" He offered.

"Yeah. If this is all just as new to you, why did you choose that word?"

"It's like a whisper through my veins. I hear it echo in my body. Just that single word when you're near. It grows stronger the closer I am to you, the more intimate I am with you." He paused. "Gwen, let's just take this one day at a time.

I might not have explanations for either of us, but I have a pretty good idea what this means. And I think you do too."

She nodded slowly, acceptance clear on her face. She settled against his chest and they both laid back in the bed. Her body shook, sending a moment of amusement from her vibrations into him. She was laughing. "You're a vet."

"Yes. So?"

"Talk about a wolf in sheep's clothing." Asher held in his own laughter while Gwen's overtook her, finding her own joke more amusing. He settled and waited for her to calm down. Finally, she did, then turned her head and rested her chin on her hand. "Unless I was in more shock than I realized and it's affecting my memory, you're much bigger than the average wolf."

"I am," he answered lazily. Her eyes rolled to the side for a moment, looking like she was thinking back.

"That night wasn't a full moon." Her aha moment burst with accusation. Asher couldn't hold in his chuckle.

"Shifting isn't dependent on the moon. I can shift at will."

"So how did you really know about Cinder being in the woods?"

Asher sifted through how much he told her. "I told you about the white wolf pup in the clearing the night I first shifted. He changed too. Not in the same sense as me, but his aging slowed and his growth matched mine. We became identical. He's my pair. That night I named him Kai. He brought Cinder to the edge of the woods. When we got here, I smelled him, and her."

"Smelled?" Her eyes widened and her jaw slackened.

"Yes, smelled. Wolves have a strong sense of smell as I'm sure you know. Kai and I have an even stronger one."

"How did you find me in the alley?" Gwen asked with

quiet suspicion. She was putting some of the pieces together.

"I was at the bar when I heard you scream. I knew you went outside and as soon as I got out there, I knew where you were and who you were with."

"Safe to say, all your senses are heightened."

Asher nodded and watched her settle back down.

Gwen yawned and sighed.

"It's a lot to take in. Sleep." He gently kissed her hair and held her close, breathing her in.

"Just one more thing." Sleep fogged her voice.

"What is it?"

"Thank you."

"For what?"

"For saving me. My white knight. My white wolf." Gwen drifted off to sleep.

FOR THE REST of the week, things felt almost normal. Since discovering Julian spying on her at the bistro, Gwen allowed Asher to drive her back and forth to work. It didn't take much convincing for Walker to let her change her schedule to match Asher's. Knowing what Julian did, and that he was now stalking her, was more than enough for him.

She was jumpy, on edge, and paranoid. Any person who walked past the bistro or came inside with their face hidden made Gwen's heart race. She never thought she'd fear him. She wanted to focus on Asher, ask all the questions that entered her mind. But she was increasingly worried about Julian. There had been two more times that week where it wasn't her paranoia. Either she or Asher spotted him. Gwen wanted to know his intentions, where his attention was. Was it on her because she reported him to the police? Or was he still trying to find the beast, find Asher?

Gwen knew it wouldn't be long until he started looking into Asher to find her with him. Asher was at the wedding and he showed up at her apartment. The connection was obvious.

Each day after work, Asher carefully drove them back to his place, often finding Julian himself first to ensure he wasn't following them. He checked his own property a few times in the evenings to look for signs of Julian, or anyone else for that matter. Gwen noticed he also often checked on his parents, who didn't live far away. Asher hadn't introduced her to them yet, but that didn't bother Gwen. Things were very new even against the standards of a normal relationship. But nothing about them was standard. Well, she was standard. An average woman in her early twenties. A simple job, life, friends, family. Until recently. It was Asher that was an odd phenomenon. And now they had connected in a way in which she wasn't prepared.

Each night in bed, they couldn't keep themselves apart. The bond was too strong. That physical, invisible line that connected them grew thicker and pulled shorter. Each time they joined, there were moments of calm and playfulness, then the rest was frantic. Neither could suppress their needs and desires, taking each other to new heights. Asher promised he was normally a controlled person. She believed him. Except in bed.

She woke each morning with minor bruises from his delicious grip. It surprised Gwen to see them fade faster each day. When she first noticed a significant change in them, she kept notes. She hadn't told Asher about her note keeping. Gwen wanted to observe things for herself. He said he didn't know what consequences biting her, marking her as he called it, would have. Maybe nothing, but Gwen monitored herself to learn exactly what the consequences were.

There was more that weighed on her mind. She felt they weren't getting to know each other well. Not well enough for the serious relationship Fate put them in. She wasn't worried about getting to know his wolf side. All those answers would come. She wanted to know what he was like as a person. She'd seen quite a bit as it was. His family was important to him, and he kept a close eye on all of them. He rescued Cinder without hesitation. Gwen believed his actions would have been the same if Cinder wasn't part of his pair's pack.

Getting to know each other seemed so far down on her list of priorities at the moment. The rest of her life kept it forced to the bottom. If Asher didn't wear her out each night, she knew she would lose sleep worrying about Julian's actions.

Gwen should feel relieved it was Friday night and she could steer clear of town and the bistro for a couple days, but she didn't. Anxiety she didn't know she had was bubbling roughly inside her chest.

"Something is wrong. I've smelled it on you all week, and it isn't getting better."

"You can smell that something is wrong?"

"Some shifter senses, like increased scent and hearing, allow me to gauge someone's emotions. Pain, sorrow, joy, jealousy, arousal." His voice dropped the further down the list he went. When he growled at like that, her body reacted all on its own, despite what she was feeling. One side of his mouth pulled up with a cocky lift. "I can also sense a lie."

"I guess that makes sense."

"So, what is it?" Asher sat on the ottoman in front of her. She was curled up with Cinder on her lap on the couch. The little grey pup had finally fallen back asleep. Gwen sighed and sank further into the cushions.

"I don't know you. And you don't know me. But we don't really have the opportunity to fix that. I can't stop worrying about Julian's intentions. I don't understand why he's been stalking me. Is he after me? Or is he still looking for you, looking for the beast?"

"I think you've underestimated us."

"What do you mean?"

"I've learned a lot about you."

"Oh, really?" she challenged.

"You're compassionate, empathetic, graceful. You're a fighter. And you're loyal. It didn't matter that Julian attacked you and tried to rape you. You thought first of hurting his parents, and you gave him the benefit of the doubt. You were willing to excuse him for that. But when he attacked you, you weren't only scared, you were pissed." His emphasis and quirk of a smile showed pride. "That anger gave you courage to move past the whole thing. You gave your loyalty to me before you even knew who I was. You were loyal to the white wolf. Not once did you allow anyone to believe Julian's claims of a beast for fear of someone hurting me. I might not know many of your favourites. I might not know any odd quirks you have. But I know your heart. I feel it as if it's my own."

"Well," she cleared her throat, dislodging the knot. Gwen swiped at a tear on one cheek at the same time Asher swiped at the other with his thumb. "I guess you proved me wrong."

Maybe Asher was right. Their bond was showing them more than what Gwen could see at the moment. This was Fate's design, it seemed. Gwen had to believe She knew what She was doing.

CHAPTER 8

"**B**ut you do snore."

"Excuse me? I do not." Gwen pulled back, a severe bend to her brow.

"You do," he said in all seriousness. "It's just a slight snore. But to someone who's part wolf with sensitive ears, it's loud." Gwen's jaw went slack, and Asher couldn't hold in his laugh any longer. As soon as it burst free, Gwen punched him in the shoulder, but he didn't budge.

"You're awful. You lie," she exclaimed, her voice lowered with mock anger.

"I'm not, but it doesn't actually bother me. It's almost cute. Almost." Asher caught her wrist when she tried to shove him again.

"Yeah. Well..." she stammered, "I have nothing." Asher used the grip on her wrist to pull her forward. He met her halfway so they didn't squish Cinder in her lap, and kissed her. He kept it chaste, then released her and returned to the kitchen.

The hairs on the back of his neck stood on end. He

opened his senses. His ears picked up crunching gravel, and he breathed deep.

"Stay inside. Don't go near the windows."

"What is it?" Gwen stood, holding Cinder in her arms. Asher didn't want to lie, but he wasn't entirely certain what it was. He only enforced his order with a look, his eyes flashing slightly. "Okay." She carried Cinder upstairs.

Asher stepped onto the deck. The scent was familiar, but he was still too far away to have told Gwen and make her worry in case Asher was wrong. But what worried him more was that Kai and the grey wolf were nearby. He hoped they stayed out of sight and that Julian did nothing to draw them out. Asher inhaled. Julian, assuming his nose was right, was coming up the lane close to the tree line, but he wasn't in sight yet. Asher bolted across his yard and into the woods. He startled the grey wolf who jumped out from the bush with bared teeth. Kai stepped out slowly and snapped his jaws at the same time Asher shushed him.

"You two stay back and close to the house. Let me know if he gets too close, but don't go after him. Don't let him see either of you." Asher watched the two wolves disappear into the bush again before moving deeper into the trees and following the line of the lane. Asher spotted him and he'd been right. It was Julian. Julian crouched to the ground and pulled out a small set of binoculars from the pocket of his hoodie. He aimed them at the house. Asher was thankful he'd told Gwen to stay away from the windows. He hoped she listened.

Asher could stop him now, he could step out and get rid of him, but he wanted to know what he would do. How far was he going to take this? What kind of threat was he going to turn into?

Asher stood still and watched. Julian had more patience

than he would have imagined. He wasn't sure how long Gwen would stay still inside the house. Asher evened his breathing and focused. Julian was thorough. He looked carefully over Asher's house, the yard and property, up and down the lane, and into the woods. He didn't see Asher or the wolves. A slight scent of frustration came from him on the breeze. He put the binoculars back in his pocket and moved out into the lane and started walking toward the house as if that was his intention all along.

Asher became unsettled as he followed Julian back through the woods and more distance separated them as he approached the house. He met up with Kai and the grey wolf. They watched Julian knock on Asher's door. Asher listened for any movement from Gwen. He heard nothing. Julian knocked again, and then a third time. With a glance over his shoulder and around the yard, Julian opened the screen door and reached for the knob. That was as far as Asher was willing to let this go. He was too close to Asher's mate.

Just as Asher took a step toward his house, so did the grey wolf. He lunged and ran toward Julian with a snarl on his lip. Asher's eyes widened. He cursed. Kai growled, but didn't follow. He stood at the ready and nodded at Asher. They both knew Kai had to stay out of sight, but Asher wasn't sure if he could take on the lone wolf alone and in human form. As a wolf, they were a close match, but he wasn't willing to let Julian see either Kai or his wolf again.

He chased after the grey wolf, falling behind on two legs versus the wolf's four. Asher made it inside the house in time to see Julian slowly getting up off the floor. His shirt torn, and the wolf snarling, ready to attack.

"Easy, bud." Asher's voice held the command of an alpha. The wolf's ear twitched back, but that was the only sign he heard Asher. He was just as much an alpha as Asher and Kai. "What are you doing here, Julian?"

"Why the fuck do you have a wolf in your house?" Asher's nose curled at the scent of terror flowing off Julian, but it didn't stop him from challenging Asher, squaring his shoulders. At least he was smart enough to keep his eyes on the wolf.

"If you want to leave here unharmed, or better yet, alive, then you need to listen carefully."

"No fucking way. I'm prepared this time." Julian reached around his back and pulled out a knife. The fucking idiot. The wolf's growl echoed and he snapped and snarled at Julian, his body becoming impossibly tense and the fur all along his back stood straight.

Asher did everything he could to stay calm. He could hear Gwen creeping along the hall upstairs. She stopped at the top, continuing to stay out of sight. The distraction she would cause could make this situation worse, or it could work out for the best. As long as she stayed hidden, Asher could call out to her and decide to use the distraction for himself. But with her so close to the danger, he was having control issues. He needed the lone wolf to listen to him as his alpha, not act on his own. With Kai, they could, but he would not bring him into this unless he had to.

Asher calmly stepped forward beside the wolf. He was unhinged, his emotions and control awry. Asher was taking a risk by reaching out to touch his neck. The wolf turned his snarl sideways, only enough to tell Asher to back off, but Asher didn't.

"You need to put the knife away, Julian. You will only get yourself hurt. You can't win against a wolf."

"I'm keeping my fucking knife. But I'm leaving."

"If you move while still holding the knife and looking

defensive, then this wolf will attack. Don't be an idiot." Asher tried to warn him.

"Listen to him, Julian." Gwen stood at the top of the stairs. Asher's body readied for an attack. Julian swung toward her, his body jerking sideways with the knife outstretched toward the wolf.

The wolf lunged and grabbed Julian's forearm from the inside of his body. Julian screeched and curled his wrist. He had just enough space for the knife to reach the base of the wolf's neck.

"No!" Asher yelled. The wolf's grip on Julian's arm tightened until he dropped the knife, a high-pitched wale escaping his throat. Asher picked it up and held it so the back of the blade ran along the outside of his arm. Julian turned to leave, holding his bloody arm against his chest, but he froze.

"The white beast," he whispered. Asher knew Kai must have come into the house when Asher yelled. Blood seeped from the cut on the grey wolf. He didn't have time for this. With the hand that wasn't holding Julian's knife, he grabbed Julian by the arm. Sadly, it wasn't his injured one. He tightened his hold and lifted. Julian hung just inches from the ground. Asher walked him to the door and threw him through the air outside. He landed hard on the ground with a rough groan.

"I better not see you back on my property. And stop following Gwen." His voice was the lowest he'd ever heard it without the tone of a wolf's growl. He went back into the house and shut the door, locking it behind him. He looked to Kai. "Watch out the window and make sure he leaves. He should be heading to a hospital to treat that bite." Kai moved to the living room and watched, but he also looked to the grey wolf who still didn't have his control in check.

"Gwen." Asher softened his voice as much as he could. He didn't look at her. "I need you to go back upstairs until I can get him calmed down." He saw her nod slowly from the corner of his eye.

Asher crouched down in front of the wolf so they were eye to eye. He didn't snarl more at Asher, but anger pulsed around him and his breath was harsh. Blood continued to seep from his wound. It needed stitching, that much Asher knew. He didn't think it was life threatening, but it could be if he didn't get the wolf calmed down and get it looked after. "Danger's over. He's gone." The wolf blinked. "You're hurt. I can help you. But you need to calm down."

The wolf shook with anger. Asher could feel him trying, but he was too lost and out of control without his shifter pair. Asher took a brief moment to hope that if anything ever happened to Asher that Kai wouldn't turn rogue and lose his control.

Asher stripped and shifted, the wolf inside happy to be let free with all the turmoil around.

Stand down, grey one. The alpha command from a wolf rather than a human seemed to penetrate. He blinked again and shook his head. He still reeked of anger, but the emotion was under his own control. *Kai? Is he gone?*

You hurt him when you threw him, but he ran as best he could and kept running.

Good. Keep the grey one under control. Asher shifted back and dressed while he called for Gwen. She slowly came to the top of the stairs. "Are you all right?" It was the first thing he needed to know.

"Yes." Her answer was barely a breath. She'd been crying. He softened his gaze, wishing he had time to console her, but he didn't.

"Think you can help me again?" He watched her

swallow and she nodded. "Good. I need you to get my bag for me from the closet."

This wouldn't be like treating a wolf pup. As he smelled her fear, he wondered if it was a good idea to bring her closer to the angry wild animal.

GWEN HAD STAYED SILENT, crouched on the floor between Asher's bed and the wall and shushed Cinder while Julian had knocked on the door. A wolf's snarl had made her jump and Cinder whimper. It wasn't until she'd heard Asher's voice that she settled Cinder on the bed and had slowly made her way out of the bedroom. She'd tiptoed down the hall and stopped at the top of the stairs, not intending to make herself known or seen. She hadn't been sure if it was the best decision to step out and speak to Julian, but hearing that he'd had a knife, she wanted to try. She had regretted that decision as soon as she'd heard Asher's painful yell.

Julian hurt the grey wolf who was dangerous from what she gathered. But it was her fault he hurt the wolf. It didn't matter how scared she was, she would help Asher in any way she could. He asked for a syringe and one of the bottles. Reading the labels, she found what he needed and slowly passed it to him. The grey wolf was eying her warily. Asher took the bottle and needle from her without taking his eyes off the wolf.

"All right, grey one. You aren't going to like this, but that cut is bad. You will let me take care of it. It's best if you let me give you some medicine first. Understand?" The wolf growled low, but nodded his head. It amazed Gwen. He actually understood what Asher was telling him.

Asher slowly moved closer to the wolf and inserted the

needle into his shoulder near the cut. The wolf turned his head and snapped at Asher, but he didn't get close to him. Neither Asher nor the other white wolf flinched. It was as if they knew he was just upset and not trying to hurt Asher.

"I'm sorry. This won't last long, I promise." The wolf huffed and laid his head back down.

"Will that put him to sleep?" Gwen whispered. The wolf raised his head and looked directly at her, his glazed eyes a thick grey.

"No. It's just a local anesthetic."

"And he's going to let you stitch him up?"

"Yes, he is." Asher spoke firmly to the wolf. The wolf switched his gaze from her to Asher. He huffed again, then laid his head on top of his paws. "There's a suture kit close to the bottom of the bag. Get that out and open it, but don't take anything out. I'm going to wash up." He left and Gwen was alone with two enormous wolves.

She reached into the bag and found the suture kit, but her eyes kept moving back and forth from the wolves to the bag. She opened the kit and waited. She saw her hands shaking, so she folded them on her lap.

"Thank you, Gwen." Asher reached in and got the needle and suture. He moved closer to the wolf and poked him with the needle. When he didn't move, Asher got to work sewing up him. The cut was long, but he was quick and efficient. His stitches were flawless. "Done. That should heal fast and I can take the stitches out in a day or so." Asher spoke directly to the wolf and laid a hand on him. It was like watching a medical physician speaking to a human patient. Asher cared. Maybe he cared more.

"He'll heal that fast?" Gwen asked. Asher turned to Gwen.

"Yes. He's the pair of another shifter."

"Another shifter? I thought you didn't know of any others?"

"New development." Asher's lips quirked, then he turned back to the wolves. "You two need to return to the pack. They don't need to be in danger from that prick because you aren't there to protect them." Both wolves looked reluctant, but they sighed and waited by the door for Asher to open it. The white wolf nudged Asher's hand before leaving.

"He's your pair, isn't he?" Gwen watched the white wolf with the same blue eyes as Asher's walk away.

"Yes, he is." Asher shut the door and turned to her.

"Do you think Julian will come back?" She couldn't begin to guess his actions anymore, so she stopped trying. Gwen never would have imagined he'd attack her, let alone enter the house of a man he didn't know, carrying a knife.

"I don't know. A smart man wouldn't. But I'm going to plan as if he isn't a smart man."

Gwen dropped onto the couch, sudden exhaustion flowing through her. Asher came over and crouched in front of her.

"Are you all right?" He wasn't asking because he needed to know. He was asking to be there for her. But the only answer she could give was a shrug. Asher scooped her up with his arm under her legs and the other behind her back. He carried her to the bathroom and slowly took her clothes off one by one. He didn't touch her other than to soothe over the goosebumps and her body's tremors.

After taking his own clothes off, he started the shower and guided her in. The heat washed over her, and she leaned her weight against Asher. He held her in the water while he gently washed every inch of her. Gwen didn't need to know his favourites or any of his quirks. She didn't need to know any of that to know who he was at heart. He was hers.

THEY DIDN'T SLEEP much that night. They didn't even go to bed. Wrapped in a blanket and tucked in each other's arms, they dozed in and out on the couch by the fire. Adrenalin was slow to leave Asher's veins. Having his mate safe in his arms helped, but it wasn't enough when he knew danger still lurked. Both Julian and the grey wolf were unpredictable. It didn't matter that the grey wolf had good intentions. He was still dangerous in his current state and without Zachary.

"You know, you make a pretty good assistant." Asher nibbled Gwen's ear. She was sitting between his legs and leaning back on his chest. His fingers traced the smooth skin on her hip. He needed to keep that contact.

"Assistant?" she asked, her voice sounding sleepy again.

"Veterinary assistant. You've helped me twice now. You did exceptionally well, especially considering both situations were urgent."

"I did, didn't I?" Pride filled her voice and she tilted her head up. She exposed the creamy line of her neck and Asher took advantage, kissing, licking, nipping up and down the column.

"You did," he mumbled against her skin. "Have you ever considered something like that as a career?" Asher felt her frown. He couldn't see her face with their current position. But with the bond they had, he didn't just sense her emotions, he felt them. He knew her face scrunched together in thought.

"I haven't. I honestly haven't thought of much. Nothing

that caught my interest, anyway. I do know that my job at the bistro isn't permanent, although I enjoy it."

"Think about it." Asher kissed her temple and leaned back, pulling her with him. They settled in to try to sleep again. He watched the flames in the fire and tried not to think about tomorrow. But there was one thing he still needed to work on. "How good are you with research?"

"Huh?" she asked, her voice soft with the beginnings of sleep.

"The grey one. He's the lone wolf that attacked the pack and attacked Cinder during the fight when she got in the way. His shifter pair is missing. All I know is that his name is Zachary, and he's from Hull Creek. So now the grey wolf is alone, angry, and worried. He's strong like Kai and I, but being a lone wolf makes him a little unhinged, a bit dangerous. I need to find Zachary, or at least what's happened to him."

"I've never tried to track a person down like that before. I can try to help."

"Thank you." They both sighed as they settled and fell asleep again.

"Asher?" He woke from the soft voice of his mate. Her image had been running through his dreams. "Asher?"

"Yeah?" He nuzzled her hair and breathed in, but didn't bother opening his eyes.

"Do you ever regret following the wind that night and becoming a shifter?"

"Never." Asher didn't hesitate. This wasn't an answer he had to think about, not anymore. He'd asked himself that same question so many times growing up and he truly took the time to think about it. And the answer was always the same. "I was lucky. I had a great home and family, and I had a great bond with Kai and his mom as a second mother, a mother to my other half. This part of my life hasn't given me hardships. And it brought me you. I'll admit, it's been lonely. I've never told anyone. I tried telling my parents as a child, but they believed it was just a vivid dream. Friendships and relationships are distant. Loneliness has sometimes been a struggle, but that hasn't been enough for me to resent the double life I have."

"You sound proud to be who you are."

"I am." He paused. "Gwen, you haven't said how you feel about me being a shifter or about being my mate. I know I said one day at a time, but does any of it bother you?"

"I can't say that it does. I'm still processing a bit, but maybe it's the bond we have as mates that makes everything feel right. Nothing feels out of place. It's a weird mixture of the excitement of a new relationship with the comfort of years of marriage."

Asher gripped her hips and flipped her over on top of him.

"You were right yesterday." Gwen's breath fluttered over his jaw when she spoke. "We know a lot more about each other than I thought."

Asher pulled her down and captured her lips. He drank in her essence while his insides screamed to make her his, again. The urge to reaffirm their bond by renewing his mark pulsed. He angled her hips and took himself in hand to align them. As soon as his head connected with her entrance, he thrust upward.

"Mine." He felt his own growl vibrate through her. Her pussy clenched, her walls tightening their grip. Slow and steady, he brought them both to the peak. They buried their faces in each other's necks. Short moans escaped Gwen and Asher growled the closer they got. He moved his hand between them, pressed his finger to her clit, and she rolled over the edge. Her orgasm pulled his forward. As he spilled inside her, his teeth sank into her skin. She cried out, starting another wave of sensations through both of them.

Asher didn't pull out. He licked and sucked his mark on her neck, then settled her on his chest. They settled for sleep with his cock softening inside her. Asher saw the sky beginning to change colour outside the living room window. The fire was burning coals, but they didn't need more heat while wrapped around each other. Asher's eyes closed and the last hour of sleep was the soundest sleep he'd had in over a week.

CHAPTER 9

"Time to go get dressed." Asher woke Gwen with a light shake. But considering the events of the previous night, she startled upward. "It's okay. My sister is here."

"Where?" Gwen looked over Asher's shoulder.

"She's driving up the lane from my parents' house."

"You know, that will take some getting used to. You know someone is coming and you know exactly who it is and where they're coming from, but there's no sign or sound for anyone else."

"I enjoy the perks." His grin was infectious. Gwen stood and took the blanket with her. She picked up her clothes and went upstairs to shower and dress. Nerves assailed her under the spray of the water. She was about to meet Asher's sister, someone in his family. They barely discovered themselves in a relationship. Meeting family was an important step. But if last night showed her anything, it showed that this was meant to be and she just needed to embrace it day by day. Fate may have put them together, but Gwen didn't have any complaints with Her choice.

Dressed in fresh clothes, she made her way downstairs. Asher was sitting on the couch, still shirtless, he only bothered to put his jeans back on, and his sister was sitting at the opposite end. They both stood when she reached the living room.

Asher's sister was a miniature, cute, female version of Asher. Sandy hair, blue eyes, although hers didn't carry the depth or have the glow that Asher's did. Gwen imagined Asher as a six-year-old boy with eyes the same as his sister's.

"Gwen. This is my sister, Madigan."

"I prefer Madi. It's nice to meet you." Madi stepped around Asher and held out her hand.

"It's nice to meet you too." Gwen returned Madi's welcoming smile and shook her hand. She was petite and about the same height as Gwen, but despite her size, she looked like she carried a bit of muscle in her compact frame.

"Asher seems to have been hiding you, even the fact you existed. But now that I know he has a girlfriend, I will definitely be stopping by more often." Madi turned to her brother and grinned, echoes of past mischief and sibling rivalry in her eyes.

"We'll look forward to seeing you." Asher's voice dripped with sarcasm, but Gwen saw, and felt, the underlying amusement. "And thanks for the heads up."

"No worries. Mom and Dad are sending them to you since you own most of the land and are the animal expert."

"Mind stopping there on your way back to tell them to do the same if anyone else shows up with similar requests?"

"Sure. See you guys later." She waved and left.

"Who's coming?" Gwen asked.

"Conservation officers. They stopped at my parents first. My sister was there picking up stuff for an errand for my

Mom before heading into work. They sent her up to tell me they're sending them here. They'll probably be here any minute."

"What do we do?"

"We talk to them."

"You sound so calm."

"I am. For now." He grabbed his shirt from the back of the chair and put it on. He paused for a second before pulling it down over his abdomen. "They're here." He walked to the door and opened it. Gwen stood back while Asher crossed his arms and leaned against the door frame.

Asher's composure amazed Gwen. Panic and fear bubbled low in her belly, but his calm invaded her emotions and forced them to subside. She wondered if it was something he was doing on purpose or if he even realized he was. Or if it was entirely the doing of their mate bond.

"Hi, Tony, Morton. How are you two doing today?"

"Morning, Asher. We're good. Yourself?" Gwen recognized the voice as one of the officers Julian brought to the bistro.

"Pretty good. Just getting around. Something I can help you with?" Asher's tone was that of talking to friends. He knew the officers personally. Gwen heard footfalls on his front step.

"We're sorry to bother you so early." The second voice held a touch of regret. "We've had a report of a wolf bite that occurred on your property. We know there are extensive woods connected to yours. It's possible this wolf travelled away from its pack. We'd like your permission to look around your property for signs of the wolf. One that would come this close and attack could be dangerous."

Asher sighed. "I've lived connected to these woods my

entire life and there's never been any dangerous wolves or any other dangerous wild animals come close to the houses. You two know that. Maybe if you explain more of what happened, I could help. You said it was a report of a wolf bite?"

"Yes. The individual has a bite on his forearm and claims it was a wolf and on your property. The marks are consistent with a wolf."

"What other injuries did he sustain from the attack?"

"Well," he paused, "none. The only injury was the bite." Asher didn't respond. Gwen saw his head tilt slightly. She was still out of sight, so she didn't see the expression he gave them. "I know." The voice heaved with exasperation. "It doesn't seem right that a wolf would attack and the only injury would be a single bite. But he's insistent and the bite is consistent, therefore we need to investigate for public safety."

"There's no public up here. Just myself and my parents. We're perfectly fine."

"We understand. Let us take a hike while we're here so we can say we've done due diligence with the investigation?" The other officer spoke, she thought it was Officer Field.

He paused just long enough that Gwen thought he wouldn't allow them. "Of course, Morton."

"Thanks, Asher," they both uttered. Gwen tilted her head around the door and saw the two officers walking toward the woods. Asher shut the door. As soon as he turned around, his fear hit her in the gut. He was afraid. But not for himself. For Kai and the grey wolf.

"Start the shower. If they come back, tell them that's where I am and that I'll call them later if there's anything they need. I'm sneaking past them and ensuring the pack is all together and far enough into their territory. Lock the door behind me."

"Be careful." Before he left her, she rushed to him and grabbed his neck. He didn't have a choice but to lean down so she could kiss him. And just as quick as the kiss, Asher left.

ASHER WALKED DIAGONALLY across his lawn rather than straight to the woods like Tony and Morton. They weren't far into the trees, stopping and looking for tracks. Asher ditched his clothes behind his shed rather than in a bush as usual. As soon as he hit the tree line, he shifted. After taking only a moment to sniff the air and get his bearings, and the whereabouts of the others, he launched into a sprint. He didn't think they'd come so far into the woods and encroach on the pack's territory, but Asher wasn't taking any chances of himself, Kai, or the grey wolf being seen. The bite on Julian's arm was distinctive of a large wolf. The only thing he had to question about any of this was leaving Gwen behind alone. He didn't worry of Tony or Morton hurting her. They were good guys. But it was difficult to leave her after the danger of the previous night.

About five hundred metres from the pack's territory, Asher found the wolf pairs.

Who are they? Kai asked. He'd already caught their scent.

Conservation officers. Get back to your territory and ensure the entire pack is there. I doubt they'll come even this far, but if they do, don't let them see either of you. All three of us are abnormally large.

Kai tilted his head for the other wolf to follow. He

paused and looked at Asher. He needed to make a decision. Hide with Kai or sneak back past them to get back to Gwen. As soon as he thought of her, his decision was done.

He looked at Kai. *My mate is alone.*

Kai nodded. Asher didn't sense resentment or sadness from Kai, maybe a little confusion, but he held no malice toward Asher or Gwen.

Asher turned and looped wide around the officers through the woods. At any point he heard them stop, he stopped. Their paths veered close, so Asher stopped his sprint and crept silently past until enough distance was between them again for him to sprint. As he reached the tree line, he heard them turn around and head back for the house. He listened to their conversation.

"I'm not sure who and what to believe, but I know wolf prints when I see them." Morton said, confidence ringing through his voice.

"Even what we consider a large wolf doesn't leave prints that big. And there's at least two of them." Asher heard the awe in Tony's voice.

"Let's go talk to him again."

Asher shifted and darted for his clothes. He dressed behind the shed, then walked normally back to the house, even though the officers still had a bit of hike to get back. He might not have needed to warn Kai, but he was glad he heard their conversation. They could turn persistent and want to set traps. He also thought he should be more aware of the tracks and trails he and Kai left.

Gwen met him at the door. "Is everyone safe?"

"Yes. But they found tracks that have made them curious. I knew there would be tracks to find, which is why I wanted to warn Kai, but I can only hope they will still let the matter drop and not chase their curiosity." Asher sighed immediately before they knocked on the door. Slowly, he opened it while Gwen went upstairs to turn off the shower. "Hello, again."

"We found tracks, very large tracks." Tony's brows rose high.

"Really?"

"Are you sure you haven't noticed anything? Maybe you could reconsider and let us set traps? We'd relocate them to a safe place for both the wolves and yourself and family."

"No, I haven't noticed anything out of the ordinary. I've had no problems with wildlife. And I'm sorry, I'd rather you didn't set traps." Times like these would be easier if Asher could tell the truth. Tony sighed and pulled out a card.

"If you change your mind, or see anything, please call us."

"I will." Asher shook hands with each of them and watched them leave. By the time he shut the door and turned around, Gwen was coming back down the stairs. "I wish I knew what to expect out of all this."

Asher'd had it easy growing up the way he did. He'd never put himself in a position of risk of exposure. And he didn't want to. He might not personally know other shifters, but they were out there. Exposing one would expose all, at least the fact that they existed, and that's all people would need. But by rescuing Gwen from Julian, exposure was becoming a possibility. This wasn't a situation in which he could go on the offensive. He needed to let it ride and ensure he was prepared.

"I never would have imagined Julian would go as far as he has. Honestly, he's surprised me with everything he's done lately."

"Gwen," Asher hesitated. What he was about to ask her, tell her, wasn't like him. Unfamiliar emotions of possessiveness and protectiveness filled him since he found her. He discovered those traits were ingrained in him and they only mattered with the one meant to be his mate. "You can't work at the bistro anymore." The demand escaped, low and pained. He hated saying it, but making the demand felt right. It soothed the emotions roaring inside to carry her off and hide her somewhere safe. That plan was already a reality in his mind. He knew it could reach that point. He knew he might have to move the entire pack, and his mate, farther into the wilderness. If the situation turned.

"What do you mean?" she asked cautiously, her eyes narrowing.

"He's been stalking you and he came here with a knife. It doesn't matter that you work around lots of people. You can't go to work anymore with him still after either one of us."

"I understand." Asher sighed inwardly, relief flooding him. But it was short lived. "That doesn't mean I agree. At no point am I ever alone, even for a moment."

"Gwen." A clear warning radiated from him. He didn't expect it out of himself. Not like this. As an alpha wolf and with members of the pack, yes, but not with his mate.

"Asher." She returned his warning. "I will continue to work. This job is still new. I'll be fine." Each step she took toward him drew his attention to her soft hips and added to his torture. Asher's jaw clenched and he breathed deep. Her scent filled him. Floral and coconut. Worry floated from her through the air, but there was more. He smelled her arousal from between her legs. He was frustrated he couldn't keep her protected, and she was turned on by it all. That's all it took for his control to snap.

As soon as she was close enough, he reached around and fisted her hair, the brown waves wrapping around his knuckles. "That isn't how this works."

"How what works?" Her breathless gasp hit the underside of his chin. He had her head tilted back and looked straight down at her while he pulled her against his chest.

"This." He took her mouth. He worked to force her to submit to him, to overwhelm, to steal her breath. He backed her up to the couch and lifted his head. Using the grip on her hair, he turned her around. He undid the button and zipper on her jeans. They were tight, but he pulled them down to the top of her knees with one hand. He needed to keep the grip on her hair, to give him the feel of control when he had none.

Gwen whimpered and her breaths were short. Asher took a moment to tune into her, to feel her, smell her. She was right there with him.

He pushed her forward over the back of the couch so her ass stuck in the air. He used his free hand to probe her entrance. Releasing his cock, he thrust in one rough motion. Gwen's scream pierced through his chest, the sensation travelling down to his balls. He controlled her movement with his fist still in her hair. She tried to move away from his initial thrust, but he wouldn't let her.

"You will allow me to protect you. You are mine. Your body is mine. Your soul is mine. Mine to protect, to love, to possess. My mate." After his speech, he finally moved within her with a punishing pace. Quickly they both reached the peak. Asher leaned forward and bit into her opposite shoulder as he came inside her. As soon as he broke the skin, a fresh heat flooded him. He felt as if they both glowed. Momentary dizziness invaded his mind, but drifted away when their orgasms faded.

He pulled her up and turned her around, wrapping an arm around her waist so she didn't lose her balance.

"Mine," Asher growled. Her eyes were glazed, but Gwen's lips twitched and she gently poked his chest.

"Mine."

Asher silently promised himself the next time wouldn't be so quick. He would take the time to worship her body the way she deserved.

⁂

ASHER CAME to pick Gwen up from work when her shift finished early Monday afternoon. Despite his insistence to protect her and his show of dominance, she'd informed him she would still be working. He didn't like it, but there wasn't much he could do. The whole scene made her love him even more. But they'd come to a compromise. She would spend time with him at the clinic when she wasn't working.

He took her back to his clinic and after a short and awkward introduction to some of his staff, she sat alone in his office and searched for the grey wolf's shifter pair, Zachary. She'd never tried searching for someone before, but she wanted to help Asher. So, she started with what he already found. She started with anyone named Zachary who lived in Hull Creek any time in the past twenty years and had moved away. She followed a few leads down that path before giving up. Asher was quite sure that he hadn't been missing as long as the grey wolf felt he had. She then extended the age range that Asher had originally searched. She sighed. They just didn't have enough information.

Asher came into his office. He wore a white doctor's coat over his button-up shirt and jeans with his name written twice with a thick blue stitch on the left side. *Dr. Ash. Dr. Morestead.* His ruffled hair and bright eyes that alluded to a boyish look playing doctor didn't match the growly wolf she knew him to be.

"Any luck?" he asked.

"No." She shook her head. "We just don't have enough to go on, but I'll keep digging. I might have to sink into some rabbit holes. It's the best we can do for now."

"I have two more appointments, then we'll head home."

"Okay. I'll keep going."

Gwen really did fall down a few rabbit holes in her search, but it was her only option. The problem was Hull Creek wasn't very big and she still couldn't find anyone that matched the right characteristics. She started on a search of people with names similar to Zachary or other variations and spellings of the name. Their search capabilities were limited, social media, news reports and public records, and family trees. What if the Zachary they were looking for didn't use any social media, was a perfect citizen, and didn't have family in Hull Creek, or no family left?

She kept notes of all the leads she followed and book-marked several websites on Asher's computer, but she couldn't stare any longer. Gwen was rolling her neck and shoulders as Asher walked into his office from the back door.

"I need to do up some paperwork and we're free to go." He nodded toward his computer.

"Perfect timing. I need a break." She stretched her arms above her head. When she stood, she saw Asher's eyes on her body and they flashed bright until they reached her face.

"You're very enticing, my mate." His hand glided from her neck and across her chest as he passed and walked to his desk. Gwen felt herself flush. Such a simple compliment, but said with a pure honesty that shone in his eyes, was a boost to her confidence she didn't know she needed.

Gwen wondered if the effects of the mate bond should bother her. After all, Fate chose this for her. She decided who Gwen was meant to be with and what kind of life she would lead. Even if Gwen was truly in love with someone, she could choose to back away based on any number of reasons. But not with Asher. Maybe she should be mad that choice was no longer hers. But she wasn't. She couldn't be. How did Gwen know how much Fate had her hand in anyone's decisions? Gwen had to believe that if this wasn't meant to be, then she would have a choice and be able to walk away. Or there would be reasons for her to walk away.

She didn't have any. With each day that passed and with each moment she got to see Asher's true self, Gwen fell more in love with him. Being thrown into an odd paranormal world wasn't as scary as some might believe. But Asher was alone in his own world. It felt safe, for the time being. And by the time they found more, Gwen hoped to be an expert on all things shifter.

There was one part of Asher she hadn't seen yet, an important part of who he was. She waited until he finished. He turned his computer off and leaned back in the chair with his fingers linked and resting on his abdomen. His eyes found her.

"You haven't shown me your wolf." She murmured.

"You've seen my wolf. I believe you called me your white knight." A smug smile broke Asher's lips.

"But I haven't seen you since. Or seen you shift."

"To be honest, I've been avoiding it."

"Why?" She frowned.

"I've only shifted in front of Kai. You are the only person

who knows that part of me exists. You're the first person I'm even able to talk to about it. This is another new first for me, just like everything else I've had to learn about being a wolf, being a shifter." He paused and his lips twitched. "Maybe I'm shy."

Gwen giggled. Being shy surprisingly suited him and she found it endearing. A big, boyish, handsome, alpha, shy, growly wolf.

"Let's go home." He hung his white coat and pulled on his jacket, then reached for her hand.

"How did you know his name is Zachary?"

"The grey wolf told me."

"Told you? How?" Gwen stopped and looked up at Asher.

"Wolves can't really talk, obviously, but we have a way of understanding each other. Even the regular pack. It's almost like thinking about what we want to say, but it's like directing or channeling our thoughts toward the other wolf."

"Do you think he could give us more information?"

"I've already asked, and he couldn't tell me more, but we can try." He shrugged.

"Maybe if we ask more specific questions, he might be able to tell us something that will help find him."

"We can give it a try." Asher helped her into his truck and went to the driver's side. Before getting in, he stopped. Gwen followed his gaze and looked across the parking lot. The conservation officers were walking toward him. Gwen waited. She didn't want to get out and draw too much attention to herself. But she lost that hope as both officers noticed her, and after wiping away minor scowls, they waved. She smiled back and moved over to the driver's seat of the truck. Asher cracked the door and passed Gwen the keys. She turned it on and pressed the button to roll down the window.

"Asher. Miss Taylor, I hope you're well?" Officer Green asked.

"I am. Thank you." They looked at her with understanding. When she last saw them, her attack from Julian had been recent and also very apparent.

"Seeing you two together helps connect the dots." He didn't comment further, but Gwen saw the common denominator as Julian. She discredited him before. Maybe that would help now. "We stopped by because we had a question for you Asher."

"Go ahead."

"Considering past circumstances and now your connection with Miss Taylor, we aren't concerned about the report from the individual who was bitten." Officer Green's eyes pointed upward. "However, there is the evidence of the bite and we found tracks near your home. We were hoping you would allow us to set up trail cams on your property, just to see what's going on and if we need to interfere further. We've placed a couple cameras on the adjoining crown land, but we hoped to see how close to your home or your parents' home the wolves are coming and how often."

"I'm sorry, Tony." Asher shook his head. "I live up there for privacy and I'd like to keep it."

"I promise they would only be temporary."

"No. But I'll keep an eye out and if I notice anything or see a need to be concerned, I will call you." Asher put his emphasis in all the right places. Gwen felt his guilt. He didn't want to push them away. He was only trying to protect his pair, the pack, and himself.

"Well, thanks for your time. Sorry to have bothered you." Officer Morison sighed and waved.

"It's no bother. Come talk to me anytime."

"Thank you." The officers turned back to their vehicle and left.

Gwen moved back to the passenger side and Asher got in.

"Fuck." Asher cursed. His muscles tensed as he pulled out of the parking lot and drove toward his home. "I need to find those cameras."

CHAPTER 10

Asher fought with himself on what to do. He needed the wolves to stay with the pack and all on their territory. It was a long hike on two feet, but the only way to find the cameras was to go as himself.

"How do you feel about going for a hike?" Asher parked the truck and turned to Gwen.

"Are you going to take them down?"

"I can't. I just need to let it ride out, but I need Kai and all other wolves to stay on their territory, or at least not travel in this direction." Asher hated this. His connection with Kai kept him grounded. Being forced to keep his distance and to force Kai to do the same hurt. It was a physical pain in his chest. He didn't want to find out what would happen if they grew apart or lost each other.

"How far away are they?" Gwen looked to the woods.

"Too far on two feet. But we only need to find the cameras and the direction they're pointing. I need to figure out their blind spots."

"Let's do it." She gave a firm nod and determination lit up in her eyes.

After going inside to change clothes, they entered the woods hand in hand.

"Was I out of line to suggest veterinary assistant as a career choice for you?" When Asher mentioned it the other night on the couch, he wasn't guarding his thoughts or words. It worried him to bring it up now. But despite that, he liked the idea of her working beside him.

"Why do you think that was out of line?" He could hear mirth in her voice.

"I don't want to be intrusive or make it seem like I'm trying to steer you in a specific direction."

"Then why did you ask?" Gwen's voice turned soft. He felt her eyes on him, so he turned his eyes on her. The brown in hers softened and her freckles seemed to dance around them.

"You handled it so well."

"But that was only twice and in strange circumstances."

"Not strange. And sometimes that's all it takes. Besides," he paused and bent to place a quick kiss on her lips, "I like the idea of keeping you next to me."

"I thought you weren't trying to steer me?"

"I'm not. But it doesn't mean I wouldn't like it."

"And who says if I did do that, I'd work for you?"

Asher raised his brow, attempting an intimidating stance, and tried to come up with a comeback to the teasing he heard in her voice, could sense in her body's reaction, and feel through their bond. His jaw worked up and down for a moment until he broke and laughed. "I got nothing."

She leaned closer to him while they walked. After walking in silence for a while, Asher realized Gwen effectively evaded him.

"You never answered my question."

"You weren't out of line. You gave me something to think

about. I've had such a hard time finding a career path for myself. I've been unsure of who I am and what I want to spend the rest of my life doing. Your suggestion was the first that I didn't immediately throw away. I've been giving it serious consideration. But nothing feels certain." Gwen watched the ground in front of her while they walked. When he looked down, he saw her brows creased together. He understood how a plan could hit so suddenly and take over the mind. It was an unexpected experience. He wanted to dig deeper into her thoughts now that he knew she was truly considering what he said, but he noticed they were reaching the end of his property.

They followed the path he and Kai often took. They moved around, but over time, a sense of security developed with their privacy. They turned lazy. At least Asher had.

"We should spot cameras soon. Don't look for them. We're only out for a hike together."

"I understand." She put on the right expression, an adoring smile looking up at him, but he sensed her tension.

They discussed her day at the bistro absentmindedly, often looking between each other and the path ahead. Asher kept his senses open, trying to smell for anything that didn't belong. These woods were his. He knew he could find the cameras.

And there they were, at least the first two. Not far past his property line. One camera faced them along the path and the other faced directly opposite. They were watching what came and what went.

"Let's walk a bit further. I want to see if there's more."

"More? You found some?"

"Two."

Asher was getting ready to set a marker for Kai, a signal they set up with each other years ago, when he heard the light hum of another two cameras. They positioned them in a way that when combined, they gave a wide angle through the woods up to the hill.

"Damn it."

"What's wrong?" Gwen asked quietly.

"They're covering quite a bit of ground. But we need to get out of their range." He looked down at her and lifted her chin. "Think you can hike further?"

"Do I look like I'm struggling?"

"No, you don't."

"Then let's go."

Gwen was panting slightly by the time they reached the top of the hill, but she wasn't waning. As soon as Asher looked down the other side, relief hit him. Kai was way ahead of him. Across the path lay three large branches. It was the marker they used to signal each other. Kai wasn't to travel past the marker toward the house, and Asher wasn't to shift before the marker.

"You're relieved. Why?" Gwen must have felt it through their bond. He made sure his body didn't change. The last two cameras could still see them standing on top of the hill.

"The three branches. It's our marker. Kai did it."

"So, he already knows about the cameras? How?"

"He probably heard them or watched them putting them up." Asher started down the hill toward the branches. Gwen kept a hold of his hand and followed. "The marker is our signal for each other. Kai isn't allowed past it and I'm not allowed to shift, or be in wolf form, before it."

Stopping at the branches, Asher openly searched the area for more cameras in case Kai missed any. They said they only had a couple up. In Asher's opinion, four wasn't a couple. Thankfully, he didn't find any. He stepped over each branch and watched Gwen to make sure she didn't trip while following him.

He let go of her hand and stepped ahead of her. It had been a long time since nervousness assailed him.

"Do you still want to see me shift?" He was more accurate than he realized when he told her maybe he was shy. He felt like he was blushing, but he did everything he could to push the heat of embarrassment away. This was just another new thing, another first, just like his first hunt, his first accidental shift in the janitor's closet at school, his first night sneaking out to meet Kai and his mother. Having a mate and showing her his life, showing her who he was, was just another first. He'd faced so many before. Why did this one feel different?

"Yes," she whispered. Her eyes widened with a smile of their own. She held the same nerves he did.

Asher pulled off his shirt and set it on the ground before he reached for his waistband of his sweats. Gwen's eyes fell to his bare skin, but she kept pulling them back up. The fight she was having with herself to be polite was amusing. Asher froze with his pants around the middle of his hips. He cocked his head.

"Your eyes are welcome to go where they please," he murmured.

"But... You... Your..." she stammered.

"Your eyes feel almost as good as your hands. Never stop looking." His voice changed to an alpha's demand involuntarily. He watched her chest fill with air as she gave her eyes free reign. He felt the pattern of her gaze down his chest until they stopped at the point of the V left from the position of his pants.

Toeing off his sneakers, he finished undressing. A few moments standing naked and a few deep breaths later, he began to shift. He watched her face. Her mouth opened and she held a look of wonder.

Asher didn't know what it looked like when he shifted, only what it felt like. It never occurred to him to stand in front of a mirror and shift. The ache moved through him as his body moved and changed. For all he knew, the sight was a gruesome one. Or maybe it looked more like an illusion. Smoke and mirrors.

Gwen's fingers fluttered over her mouth.

"Wow." She let her air out in one quick breath. "That looked both beautiful and painful at the same time. That whole experience a contrast to itself." She took a hesitant step toward him and Asher met her halfway, pushing his head under her hand. "You're beautiful."

He closed his eyes while she ran her hands through his fur. Then he turned, facing deeper into the woods, and crouched to the ground. He nodded to his back with his snout.

"What? You want me to get on your back?" she asked in surprise. Asher nodded. "Can you hold me?" Asher huffed and nodded again toward his back. When standing, he reached her ribs, and he had a larger girth as a wolf than he did a man.

He watched her swallow before slowly climbing on his back. He stood and gave her a little bump. She yelped and seemed to get the message. Her arms wrapped around his neck and her thighs squeezed his flanks.

Asher started with a trot, but soon picked up speed, enjoying Gwen's laughter in his ear. He didn't hit his full speed, but they moved at a steady sprint, covering ground much faster than before.

GWEN SQUEEZED her eyes shut as they picked up speed. Exhilaration shot down her spine. She laughed while clinging to Asher, laying her cheek against his soft fur on the back of his neck. His muscles moved beneath her. His strength made everything he did look easy, in human form or as a wolf.

After a while, her limbs weakened from holding on so tight. Asher must have sensed her fatigue because he slowed down to a jog. His tongue hung out and she swore he smiled. She loosened her grip and propped herself up a little to see where they were. Looking over her shoulder, the hill with Kai's marker was no longer visible. Asher slowed even further and Gwen sat up fully, taking in her surroundings.

She was city raised, it was a small city, but a city nonetheless. The odd camping trip with family or friends wasn't the same as what she felt now. There was something different about this wilderness compared to campgrounds. Campgrounds, no matter how far into nature, were safe. As safe as they could be. This, where they were now, was territory. Somehow, she felt it the moment they crossed the pack's lines. Something changed. It was a sense. Her body became more alert, her mind more aware.

The sounds were faint, but she heard birds in the trees, rustling the leaves as they took flight and landed. A bird of prey in the third tree ahead of them on her left. She looked up and saw she was right. A falcon eyed them carefully as they sauntered through the trees.

Gwen didn't feel different. She hadn't changed, but her senses increased. Being out here and on the back of a wolf cleared everything from her mind so she could feel. The gates opened and her newly heightened senses kicked in. She doubted they matched Asher's capabilities. It had to do with the mate bond. The bites. It connected them in other ways, their emotions, the rhythms of their bodies. Why not their senses? As soon as they returned home, she needed to write this all down. And she'd write more. She wanted to remember what it felt like to ride on Asher's back for the first time.

Wolves appeared. Some stepping out, others only poking their heads out to look and then going back to their business. Pups ran out toward Asher. They nipped at his legs, but he kept walking until they met up with Kai, the grey wolf standing beside him. Asher looked down at all the pups and they nipped at each other and ran off to play, leaving Asher alone. He looked back at her before crouching down. Once one foot touched the ground, she lifted the other leg and stood beside him. But she couldn't bring herself to let go of his fur.

The three wolves stared at each other with the occasional head movement. Gwen was confused for a moment, but soon figured out they were talking to each other. She waited while running her fingers through Asher's fur.

Suddenly, Asher moved out from under her hand and charged at Kai. They nipped, pawed, and rolled, moving further away. Gwen laughed when she realized they were playing. She wouldn't have thought adult alpha wolves were playful. The pups ran back out to join them. As soon as they noticed them, the two white wolves eased up and included the pups. Kai's personality matched Asher's, but at this point she couldn't tell them apart. They really were identical.

Gwen realized she stood alone with the grey wolf. So far, he hadn't seemed as calm as Kai, but at the moment he wasn't angry. He looked sad. Seeing Kai and Asher together made her hurt for him. He missed that right now. And from what Asher said, his bond with Kai was extremely important to him. She assumed the grey one and Zachary had the same connection. Gwen would bet money that their personalities also matched.

"Can I touch you?" Gwen asked softly. She wanted to provide some comfort to him. He eyed her for a moment, then bowed his head once. She took the few steps toward him and slowly extended her arm. She was suddenly nervous, unsure of his mood, but he leaned the rest of the way so her hand touched the top of his head. She stroked down and watched his eyes close.

Gwen moved to the closest tree and sat with her back against it. The wolf watched her move then followed her. He towered over her, his size similar to Asher and Kai. She swallowed, realizing the vulnerable position she put herself in. But again, he bowed his head then lay down next to her. He studied her a moment before hesitantly setting his head on her lap. She would have laughed at his cautiousness if she didn't feel his sorrow. A somber wolf in contrast to the two playful white ones.

"We're trying to find him." She hoped to help. He sighed, his hot breath brushed over her legs. "Maybe you can tell Asher about you and Zachary. How long ago you met. How old he was. Did he have a name for you?"

Gwen sighed. Talk about a language barrier. When she looked up, both white wolves were staring at the two of them, the pups still trying to play, nipping and swatting with their paws. One leapt up and grabbed an ear, pulling their attention away from Gwen and back to the game. She laughed, joy bubbling up. She swore she saw the two roll their eyes, but they jumped back and crouched low to excite the pups.

"No matter what, you'll be all right. I promise." Gwen kept stroking his dark, grey fur and soon heard his light snore. She watched Asher and Kai play more themselves after they'd worn out the pups, each one walking away with flagging energy. She knew Asher regretted not bringing Cinder out to visit her pack, but the cameras would have seen them carrying a wolf pup.

Two beautiful white beasts slowly walked toward her. How many people got to say they spent an evening with wolves? She got to enjoy being part of their world. One contentedly sleeping on her and two that towered over her. All her nerves and uncertainty vanished, a sense of home filled her heart. Maybe that came from Asher, but she liked the feeling. She embraced it, just as she embraced Asher.

Gwen looked between the two, comparing every inch. She studied their eyes and sure enough, they both held the same deep colour and glow.

"I can't tell you two apart."

One of them sat down heavily and sighed, cocking his head. Gwen laughed.

"Okay, now I can." Asher stood and walked over to her and stuck his nose in her neck. His cold, wet nose. She squealed and tried to move away. But the grey wolf stirred and lifted a paw onto her lap to keep her still.

In that moment, Gwen wasn't worried about Julian, the conservation officers, the cameras, or what the future held for her and Asher. The wolves and their world charmed her. Her world now.

ASHER HADN'T ALLOWED himself to be free and relax in this home since his life and Gwen's were threatened. He took for granted the feeling of safety when surrounded by the pack, but now that that safety extended to Gwen, Asher held a different appreciation for it.

The lone wolf on her lap made him nervous. Asher knew he wasn't dangerous, but he was unstable. It seemed Gwen calmed his soul.

"Asher?" He lifted his head. "Can you ask him more about his life with Zachary? Maybe if he knows how old he was when they met or if Zachary had a name for him?" Asher looked to the grey wolf who raised his head as soon as Gwen spoke. Asher should have thought of more specific questions. He'd been too caught up in the knowledge that there was another shifter, another wolf shifter out there.

Well? He raised a furry brow.

I remember him saying he just turned six the night we met.

I was seven when I met Kai. Do you know how old he is now? Any age and timeline would help, even to just narrow down the possibilities.

No. I've been alone for at least two winters, maybe more. Some time before he went missing, he said something about turning twenty-eight.

That's okay. That still helps. What else can you remember about the night you met? Asher wanted to ask Zachary the same question when they finally found him.

Not much. I ran into a kid in the woods. And the wind was grey.

Did he have a name for you? Asher named Kai as a child. Guilt settled when he realized he didn't ask this wolf what his shifter named him. Of course a child would name any animal with which they had a bond.

Smoke.

Okay. Kai told me he's welcomed you into the pack until we find him, and even longer if you choose. Asher hoped it was longer. He hoped he could convince Zachary to stay nearby, or at least keep in touch.

Smoke tilted his head in appreciation and acceptance. Asher stepped back and shifted. He stretched and rolled his muscles before settling on the ground next to Gwen. Her flushed skin and wide eyes didn't escape his notice, but he let it go.

"Zachary was six when he first shifted. He's at least thirty now, but no more than thirty-five would be safe to say." Asher looked at the lone wolf once again resting against Gwen. "And his name is Smoke."

"I can see why a six-year-old would name him that."

"It probably had something to do with the wind. He said the wind was grey. It probably looked like smoke."

"So, did you and Zachary follow the same wind as children, but it changed colour?"

"I don't think so." He hadn't told Gwen about the bear he smelled outside the bistro a couple weeks ago. Or the auburn wind that went with him. "We should head back soon. You're hungry."

"You can't possibly feel my hunger."

"No, but I can hear your stomach." Gwen tried to suppress her smile and covered her face with her hand. When she looked up again, she was blushing and had laughter in her eyes.

"Yeah, okay. I'm hungry."

Asher stood again and stepped back to shift while Gwen stroked Smoke's head.

"Bye, Smoke." He let her go.

Asher called to Kai. *Stay safe. We'll check in whenever we can.* He crouched down and waited for Gwen to climb on his back. He didn't move until she had a firm grip. He raced to the marker of branches. Gwen buried her face in his fur and the wind rushed over them.

Darkness was creeping across the sky by the time he dressed, and they walked hand in hand past the cameras. Asher hated how quick unease settled across his skin after leaving the safety of the pack. Down here, Gwen was vulnerable to Julian, and he was vulnerable to discovery. He needed the comfort of the pack, needed others like him. *They* needed it. Without more shifters, Gwen would be left in a world alone, instead of him.

Sitting by the fire after eating leftovers, Asher felt a question burn on his tongue.

"What does it look like when I shift?"

"You don't know?" She turned her head over her shoulder.

He shook his head.

"It looks painful at first. Is it?"

"Not as a child, but in my teens it was. It's not that bad anymore. More of an ache."

"Your body moves and changes shape itself. Then your white wind swirls through you, or more like it comes out of you, to finish what your body can't."

"My white wind? You saw the wind?" Asher straightened, knocking Gwen off his chest.

"You didn't?" She moved to sit beside him.

"No. I didn't know it showed up every time I shift." He narrowed his eyes and looked out the window. Seeing the white wind was rare for him. Only when it needed to tell him something it seemed.

"I don't think it does. It looked like it was a part of you." Her hand on his wrist forced him to look at her. It turned out he didn't need other shifters to help answer some of his questions. A mate could answer them too.

CHAPTER 11

Things ran similarly for the rest of the week. Asher would bring Gwen to the clinic each day after work and they would leave when he finished with his last appointments. They ate a quick dinner then left for a hike through the woods. As soon as they reached the marker, Asher shifted and they raced to the pack. It quickly became the favourite part of Gwen's day.

But each night they left, something pulled at her. It was Smoke. His heartache was visible and it hurt Gwen each day she saw it. She decided it was time to ask Asher about her plan to find Zachary.

"Asher, Smoke is getting worse."

"I know he is." Asher sounded just as saddened by it as she was.

"I've gone down so many rabbit holes searching for Zachary."

"I chased a rabbit down a hole once." He spoke so quickly after her that it took her by surprise.

"Huh?" When she looked up at him, he shook his head and started to chuckle.

"Sorry. I didn't realize I said that aloud. I find memories of growing up like to pop up when we talk."

"So, you literally chased a rabbit down a hole?"

"I did. I was still technically a pup. I got stuck." He laughed to himself, off in his own memories.

Gwen made a mental note to get the full story and write it down with everything else.

"Anyway, you were saying?"

"I can't find him, at least not anyone I'm certain about. And I've shown you everyone I suspect." She took in a deep breath and forged on. "I want to go to Hull Creek to search for him in person." Her words rushed out in one long breath.

Asher stopped and turned to her, his expression cast downward. "Can you clarify that a little?"

"I want to go to Hull Creek."

"Alone?"

"Yes," she answered quietly.

His full height above her held a menacing stare. This wasn't a look she saw on him often. "No. I won't let you go alone."

"You're busy at work. And I've seen what you have coming up. You can't reschedule."

"I can't let you go anywhere alone when Julian could still be after you."

"How is he going to know I'm in Hull Creek?" She paused and he couldn't give her an answer. "Asher, I need to do this for Smoke."

"We don't know what kind of man Zachary is." He let out a long sigh and his eyes slowly closed. "Let me think on it?"

Gwen could feel his struggle. She struggled with it

herself, but Smoke's pain battled within her too. "Of course." She was only thankful he didn't continue to refuse.

Later that night, Asher woke her. The room was dark and the moon was high. She had difficulty waking with the warmth of him around her, but she rolled over in his arms and forced her eyes to open.

"All right. You can go. I'm worried about what will happen to Smoke if we don't find him. But I won't be far behind you. I'll follow you up. We'll search with short trips together whenever we can."

"Thank you, Asher," she whispered and stretched to place a soft kiss on his cheek, feeling his stubble under her lips.

In the morning before leaving for work, Asher handed Gwen the keys to his truck and put her packed bag in the back seat. He gripped the back of her neck. The heat and pressure of his hand sparked, then seemed to calm her senses. She breathed deep and opened her body and mind. But as she felt calm blanket her, Asher fought. His grip tightened and his jaw locked. His eyes deepened and the blue swirled.

"Be careful. If you find him before I get there, and I will be there, don't approach him."

"I'll try."

"You'll do better than try," he demanded. He was generally such a patient and kind man that Gwen always found it amusing when he growled, not that she wasn't taking him seriously, but the contrast got to her. It got to her in ways she never thought it would. Just the sound of him started heat pooling low in her belly. "Gwen, promise me."

"Okay, I promise." She hoped she kept her promise. If she found him and thought she would lose him, she wouldn't have a choice but to talk to him. She understood Asher worried about her, but she was doing this for Smoke. Asher relaxed, only marginally. "You're sexy when you're growly." Gwen gave him a lopsided smile.

"I'm only growly like this with you." She held onto him as he kissed her. Gwen fed on his strength. She wouldn't admit this to him, but she felt nervous searching for a shifter alone. Although, she suspected he already knew. "Call me often. I'll be there no later than tomorrow morning."

Asher opened his truck door and helped her in. Before closing the door, he tried to say something else, but he stepped back. Gwen felt it. She felt the words. They spurred on her own urge to say the same to him. It wasn't the right time. She wasn't sure why. Their circumstance was unlike any other. The same unwritten rules of relationships didn't apply.

But she still couldn't bring herself to say it. Instead, she let the feeling move through her and allowed him to feel the same from her too. His nostrils flared and his muscles around his jaw twitched. Gwen waved, just her fingers moving, and started the truck. It would be easy to get lost in thought for the three-hour drive, but she forced herself to think about anything but her life. Sometimes a mind and body needed a reset. This might be her only chance for a while.

IT TOOK effort for Asher to work through his day. Several times he had to remind himself that he loved his job and his patients liked him and continued to come to him for a reason. He used that to push his worries about Gwen away from his mind. Receiving her texts and a phone call once she had arrived helped.

After seeing his last patient, he asked Laura to finish up some paperwork and to leave notes for anything he needed to do himself. He left her to lock up and started walking. He had walked to the clinic that morning and planned to rent a vehicle to get to Hull Creek. He would return it there and drive back with Gwen at the end of the weekend.

He caught the scent as he hit the corner that rounded into town. It caught him off guard and Asher stopped before he tripped over his own feet. They had passed each other. Asher hesitated, unsure if he should say anything. His own curiosity won.

"Excuse me." Asher turned and called back. The bear slowly turned around and just as slowly raised a single impatient brow. "Asher Morestead." He straightened confidently and held out his hand. The bear slowly looked him over, his nostrils flaring mildly. Asher slowed his breathing and stayed calm. He needed him to know he meant no harm. Finally, the bear took his hand.

"Nathan Marks."

"It's good to meet you." They let go of each other. "I believe we've crossed paths once before."

"Yes," he agreed, although not enthusiastically. He didn't want to be here or have this conversation, but Asher sensed no hostility.

"We have something in common. I've never had the opportunity to meet someone with the same... trait... as we have."

Nathan's lips twitched and his gaze slid to the side for a moment. "I've noticed a few. Never met any."

"Really. I've figured we're a small group." In his twenty-two years as a shifter, he'd never noticed any others until he smelled this bear.

"I wouldn't say small. Just spread out."

"That's interesting. Maybe we can sit down some time, compare notes."

Nathan shrugged. "Maybe. See ya." He nodded once and turned, continuing around the corner.

Asher tried not to let his frustrations get to him. It was more information than he'd ever discovered on his own. He'd lived his life to suit himself, never leaving home to search for others. He couldn't blame another shifter for keeping to himself as well.

He shook himself off and finished the walk to pick up the car rental. He dialed Gwen, set his phone in the cup holder, and started the drive home.

"Hello?" Her sweet sing-song voice came through the speaker of the car.

"Hi. How are you doing so far?"

"Well, I've checked into the hotel and I've started by going out to lunch and now dinner at smaller restaurants. The ones that are run by locals. The kind of people who would know everyone who grew up here."

"Good idea. I'm on my way to return Cinder to the pack and grab my bag. I should be there in four hours, five at the most."

"You don't need to rush. Take your time with Cinder and get some sleep."

"Not possible. I'd never sleep. I'll be there tonight."

"Okay." Gwen's voice softened and the sound fled straight to his groin. Just as they had that morning, words that felt natural bubbled up, but he held them back. Forcing them down caused bile to swirl in his stomach.

"Bye, beautiful."

"Bye." Her goodbye was breathy. She'd had the same urge as him, both that morning and now. Even through the phone their emotions could affect one another. He couldn't physically feel it unless she was next to him, but apparently their bond was intuitive.

When Asher arrived home, he put his already packed bag in the rental, then went back to gather Cinder.

"Time to go home, beautiful girl." They'd kept her here longer than Asher planned. Gwen had grown an attachment to the little pup. Although her leg hadn't fully healed, it was past time for her to go home. He kept the splint on her leg and would check on her often to remove it when he could. He knew Kai would make sure she didn't knock it off. The circumstances were definitely unique. For any normal pack, there stood the chance that Cinder might never have been released to the wild. She also wouldn't be returned until her leg healed, ensuring her time spent with humans was longer.

He picked her up and scratched her ears. Cinder nipped playfully and licked his cheek. He wouldn't say he'd miss running back and forth from work and home to check up on her, but he will miss having her so close. She has a sweet soul.

Asher locked up behind him and started the hike through the woods, but he took a longer route to bypass the trail cams. He still didn't shift until he made it around to the marker, just in case. After he shifted, he picked up Cinder by her scruff and broke into a slow run.

Kai stood and met Asher outside the den that held the rest of the pups. The litter had grown and didn't spend as much time in the den as they did even a few weeks ago, but it would still be in use by the pups for a little while yet. Enough time for Cinder's leg to heal.

Asher set Cinder down and nudged Kai, a greeting and goodbye in one. Kai picked up Cinder and took her into the den. Asher was about to leave when he heard the sound of a rough engine. He froze, adjusting his ears. Kai suddenly appeared beside him and just as quickly, so did Smoke.

It could be Tony and Morton. It could be a stranger. It could also be Julian. Asher tried to calm himself so Kai and Smoke didn't feed off his energy, but his senses were firing. Telling himself it was only the conservation officers, he looked to Kai.

I'll check it out. I'll come back to give you the all clear before I leave.

Neither Kai or Smoke spoke back. Their heightened states infected Asher. They didn't believe it was the conservation officers any more than Asher.

Asher started back with a run then slowed to stalk up onto whoever it was. He sighed inwardly when he sensed Kai some distance behind him. Asher moved silently with each step. The scent of the vehicle grew stronger. Knowing he was getting close, he crouched low and searched around him. A few moments later, Kai crouched beside him.

I wish you stayed with the pack.

No. I'm with you.

Seeing nothing, Asher skulked from his hiding spot. Julian. He could smell him. It was faint, clouded by something else, something foul. Despite his stomach revolting, Asher followed the rancid scent. His senses were strong enough to smell the worm beneath it. He rounded a bush. What he saw stood his fur on end down the full length of his back. Chills crawled over his body. A quad sat there with a trailer, but the cage on the trailer sent fear and anger racing through his blood.

He took one more step and he felt a sudden sharp sting

in his hind quarters. He turned his head and saw a tranquilizer dart sticking out.

Fuck.

Alcohol, over the counter drugs, and even prescription drugs never had an effect on him, at least not at normal or safe levels. One night when he'd been seventeen, he'd wanted to see what it took for him to feel the effects of alcohol. Turned out to be way too much before he had even started to feel slightly inebriated. It was too expensive and not worth it.

He hoped the same applied for the drug inside the dart.

Kai burst from their hiding spot. Asher felt the rush of another dart fly past him. He reached around, stretching further than his body allowed, and pulled the dart out. He looked back and Kai was still running toward him, a dart stuck in the ground behind him. Asher searched, not seeing anyone. He heard a faint whoosh just as Kai slammed into his side rolling the two of them together and into the cover of the closest bush.

In the tree, said Kai. Asher looked up and there he was. The fucker was perched pointing the tranquilizer gun toward the bush. *He hit you.*

He did.

Feel anything? Asher hadn't felt this much worry from his pair since they were pups.

No. He probably planned for a normal wolf. But now he has us pinned. Or so Asher thought. A dart flew through the bush and landed in Asher's shoulder. Kai was quick to pull it out of him. A second dart came through and hit Kai. Asher did the same, gently and quickly gripping the dart between his teeth. Asher knew the drugs had already been released, but it was better than leaving them in. This was ridiculous. They couldn't hide while Julian shot at them through the bushes with darts. *We need to divide his attention.*

Got it.

We're strong enough to shake the tree and make him lose his balance. First one to get there gets to choose the next hunt. Asher threw the competition down to ease the tension.

You're on. Kai loved taking Asher on hunts. He bolted, running in an erratic pattern to the next bush. While Asher thought Julian would be occupied following Kai, he started in the other direction. But as soon as his body cleared the bush, he was struck with a dart.

Son of a bitch. The fucker was smarter than he gave him credit for. He ignored the dart and moved to the next hiding spot. He saw Kai in the distance move again and Julian pulled the same move on him. *Kai!*

I'm fine.

A vicious snarl snapped Asher's head back. Smoke. With gnashing teeth, Smoke bolted for the tree where Julian sat. Julian's attention changed forward and he fumbled with the gun to load it and raise it toward Smoke.

Now! Asher and Kai yelled in unison. All three wolves lunged for the tree. Hitting it with the force of three giant sized wolves jarred the trunk and shook the upper portion. Julian's hands and focus had been on his gun, leaving his balance unstable. He fell, reaching for branches and the tree trunk on his way down to lessen his impact.

Kai grabbed the fallen gun and threw it away. The three wolves rounded on him. Asher shook his head. His eyes crossed. Julian blurred in front of him. Fucking drugs. He must have hit him with enough, but Asher knew they wouldn't last long. Just how long, he wasn't sure.

Checking on Kai, Asher saw him struggling. They both

stumbled over their feet. Asher was conscious long enough to see Julian pull a tiny pistol from the side of his leg.

Get the fuck out of here, Smoke! Now!

Protect the pack, Kai added.

Smoke backed away slowly, looking between Asher and Kai, and still snarled at Julian. When Julian raised the gun, Smoke bolted. Asher sensed his guilt and he hurt even more for Smoke and what he was going through missing his pair.

Asher wouldn't be getting to Hull Creek tonight. He needed Gwen to be safe. Asher locked eyes with his pair. Because they weren't.

GWEN'S COURAGE TO search for Zachary on her own was fading. With so little to go on, she didn't know where to go from here. At least she got a feel for the town. It wasn't so big that searching for someone would be difficult, but it wasn't a cozy small town either. This could take a bit of work. Asher's nose might help, if Zachary was in town.

People were friendly. She found it easy to strike up conversations and the residents loved to talk up their town and people, but when it came to asking, "Do you know a man named Zachary between the ages of thirty and thirty-five and might have had a pet named Smoke? Oh and no, I don't know what he looks like," seemed strange. If someone asked her a question like that she would wonder about the person's intentions.

Leaving the restaurant, a small tremor took over her body. She took a breath to steady herself. All of her senses pulled together then expanded, searching her surroundings. The whole process was out of her control and it left her reeling. Taking short breaths was the only way she managed to stay standing. As her senses reached, she felt eyes on her back. Someone was watching her. Gwen spun around. Grey eyes flashed, but quickly moved away.

Damn it. She found Zachary, or he found her, but that wasn't the cause for her body going haywire. She didn't have the strength, or the urge, to follow him. Zachary would have to wait. She needed to call Asher.

Slowly, Gwen made her way to Asher's truck. Maybe she shouldn't drive while struggling for control, but all her senses were on high alert. She decided to trust them and let instinct help her through. She made it back to the hotel and splashed her face with cold water. Steadying herself with the bathroom counter, she breathed in slowly. She took some yoga classes a few years ago, not her thing, but the one thing she took away from them was the breathing, feeling her breath enter her body, filling her body, and slowly exhaling through her mouth, focusing on the sounds.

Feeling as if she at least understood her own body, Gwen sat on the bed and dialed Asher. He didn't know anything about what the mating bond would do to her, but maybe he could help her figure it out. She needed to tell him how her senses had been reacting at certain times. But what made her react this time and so severely? Not Zachary. She knew that without a doubt.

The call went to Asher's voicemail. Gwen didn't bother leaving a message. She hung up and waited. Maybe it was taking him longer to return Cinder. He would be back soon.

She watched the clock, waiting exactly ten minutes and tried again. It went to voicemail after several rings. Her body was firing, sending shocks through her system. Something wasn't right. The sensation wasn't painful, but uncomfortable. Her skin felt sensitive as whatever the impression was, it originated from her chest.

This time, she waited fifteen minutes and called Asher again. She slammed her phone down on the bed when his voicemail answered, but then she brought it back up to her ear and left a message.

"Asher. Something isn't right. Call me soon." She laid down on the bed, clutching her phone to her chest, and tried to rationalize. Maybe he forgot his phone, or the battery died and he didn't notice. He could have gotten an emergency call from work.

She closed her eyes to rest, knowing the futility of the effort with her body fidgeting and urging her to move. With her eyes closed, her body and mind entered an altered state. She grappled within herself while she had no idea about the time passing.

Gwen wasn't sure if she fell asleep. Maybe it was some form of rest, but her senses won the fight. She bolted upright and looked at the clock. Only thirty minutes had passed. She called him one last time while she grabbed the keys and her bags. Still nothing.

She didn't wait to check out of the hotel. She tossed her room key on the desk and kept walking. Hairs on the back of her neck made her stop suddenly. She searched and there, flashing grey eyes off in the distance. As soon as she found them, they disappeared. He must have followed her and discovered what she is to another shifter, or it was possible he smelled Smoke on her, but he didn't want to talk to her. He stood too far away and she didn't have time. She would come back. They would come back, her and Asher.

Poor Smoke.

Guilt gnawed at her. She should try to confront him. She took one step toward the direction of those eyes but an ache in her body pulled her back to the truck.

Caution called to her. She assumed the grey eyes were

Zachary, but there was a possibility it was a different shifter. It would be best to come back with Asher. At least they knew where to find him.

She threw her bag across to the passenger side and climbed in the truck. Gwen didn't stop the entire drive back to Asher's and the closer she got, the harder her heart pounded.

CHAPTER 12

Asher breathed deep to expel the last of the effects of the tranquilizer. He let out a huff and shook his head, relieved to have fur covering his body. He hadn't known what his body would do in a drug induced unconscious state. It occurred to him at the last second that he might lose control of a shift. He looked at Kai. He lay beside Asher, still unconscious, but he groaned and his eyes squinted.

Metal was solid beneath him and he noted the surrounding bars. They were in the cage on Julian's trailer. At least he and Kai were together.

Pushing himself up, he braced himself on his front legs. Julian had parked outside of Asher's house. His front door was open, and he heard Julian yelling inside.

"Gwen!" He gave his thanks to Fate that Gwen convinced him to let her go to Hull Creek, but he wasn't sure what she would do when he didn't show up. At least she didn't expect him for a few more hours.

Julian came out. He slammed the door behind him and stalked toward them. Kai woke and watched Julian with narrowed eyes.

"Two fucking beasts. I don't get it and I don't understand why one of you was at that wedding. There's so much I could do with just one of you, let alone two, two identical beasts." He repeated with awe. "But I've been turned into a fool. I'm turning you two over to Fish and Wildlife. Then I'm going after Gwen. The lying bitch."

Asher and Kai growled low.

"You don't scare me, not from inside that cage. But keep growling. Show them exactly how dangerous you are." His words didn't stop them. If the drugs hadn't left them weak, they'd try to break free from the cage now, but the last thing they wanted was for Julian to load them with more darts. If Asher still felt the effects, then so did Kai. It wouldn't last long, but by the time they had their full strength back, they could be moving.

Julian drove down past Asher's parents' house and to the end of the road where Tony and Morton waited. He cut the engine and pulled off his helmet.

"There!" He pointed at the cage. "I'm not crazy. And there's two of them."

Asher and Kai lay still beside each other, their strength beginning to rise. They kept their eyes on Julian. The conservation officers didn't worry them. Julian's plans did.

"Amazing." Both Tony and Morton whispered simultaneously. Asher had known both Tony and Morton for a long time. They all went to school together. He knew the love they held for animals. He also knew how excited they were to see wolves such as Asher and Kai up close.

"They're massive." Tony walked around the cage.

"They're beasts," Julian snapped. "I hope you do the right thing and get rid of them."

Asher saw the officers frown from the severity of his suggestion, but they nodded to Julian.

"Good." Julian unhitched the trailer and put his helmet back on. "They're all yours." He drove off. Asher wasn't sure where, except he was in search of Gwen.

"We're releasing them, right?" Morton crossed his arms.

"Yeah, of course. We should give Asher a call first, let him know someone captured wolves close to his property and ask if he can come look at them." Tony sighed as he reached into his pocket for his phone. "He had to have known about the wolves and chose not to tell us." Asher hated hearing disappointment from his friend.

"Who knows how many darts that kid hit them with or what he did to them after."

Asher's ears perked up. Were they assuming Julian used darts, or did they know?

"That grey wolf is just as big as these two." The trail cams have live feed. They saw most of what happened. Tony lifted his phone. If he was calling Asher now, he was going to be disappointed. "No answer."

"Can I help you?" Asher heard his father's voice echo from the lane. The officers waited until he reached them.

"Sorry if we've disturbed you, Mr. Morestead."

His father tilted and looked around them to see the cage. "As I said, is there anything I can help you with?"

"Do you know where Asher is?" asked Tony.

"He's out of town for the weekend. Have a couple wolves?" Asher's father walked around the officers and came close to the cage.

"We're hoping he could look at them to make sure they're okay."

"Oh, they're fine." He reached his hand into the cage and toward Kai's head.

"No! Don't do that, sir." Morton yelled and stepped forward with an outreached hand. His father didn't listen.

He gently stroked Kai's head, then Asher's. He was nervous, Asher could sense it, but he forced himself to be outwardly confident. Asher pushed his head into his father's hand. The man knew something.

"I'll be damned," whispered Morton. Asher and Kai were too big for the cage and unable to stand up, but they both propped themselves up to show their strength.

"There's always been wildlife in these woods. Wolves have never been a problem." His father turned to the officers.

"You see them often?" Tony stepped closer.

"No. In fact, it's been a very long time. Before Asher moved out." His eyes turned to Asher.

Damn it.

Don't beat yourself up, Asher. We must have been pups.

"I'd appreciate it if you'd let them go."

"We will. I'd feel better if they were looked at first. They were both shot with several tranquilizers. Then we'll get them back into the woods and release them there."

"If they're awake, they're fine. And it'll be safe to release them here."

"Is there something you know that we don't?" Tony narrowed his eyes.

"Probably a lot of things." His father's lips lifted at the corners.

"Thank you for your input and help, Mr. Morestead." The officers dismissed him.

"You're welcome." He looked back at the wolves one last time and walked away. There wasn't anything he could really do to help them.

We don't have the time to wait around for another vet or for them to drive us back to the woods. Besides, I don't want a vet to touch us. We're too atypical for someone to ignore. Even the officers may want to track us.

Then let's break out. Kai pushed his legs beneath him and braced himself in a crouched position. Asher followed suit. Pulling back, they lurched forward, ramming the cage door. Twice more and they bent the bars, allowing the door to release. Tony and Morton stood in defensive stances, their jaws tense, staring at the two wolves standing their full height behind the trailer.

Asher looked at his father, who had turned around at the noise. His chin lifted and his eyes sparked with pride.

Let's go, Asher said to Kai. They darted into the woods and hoped no one followed them. He also made a note to get them to remove the cameras. They turned out beneficial for now, but when this was over, Asher wanted the freedom of his woods back.

GWEN PASSED the Fish and Wildlife truck on the way to Asher's. They pulled a trailer with a broken and empty cage behind them. Gwen's stomach dropped. She pulled into Asher's driveway and parked beside the rental car. She sat, knuckles white on the steering wheel, unsure where to go or what to do.

She stepped out of the truck and started for the house, calling Asher's name.

"Asher?" There was no response by the time she reached the doorstep. Standing still, she listened, her senses still scopic, but she couldn't sense Asher. A split second decision had her running back to the truck. If the conservation officers had been here, Asher's parents might have seen something. She didn't have time to feel nervous or awkward about introducing herself to his parents without Asher. This was more important. Although she didn't know what was going on, only that something was wrong, either with her or Asher.

Gwen parked the truck and jogged to their front door. It swung open before her knuckles reached the wood to knock.

"You must be Gwen." An older version of Asher looked down at her with the same kind smile his son had.

"I am. Gwen Taylor."

"I'm Theodore. My wife Molly is inside. Come in." He stood back to let her in, but she shook her head.

"I'm sorry. I wish I had time to visit, and I'd like to very soon, but I need to find Asher. It's urgent."

"I'm sure Asher is fine. I haven't seen *him*," he stretched out the word and his brows, "but I did suggest to some young conservation officers that they release a couple white wolves they caught. However, the wolves beat them to it. They ran off safe and sound." His lips twitched while he explained what happened. Asher told her his parents didn't know what he was, but it seemed his father was more vigilant than Asher realized.

She sighed inwardly, knowing that Asher was fine, but her insides churned, still in turmoil. "Thank you." She attempted to smile at him, but was certain her expression didn't resemble what it should. "I promise I'll come back and introduce myself properly, or make sure Asher does."

"You're welcome to stay and wait for him here. I'm sure he'll be able to find you." Another piece of knowledge reflected in his tone. Gwen hesitated. It would be smart to stay in one spot until she found out what was happening, but her body wouldn't sit still. She needed to move. She needed to run. She needed her mate. To think that way herself had become innate. The word rang through her the same way Asher described it did for him. It didn't matter that she wasn't a shifter. Fate made her a mate and pulled her into that same magical world.

"Thank you. That's very kind. But something isn't right. If I can't find him, I'll come back to wait here."

Gwen walked back to the truck. His eyes followed her. She didn't want him to worry overmuch. She waved before driving back to Asher's house.

He was probably still in the woods with Kai. She started for the woods, mindful of the trail cams, but stopped when her ears picked up something inside the house. The foreign oversensitive hearing put a low hum between her ears. She winced whenever a sound jumped across that humming bridge. Gwen cocked her head with the faint sound of a door closing and heavy footsteps. She never heard Asher be anything but graceful and silent when he moved. Something was wrong, even if she didn't know what. Maybe he felt just as off as she did. She walked back to the house and called his name again.

"Asher? Are you in there?"

As soon as her hand landed on the door handle, her gut twisted with nausea. Her stomach coiled tight and an instinct tried to pull her away. A pressure along the length of her spine curved her back, like an arm wrapped around her ribs from behind.

Before she could react, the door swung inward, her grip on the handle jerking her forward. A hand wrapped around her wrist, the grip painful. She looked up and Julian's eyes looked back at her with a disgusting evil. Gwen twisted so she could pull back toward herself. Flexing her fingers, she yanked suddenly, surprising Julian and breaking free. She turned to run out of the house, her intention to find Asher,

Kai, or even Smoke, but he fisted her hair and pulled her back. She screamed as he threw her into the house and landed on her back on the floor. Julian shut the door and locked them inside.

"You fucking, lying, cunt. You saw the white beast and made me look like a fool. But not anymore. I've caught it and handed it over to the conservation officers. Now it's your story that has been discredited. They all know you lied. Do you really think they'll believe I attacked you?"

If she didn't just hear from Asher's dad that the wolves escaped, she would worry. Julian frightened her, she couldn't hide that, but Asher was free. He would come back.

Julian looked around the room, shaking his head. "You barely know this guy. Why the fuck would you hook up with him, but not me? We've known each other since we were kids. It's natural for us to end up together." He kept talking, not really caring if she had an answer. "I tried so hard to get your attention. If you had just let me fuck you in the alley, you would have seen we are good together."

"You're insane."

"Don't be rude, Gwen. It's not like you."

He obviously had no idea what kind of person she was. She was only just learning that herself. No wonder she didn't know what to do with her life. She'd been waiting to find Asher. With Asher, she saw herself more clearly.

Her problem right now was that she hadn't really known Julian either.

ASHER AND KAI raced into the woods, only long enough to ensure Tony and Morton weren't trying to follow them. Asher wouldn't put it past them. The wolves stopped over a hill and watched. The officers froze with shock. After some time of discussing what to do, they shook themselves off and closed the cage, tying it in place to keep the broken door from swinging. The wolves didn't move until they saw Tony and Morton drive off and turn away from Asher's property.

When they'd escaped, they had run in the opposite direction of Asher's home, but now they circled back taking a wide berth. Knowing Gwen was safe in Hull Creek helped Asher stay calm, but he needed to call her and tell her he wouldn't be coming, at least not right away. He needed to deal with Julian. Images of what he would do to Gwen if he found her haunted his mind. The man was unpredictable, and Asher didn't know what lengths he'd go to or what his intentions were.

Shut up. Kai spoke to him.

I didn't say anything, Asher said, confused.

You didn't need to, but I don't need to see your thoughts. Gwen is your mate, so she's pack. I won't let anyone hurt the pack.

I didn't know you could see my thoughts. They slowed down to a trot.

I didn't know that either. It was just now. Kai shook his head as if to shake out the images Asher unintentionally placed.

I haven't talked to you about Gwen since I found her. Between everything happening and his own cowardice, Asher hadn't brought it up in conversation.

There's nothing to talk about. She's your mate. It's uncontrollable, not that that matters. How else would your species live on? His pragmatic explanation made Asher stagger.

There's no way to know how our offspring would turn out. Asher stopped and waited for Kai to stop as well. Kai turned around and they stood looking at mirror images of each other for a silent moment.

My mother used to say we were created for a reason and that reason didn't end with us. Kai paused, a moment of grief flashing through both of them. *Of course your offspring will be shifters.*

Shifters without pairs. Asher's kind could live on, but not Kai's.

I don't know.

Eventually, they moved again, walking until they heard a vehicle drive along the adjacent road. A vehicle that sounded exactly like Asher's truck. Asher didn't understand why Gwen would be back now. She wasn't expecting him for another hour or more. Then suddenly, the sensations hit him. Her body was panicking. That still didn't explain why she wouldn't have waited for him in Hull Creek, where she was safe.

At least Julian had left to search for her elsewhere. But what if he was wrong?

As if to justify the rising panic inside him, the white wind appeared suddenly in front of them. It shook with its own form of panic then darted off through the trees in the direction of Asher's house. It disappeared entirely once it was out of sight, but that was all the warning Asher needed. If the wind was upset, then Asher should be too.

Run. Now! Asher and Kai bolted toward his house. The closer they got, the more chaotic his insides became.

By the time they reached the tree line outside his home, they heard screams and the violent sound of a thrown body. Asher lunged for the house, but Kai gripped his shoulder in his jaws.

Calm down.

You expect me to fucking calm down? That's my mate and I can smell the bastard who has her.

Smoke is almost in the house.

Asher swung his head and opened his senses past Gwen, it took a lot of effort to the point he wasn't sure he could, but then he spotted Smoke. Fur on end, teeth bared, ready to break through the door and kill Julian. Asher knew he would, he felt the urge himself, but that wouldn't do them any good right now. Not that Asher knew of a better option for Julian's fate. He'd figure that out after he saved Gwen.

They darted across the yard toward Smoke and called after him. He looked back and snarled.

We work together. Understand?

Smoke growled at Asher, but his head bobbed up and down. *Got it.*

Spread out.

CHAPTER 13

Gwen braced her hands on the floor and tried to stand. Julian swung his leg, his foot striking across her face, throwing her back down. She gritted her teeth at the tears that escaped with the pain.

"Oh, the things I want to do to you." Julian spoke through his teeth. His lips curled with a repulsive enjoyment. He hardened and bulged beneath his black pants. "First things first. We're going to get out of here before your lover boy comes home."

He grabbed her arm and tried to pull her up. Gwen kept her weight dead and lifted her legs. She kicked, her foot landing in the crook of his arm, breaking his bruising grip. He twisted away from her and landed with his knee on her chest. The air heaved out of her. The impact left her gasping while Julian pulled a knife from behind his back and held it against her throat.

"Don't fucking fight me this time."

The cold, stinging sharpness of the blade pressed against her skin. Her body shook and she whimpered. The fight left her in favour of preservation.

"That's right. You should be a scared little cunt." Keeping the knife against her neck, he lifted off and pulled on her arm. This time she braced herself and followed him up. He moved the knife to her side, wrapping that arm around her so her back was against his side. He moved toward the back of the house. Gwen's feet scurried to keep up with him. She feared if she slipped, so would the knife, and in the wrong direction.

Gwen hated herself for not knowing how to handle this. For not knowing how to fight against him and free herself. For not knowing if she needed to stall and keep him there until Asher and Kai made their way back. For not knowing if she needed to let him take her and get far away to make sure Asher and Kai didn't get hurt.

Just when she thought her life was taking shape, her options and new interests laid out, new opportunities showing themselves, Julian happens. What life would she have after being taken away from Asher? Would she have a life at all? She didn't think Julian planned to kill her, but what did she know.

Gwen searched for some of Asher's confidence to believe this would be over. It had to be. Where was Fate right now? Gwen promised herself she would learn. Learn how to defend herself and learn what to do in a situation like this. And that was how she needed to look at this. A lesson to be learned, because she refused to let Julian win in any way.

He pulled her through the back door. Asher's back yard was bare for only a short distance until it hit more trees. A quad was parked and waiting with two helmets.

Julian's grip changed as they approached the quad. Smoke leapt onto the seat of the vehicle, knocking off the helmets, his huge front paws covering the leather and his back paws behind the seat. His balance was steady while he crouched and snarled at Julian.

No. Not Smoke. Gwen couldn't stand the thought of him getting hurt, not when they were so close to finding Zachary for him. She suddenly wished she could speak to him the way Asher did when he was in his wolf form. She wasn't sure what Julian would make of her speaking aloud to a wolf. He didn't know about shifters, and Gwen wanted it to stay that way.

"What is it with this place and fucking wolves?" Julian tightened his grip. She felt the knife slice through her shirt and prick her skin. She winced and Smoke snarled and snapped, having scented the blood. Similar sounds from behind them forced Julian to swivel. His attention was no longer on what he was doing with the knife at her side, but with his grip tightening with tension, the prick in her side turned to a longer cut. She gasped, but Julian noticed nothing except the three wolves surrounding him.

But the wolves noticed. Their nostrils flared further and their growling deepened. Julian whipped back around, sending the knife through the cut again.

"Ahh," Gwen cried out, unable to hold it in.

"Shut up." His attention wasn't staying on one wolf. As soon as he turned back around to face Kai and Asher, weight landed on his back. He hunched over, pushing her into the blade before he let go. The knife dropped and his arm loosen. Gwen pitched herself forward and to the ground, her arms blanketing her left side. A quick glance back and she saw Smoke's jaw latched onto Julian's shoulder.

Asher and Kai moved close and barked until Smoke let go. Blood coated Julian's shirt. His body sagged once he stopped fighting. His eyes fluttered as he rolled onto his back and eyed the three wolves.

"Why the fuck aren't they attacking you?" His voice cracked.

"I didn't look threatening carrying a knife." Her voice didn't sound much better. Even she heard her weakness. And she wasn't hurt as badly as Julian. At least she didn't think she was. Her side and her hands were wet and warm.

With the wolves all on one side of him, Julian tried to scramble toward Gwen. "We're going to crawl to the quad and get the fuck out of here." He reached for her ankle. She pulled her foot back.

"I'm not going anywhere with you."

The bite on his shoulder was deep. Blood continued to flow, and his strength was draining fast. He wouldn't be able to keep a hold of her, let alone drive away on anything.

Asher came over to her but didn't shift. She assumed that was because Julian was still conscious. They all waited and watched while Julian's eyes finally closed, and he fell fully to the ground.

ASHER'S HEART POUNDED. Gwen was hurt. Julian was bleeding out. He needed to be the alpha he was.

He nudged her arms away from her abdomen and nipped at her shirt to lift it. The deep cut needed stitches, but putting pressure on it would stop the bleeding for now. Julian's injury was more severe. As much as he wanted the fucking ass nugget to die, that could create more problems. But so could a vicious attack by a wolf on private property.

Asher shifted.

"Gwen." He breathed her name and pressed his lips to her head. "Are you hurt anywhere else?"

"No." Asher helped her sit up and gently pulled her shirt over her head.

"Use this and keep pressure on it."

He stepped over her and went to Julian. He felt for a pulse. It was slow, but it was there. Asher ripped Julian's shirt off him. Damn, Smoke bit hard, but he had the self control that Asher probably wouldn't have had to keep the bite from puncturing something vital and killing him a lot faster. He lost a lot of blood and must be in a lot of pain for him to pass out the way he did.

Asher had a decision to make. Probably the hardest decision of his life, so far. He looked at Smoke and then Kai.

"You two need to get as far away from here as possible. And move the pack. Move deeper, toward the mountains. I'll find you when it's safe. I'm calling an ambulance. Stay on him until I get some clothes and get my phone."

He couldn't let him die, but he couldn't treat him himself and let him get away with hurting Gwen.

"Asher. You can't. You can't put yourself in danger, or any of the other wolves. And what about other shifters?"

"Gwen, do you know what the other option is? He'll have to die and disappear."

Tears coated her cheeks.

"We'll get through this. It will pass."

Asher had to think of the best future for himself and his mate, for his pack family, and for other shifters. They needed to be clear of this and allow authorities to move on, knowing they wouldn't find anything suspicious. He ran inside and dressed and grabbed his phone from the rental car. When he got back, he checked Julian's pulse again. The bleeding slowed with his own shirt wrapped around the wound.

"Okay, you two. Time to go. Disappear. Cover your tracks."

Kai growled, a low, painful, frustrated sound, and closed his eyes. Asher felt the pain coming from him as if it was his own. It was his own. Kai laid his head on Asher's shoulder. He started a sorrowful howl. Asher allowed himself to begin to shift enough that his voice changed, and he joined in the song that echoed. The breeze came rushing through the trees and gradually turned to white. The wind danced around them until their song finished, then pulled Kai away.

"I will find you! Soon." Kai nodded and ran, following the white wind. Asher looked behind him and saw Smoke laying his head on Gwen's chest with his eyes closed. He took a deep breath and abruptly stood, following Kai and the wind.

Some of Asher's worries eased, knowing they had the wind to follow. It would keep them safe.

Knowing he was making the best decision to keep them all safe, he dialed 911 and requested an ambulance and the RCMP.

A SMALL SUV skidded to a stop as the paramedics pushed Gwen toward the waiting ambulance. The doors of a second ambulance surrounded by RCMP officers closed. Asher left her side and met his father getting out of the SUV. He brought him over.

"Gwen, I'm sending my father with you. I need to stay and talk to the police, but I will be there as soon as I can." He squeezed her hand and brushed her hair back. The paramedics continued to push her along and were getting ready to lift her into the vehicle. Asher didn't let go of her hand as the distance stretched. Pain settled in her heart as they pulled them apart. She was being silly. He would follow her to the hospital as soon as he finished with the police.

"It's all right, sweetheart. I won't leave you." Theodore climbed into the ambulance and took her hand, patting the back of it. His knuckle swiped down her cheek and she realized she'd been crying.

"Thank you," she said with a hoarse whisper.

Entering the emergency wing of the hospital was hectic, and it was the first time she feared being here. As they pushed her through the doors, she saw Julian disappear down the hall, followed by two police officers. Gwen shuddered, but Theodore patted her shoulder.

"He won't be coming near you again." He sounded just like Asher with his growly demands. "Is there anyone you'd like me to call for you?"

"Yes. My parents, please." Theodore followed them to the exam room, then stepped outside to make the call. When he tried to step back in, the nurse stopped him.

"Please let him in. I want someone with me." Gwen's voice was a cracked plea. The nurse eyed them both.

"Only immediate family."

"He's my father-in-law. He came with me in the ambulance." Theodore nodded firmly at the nurse, confirming her lie as the truth.

"Well, all right." She allowed him to pass. He moved to her side and winked just before the doctor entered the room.

A few questions and a quick inspection, the doctor confirmed Asher's opinion. Her wound wasn't too deep to cause serious damage, but needed several stitches, and they didn't suspect a concussion.

Chaos erupted as Gwen's parents barged into the room. Theodore bent down to speak in her ear.

"I'll wait outside for Asher." He squeezed her hand and nodded at her parents as he passed to leave. An odd look passed between him and her father, but neither said anything as their attention moved directly back to Gwen.

"What happened?" her mother cried.

"Julian." Gwen didn't have the energy to say more, not yet. Seeing her parents allowed the tears and fear she held in so tight to escape. Her mother bent down and held her. Gwen wrapped her arm around her mother on her free side while the doctor was working on her cut.

"Where is he?" The menace from her father had the doctor and the nurses looking toward him.

"Here. With police." She watched her father struggle. He shook on the spot, fighting with himself to stay or leave to find Julian. He ran his hand over his face and moved to stand beside her with his wife. They stayed with her while the doctor finished.

The doctor left, and she heard voices outside her room. The voices triggered her sensitive ears and she recognized Asher. The ache in her heart she didn't realize was still there, faded away.

Asher came into the room and stopped short at the sight of her parents. Lines creased his face that hadn't been there when she saw him the day before. She felt every wave of anxiety pour out of his chest and crash against hers as if he was screaming the emotion directly at her.

"Who are you?" Demanded her dad.

"I'm Asher Morestead. I've been seeing your daughter." He moved to the other side and rested his forehead to hers.

His eyes bored into her and she closed hers, soaking in the warmth and safety.

"Gwen?" her mom asked. Gwen sighed, unsure what to say, but she was saved from explaining when the RCMP officers that followed Asher from his place stepped into the room.

"Miss Taylor, the doctor says you're all stitched up and are going to be fine. Do you feel up to talking with us?" Gwen nodded. The officers looked to her parents and Asher. "If you'll all excuse us?" No one moved.

"Mom, Dad, please?"

"Dr. Morestead as well."

"No." Gwen gripped onto Asher's arm. "I need him here." The officer nodded, then held the door for her parents. They hesitated, but left without a fight.

"Well, Miss Taylor. We've talked to Asher and to the conservation officers involved, but we need to hear what happened tonight. Can you talk us through that?"

Gwen swallowed and walked them through the night, explaining a gut feeling that brought her back earlier than planned. It terrified her to talk to them. Asher had told her to tell the truth, but as she saw it. She saw three wolves rescue her from her attacker and then disappear once she was safe. She didn't want to put Asher or other shifters in danger by bringing attention to the abnormal wolves.

Just as the first time Julian attacked her, her mind only focused on protecting the wolf, or wolves. She hadn't considered the trauma she went through until fear struck through her chest when she had to tell the officers how he'd pulled her into Asher's house, kicked her, had to remember the knife at her throat, the sharp edge easily cutting her side.

Asher's muscles tightened and his eyes flashed deeper

and brighter as she spoke. They changed enough he had to hide them. He looked downward or buried his face in her neck until he regained control.

Between what Asher told them at his house, the reports from Fish and Wildlife, and Gwen's recounting, they had more than enough to arrest and charge Julian. As soon as he was treated and discharged from the hospital, they would take him into custody.

They allowed her parents back in the room and the tension instantly rose thick in the air. Her mother looked at her and her father watched Asher with narrowed eyes, both demanding answers.

"I've been seeing Asher for a couple weeks. Julian has been stalking me and came after me at Asher's." She didn't want to say more. How would she explain wolves to her parents?

"You let this happen to my girl?" Her father sneered at Asher.

"Don't." Gwen snapped. "Don't say another word. This is not his fault and I'm too tired to deal with any more. I'm done." Gwen couldn't fault them for placing blame at Asher's feet. She hadn't told them about him. They didn't know she was seeing someone, let alone practically living with him. But she wouldn't allow them to outwardly blame him, and she meant it when she said she didn't have the energy.

The tension hadn't dissipated by the time the doctor came back in to discharge her. Her body still felt panicky, so she insisted on leaving with Asher rather than her parents. They tried to fight her. They tried to fight Asher. They even tried to fight the doctor. But Gwen stuck to her decision. It was Asher, her mate, that she needed.

Exhaustion weighed heavily on Gwen as Asher carried her into his house.

The RCMP officers notified them before they left that Fish and Wildlife would put up more trail cameras, and a thorough search for the wolves would begin the next day. That worried her as much as it did Asher. He trusted Kai to move and cover their tracks, but Gwen knew how much it was hurting both Kai and Asher.

It had been hours since Asher called 911 and they'd yet to have a break. Asher sat down on the couch and held her. His arms wrapped around her and she soaked in his determination while she tried to lend strength to his hurting heart.

"What about Cinder? She still has the splint on."

"Kai will take care of her." His voice was hoarse.

"What do we do now, Asher?"

"We wait. We just wait until this blows over and we hope it doesn't take too long." He placed a knuckle under her chin and tilted her head back to look up at him. "With things so calm, maybe we'll get to date each other properly."

"I think that sounds like a great idea."

"Let's go to bed." He stood and lifted her with him. She could walk on her own, but he insisted she didn't at the hospital and she didn't want to argue with him about it now. Gwen selfishly enjoyed being taken care of.

Asher divested them each of their clothes, being gentle with her, then helped her into bed. Once they settled, her laying on her right side with her cheek on his shoulder, her eyes closed. The worry, anxiety, and fear weren't enough to keep her awake, but she fell asleep with one final thought.

"I could use a bit of normal for a little while."

CHAPTER 14

Asher's body finally took over and forced rest upon him not long after Gwen fell asleep, but he woke with her last words ringing through his head. She wanted normal. There had been a time he would have been able to give her normal, at least something resembling normal. He was a shifter who had a wolf for a best friend, but that was the only abnormal thing about his life.

Except not anymore. He wouldn't be ignorant and live life to suit himself. Other shifters existed and he needed to find them. It was time he discovered how and why shifters were created. Life wouldn't be normal again.

He wondered if it was possible to separate bonded mates. And the strength of their bond that fused them together was a heavy aura. But he wouldn't force her if she truly wanted out.

Asher kissed her awake, running his lips along her collarbone. He ran his fingertips up and down her side and over her hip. She sighed and moaned, and Asher soaked up every sound she made.

"Morning." Her sleepy voice was an aphrodisiac he

didn't need. She was too sore for him to take, despite what his body wanted.

"Morning." His desire leaked through unintentionally. They said nothing else to each other. He placed a gentle kiss on her forehead and helped her out of bed and to the shower. He refused to let her shower alone, helping her with her bandage and washing around her wound. When they finished, he applied a fresh bandage and gave her one of his t-shirts to wear.

Sitting by the fire with coffee, Asher felt it was the best time to talk. He sat on the table in front of her, the position becoming familiar.

"Gwen, why did you come back from Hull Creek so soon?"

"It was a feeling I'm not sure if I can even explain. I was dizzy. My insides were in utter panic. All I knew was that something was wrong. At the time, I didn't know if there was something wrong with me or you. Now I know it was you."

"The mate bond," Asher said, giving voice to the obvious explanation.

"My senses went into overdrive and I couldn't control myself. I wasn't sure if I could drive, but my focus was heightened. It's something I've noticed recently. I haven't said anything because I wanted to keep an eye on it myself to see if I could figure it out."

"What is it?" Asher leaned forward and took her hand in his.

"I've had increased senses, smell and hearing, ever since you bit me. They aren't constant. They're active when we're out in the woods together, around other wolves, and apparently when they're needed. Like last night." Gwen spoke slowly.

"I wonder if it's the mark or the bond." Asher had

wondered if something in her would change. He had no way of knowing and he'd had no way to control it. He couldn't have stopped from marking her even if he wanted to. The satisfaction that followed and the euphoric state the marking put both of them in turned the mating into what it was now. It would be hard to let her go.

"I think it's the bond. The bite just seals it. But what do I know?" Gwen shrugged, then winced when she lifted her left side too suddenly. He reached his hand out to soothe over her wound.

"Easy. You know as much as I do." That shouldn't be the case. Asher should have more knowledge about his own species.

"I might have found Zachary."

"What?"

"If it wasn't him, then it was another shifter. I think he followed me from the restaurant, but I didn't stick around long enough for him to confront me. I couldn't. He was spying on me when I left to come home. He was far away, but I saw his eyes flash, the same way yours do. Also, my smell and hearing were going wild, so I knew what he was."

"While we're waiting for this to blow over, we'll go back. Together this time." He looked down at his hands. "If we are still together."

"What did you just say?" Gwen tilted her head, her brows falling together.

"Gwen, you said you wanted normal. And before we met, I could have given you normal, or at least as close to normal as possible, but I can't guarantee that anymore. I need to find other shifters and dig into the past. I don't know what sort of life this will shape out to be. I won't force you to stay with me if it isn't what you want."

"What a drama queen." Gwen shook her head and she laughed. Asher straightened.

"Excuse me? Drama queen?"

"I said I could use normal for *a little while.* That didn't mean I wanted to end our relationship, or worse, break our bond. I'm not sure about you, but I think it would be terribly painful for us to break that bond."

Gwen was still smiling at him and he felt a wave of relief followed by embarrassment.

"Drama queen, huh?" He tried not to let his lips twitch.

"Well, you jumped to the worst conclusion when all I meant was it would be nice to have a couple calm days to recover."

"Then that's what we'll do."

🐺

"I WANT TO CHANGE." Gwen sat in the passenger seat of Asher's truck on the way to work a week later. Asher hadn't been able to reschedule all of his appointments, but he took most of the week off to spend with her while she healed. She hadn't healed yet, but she didn't want to sit around any longer. She called Walker and asked if she could work short shifts and light duty. Asher wasn't pleased, but at least he understood and didn't stop her.

"Change? We're halfway there. You look beautiful, Gwen." Her heart thumped hard. He truly meant it every time he said it, and he'd been saying it a lot over the past week. He could brush her off and use average words, mundane words, but no. He said exactly what he thought with her.

"I'm not referring to my clothes. I'm referring to me."

"How do you want to change?" Asher glanced at her

quickly, his face creasing, before he looked back to keep his eyes on the road.

"I made a promise to myself during Julian's attack. I promised I wouldn't be helpless in that situation again. I want to learn to fight, to defend myself and others around me."

"All right." He nodded.

"Really? You don't have a problem with that?"

Asher laughed. "No, I don't." He sobered. "As much as I hate you needing it, I can't always be by your side. Life happens. It will be a comfort to know you'll be okay, at least until I get there." He paused, his features somber. "Besides, life will change from here on out."

"About that, I want to help with that too. Have you written everything down that's happened to you or all the things you've learned?"

"No."

"I want to keep a log, write the stories and legends we discover along the way."

"I don't know. There shouldn't be proof we exist."

"Think about it. There are ways around that."

"I'll think about it." Asher parked at *Woods Bistro* and stopped her from opening her own door. After he stalked around his truck and opened her door for her, he reached in and lifted her out. "You will let me take care of you how I see fit." He scowled before setting her down so her feet touched the ground.

"I can't argue with you when you get all grumpy about it." She leaned up on her tiptoes, a little strain pulling in her stitches, and quickly kissed his cheek. He only frowned harder.

"You better not push yourself like that at work." He'd felt the same strain she had. Ever since she felt the trouble while in Hull Creek and it brought her back to him, their bond only strengthened by the day. They weren't reading each other's thoughts, but they felt almost everything the other felt. Some days locked up in the house alone with him were harrowing. Emotions ran high after Kai went into hiding, but things evened out.

The pain still lurked, but they'd learned how to suppress it for now. A week wasn't long enough for things to blow over. Gwen hoped it didn't take more than a few months. She feared for Asher and she feared for Kai and Smoke. Finding Zachary was still a priority, but it had to wait.

"I'll be careful."

Asher escorted her into the bistro and all the way to the counter, practically handing her over to Walker who stood waiting, his eyes taking in every inch of her with a rough grimace on his face. The two men nodded at each other.

Asher spun her around and kissed her. It wasn't long, but it didn't need to be for the heat and promise he held to soak into her. Determination and tension were tightly wound coils inside him beneath everything he felt for her. She knew they were there because they were starting their own coils in her gut.

He straightened and ran his thumb over her wet lips. Heat pooled in her core and she closed her eyes while he stepped back. The entire exchange only took seconds, but the depth of those seconds would stay with her while she tried to resume her normal life over the next few hours.

Walker didn't baby her, but neither did he stop watching her like she would faint and fall flat on her face from pouring too many cups of coffee. Gwen did the best she could to ignore the behavior and poke fun at him every chance she had, which just increased his focus. She had to admit, it was nice to have someone watching out for her when she couldn't be with Asher. Now that she was here, she felt nervous. Julian was locked up. He couldn't come for her. Her mind knew that, but her body was responding to irrational fears.

Gwen made it through with no blunders or without panicking, although she was tired by the time Asher came in to pick her up. On the drive back to Asher's, her cell rang.

"Hi, Mom."

"Hi, hun. How are you feeling?" Her parents were only just getting over the shock that Julian could do what he did. Even after the first attack, they said the same things Gwen had. Something was off and everyone gave him the benefit of the doubt, willing to forgive him. But seeing Gwen in the hospital with a knife wound sealed their new opinions of Julian.

"I'm good, Mom. Finished my first shift back at work. Asher just picked me up." After their tense introduction at the hospital, she had been avoiding a more formal one. Despite its strength, their relationship felt raw.

"Should you be back at work so soon?"

"It was very short and very light work. I needed to get out."

"We haven't seen you since you got out of the hospital." Her mother's voice softened. Guilt crept up Gwen's sternum. "And we haven't really met your new man. Nor did we know about him until a week ago." Gwen had been so wrapped up in their relationship and everything going on with Julian, and then Smoke, she hadn't even thought about telling her family that she'd met someone.

"I know. I'm sorry."

"Bring him to dinner tonight then. We need to see our daughter, Gwen."

Gwen looked over at Asher, who was driving with a considerate tilt to his mouth. He nodded.

"Okay. We'll be there."

"One more thing. A man came here looking for you earlier. He didn't say who he was, just that he needed to speak with you. I didn't tell him where to find you." She paused. "He seemed nice."

Gwen and Asher looked at each other. "Okay. What did he look like?"

"Oh, tall, wearing a leather jacket, handsome. Dark." Her mother's husky tone didn't say that as if it was a bad thing.

"Mom." Gwen squeezed her eyes shut.

"Sorry." She didn't sound sorry about it.

"Okay, Mom. Call me if he shows up again."

"Will do. Bye, hun. Love you."

"Love you too, Mom." Gwen set her phone down on her lap.

"Any idea who would be looking for you?" asked Asher.

"None." She hadn't lived with her parents for years. No one she knew would bother looking for her there. Gwen shrugged and put her thoughts to better use, like introducing Asher to her parents. Properly.

◢

"Mom, Dad, this is Asher Morestead. Asher, these are my parents, Doug and Dianne Taylor." Gwen made the show of a formal introduction despite their own introduction at the hospital a week earlier.

"It's nice to see you again, Asher." Her mom smiled and held out her hand. Her father said nothing, but shook hands with Asher, unlike what he did at the hospital when he said her injury was his fault. "And it's good to see Gwen so well taken care of. You look so much better, hun." Her mom pulled Gwen into her embrace, and she realized that she was missing their comfort. She hadn't noticed it, but after being held, even briefly, her heart hurt. If it weren't for the bond and growing relationship with Asher, Gwen might have liked going home with her parents after the attack. But it would have hurt all the same to separate from Asher.

When she stepped back, Asher squeezed her hand, telling her he understood what she was going through.

Her parents took them to sit in the living room while her mother cooked across the room in their open concept main floor. It took her mother years, Gwen was in her late teens, to convince her father to renovate the house so she could socialize with them while she cooked and cleaned. She finally wore him down and he surprised her for Mother's Day by giving her a mallet and letting her make the first swing. It was one of the happiest times she'd ever seen her mom.

"So, Asher. What do you do?" Her mom called from the kitchen.

"And, how old are you?" Her father followed on the heels of her mother's question and glowered.

"I'm a veterinarian. I own Morestead Veterinary Clinic. And I'm twenty-nine." Asher spoke smooth and calm and it surprised Gwen he felt that way. She thought her nerves would be spiking, had felt them jumping like crickets in the truck before coming in. She wondered if Asher could project his feelings onto her.

"Is something wrong, Gwen?" her father asked, making her realize she was staring at Asher. She shook her head and smoothed her features.

"Of course not, Dad. Sorry. I must have been lost in

thought." She'd missed their entire exchange after Asher answered their initial questions.

It wasn't long and her father's scowl turned to a grin. Asher had won them over by asking questions about her father's businesses, then asking more specific questions of interest that he could use in his own business. Her mother was happy enough to see them getting along that it surprised her when he paused in the middle of a sentence to compliment her on the scents coming from the kitchen.

"Oh, thank you. I hope it tastes as good as it smells."

"I'm sure it will, Mom. I'll come help." Gwen felt comfortable leaving Asher's side. He reached out and gently gripped her wrist. His heat seeped into her sensitive skin from each of his fingertips.

"Take it easy."

She reassured him with a soft smile, and he let her go.

"He's handsome." Her mom whispered conspiratorially to Gwen when she sidled up beside her. Gwen pinched her lips between her teeth to keep from showing a wide-toothed, giddy grin, knowing Asher would most likely hear everything they said.

"Yes, he is."

"And a little older. Does that bother you?"

"No. I didn't really notice it at first."

"Your father and I have been surprised. Everything seems to be moving very fast. You barely know each other." Her mom was echoing some of Gwen's earlier fears that seemed so silly to her now.

"I knew Julian almost my entire life and look how that turned out. I've learned time isn't a requirement to get to know someone." Gwen absently stirred a pot on the stove. Her mother paused and straightened.

"Well, I suppose you're right." She sighed, then pulled

out dishes to set the table. After setting the table, she stopped beside Gwen and laid her hand on her cheek. "As long as you're happy and safe, then we're happy for you."

"Thanks, Mom." Gwen kissed her cheek. She never lacked for comfort and support from her family.

But the entire evening felt too easy.

ASHER LEARNED the mate bond gave him similar capabilities as it did with wolves and other animals. He could project his feelings onto Gwen. She had been mildly nervous about this dinner, not that she had to say anything. It didn't worry Asher. He understood the speed of their relationship would be a concern, but it would be one they would get over with time. There wasn't much either of them could do to soothe her parents' fears.

With both of them calm and happy, a new state for their relationship lately, the night ran smoothly. Asher helped clear the table and do dishes before they all moved back into the living room.

Halfway down to the couch, Asher's skin prickled all along his spine. His senses snapped, like a spark from a live wire. He smelled a wolf. The scent almost familiar. Almost.

Gwen shivered on the couch and Asher finished sitting, wrapping an arm around her. Doug and Dianne turned when someone knocked on the door, but Gwen and Asher were already looking. The scent was much stronger now. Which also meant if Asher could smell him, then he could smell Asher.

Doug stood and answered the door.

"Hello. I stopped by earlier, looking for Gwen. I was wondering if you know where she might be?" Asher heard the rough voice. His question was polite, but misleading. He knew exactly where Gwen was. Asher tensed.

"And who are you?" Doug asked cautiously and not so politely. He might be a supportive father, but he was also protective.

"Just a friend."

Asher followed Gwen to the door. The wave of anger flew across the room and hit him in the chest. Gwen must have sensed the volatile situation that was brewing.

"It's okay, Dad. We'll be right back." Asher didn't allow Gwen out of his reach as they stepped through the door, forcing the shifter, the wolf shifter, back. Gwen's parents frowned, but didn't question them further.

The shifter emitted a low sound that vibrated from his throat. Bones began to pop. His canines lengthened and his eyes flashed. Asher's body followed his. His own chest rumbled and his teeth showed. The shift moved through his body, an instinctual reaction to the aggression from the other shifter.

Gwen stepped between them and laid a hand on each of their chests. The other wolf snapped at her hand and Asher snapped at him. His brave little mate barely flinched. Gwen gasped, barely audible, but she forced her hands to stay connected to the wolves. Before he could grab her and pull her behind him where she was safe, she said the words both shifters needed to hear.

"Calm down. You're in public and there isn't anywhere to hide a large animal fight. Get it under control and talk like the adults you are."

"Where is he?" The wolf was no longer on the verge of shifting, but his anger still hovered between them. "Where is he?" He ground each word through his teeth, barely moving his lips. All the sound came directly from a growl in his chest. His eyes widened and flashed. Gwen gasped.

"Zachary." She let his name out on a breath. "You're looking for Smoke."

"Where is he?" he asked, a little calmer, recognizing that Gwen understood.

"He's safe, but he isn't here anymore," said Asher. "Give us a few minutes to finish here. We can't just abandon Gwen's parents. Then you are welcome back at my place and I'll tell you everything I know." He paused. "And I hope you'll do the same."

Zachary grunted and walked away to stand next to a motorcycle parked behind Asher's truck.

Asher guided Gwen back inside, but didn't turn away from Zachary until he shut the door between them.

"I'm sorry. We need to go. I promise we'll come again soon." The hope in Gwen's voice pinched Asher.

"I apologize. He's a friend of mine and we have something we need to discuss." Sure, a vague description like that would comfort the parents. He inwardly shook his head at himself and offered a weak smile.

"Why did he come here looking for Gwen?" Dianne looked between the two of them for an explanation.

"He must have thought it easiest to track me down through her. Again, we're very sorry." Asher shook their hands and waited for Gwen to hug them both before opening the door for her. As soon as the door closed, Asher put Gwen behind him, ensuring she didn't become a target for Zachary.

Asher considered leaving Gwen with her parents. Zachary vibrated with hostility. Asher wondered if he'd be the same if he lost Kai. Assuming that was Zachary's only reason for being irate, Asher kept Gwen by his side. She spent a lot of time with Smoke. She could help. As long as Zachary was willing to listen.

"Follow us." Asher helped Gwen into the truck while Zachary got on his bike.

Once in the driver's seat, Asher watched the rear view mirror for him to pull out. With the driveway clear, Asher backed out and drove home, watching closely for his tail.

Driving up his road, he took in his parents' house. Only a couple lights were still on. They were so close to any danger that could come here because of Asher. First Smoke in his initial rage, then Julian, and now Zachary. Asher was holding on to faith that things would work out with Zachary, but what other shifters would Asher find? And what if they aren't all friendly?

It wasn't something he had time to worry about at the moment.

Parking his truck, he got out and went around to help Gwen. Zachary parked beside him and got off his bike. Removing his helmet, he set it on the seat.

"Come on in."

"I'd rather you just answer my questions." He crossed his arms, pulling the leather jacket tight.

"Unfortunately, that isn't something I'm comfortable doing out here anymore. I promise I'll explain everything inside." There weren't trail cameras in his yard, but they weren't far into the trees. Asher didn't trust that none of them weren't facing his house and he hadn't dared to map them out yet.

Zachary glared and sighed. "Fine." He matched his stride to Asher's, neither of them willing to put their back to the other, but Asher was forced to when entering his house.

"We're in. Now, where is he?"

"He's in hiding with my pair and the pack. I don't know

where. It's too soon to track them. There are trail cams surrounding my house and going deep into the woods. Before Fish and Wildlife set them up, I sent Kai, my pair, and Smoke into hiding."

"Where the fuck is my wolf?" Zachary yelled.

"Zachary," Gwen tried to step in front of Asher, but he blocked her with his arm to the side. "Smoke is well and he's safe. He helped save my life."

The glow of Zachary's eyes snapped to Gwen, then dulled until a steel grey settled around the centre. He shook his head and took a slow breath. "Okay."

Between Gwen and himself, they explained how they found Smoke, or how he found them, and their subsequent search for Zachary. They explained his initial attack on Julian, causing the first wave of trail cams and then Julian's final attack. Asher defended his decision. He stood by it, but he worried that Zachary, in Asher's shoes, might have done something different.

"I probably would have killed the bastard," Zachary said absently after Asher finished. "But you probably did the right thing." Even though he agreed, he still rolled his eyes, then glanced at each of them with a frown. "You wouldn't have been able to find me with the way you were looking."

"Why not?"

"My name isn't Zachary. It's my middle name. There aren't many people that know that, and only a few that call me by my middle name. Smoke only knows that name."

"So, what is your name?" Gwen asked.

He narrowed his eyes and looked at each of them. "Nah. You guys already know me as Zachary." He shrugged and changed the subject before Gwen asked a second time. "When will it be safe to search for the wolves? Or is there an alternate route we can take to search?"

"I've thought of searching from the opposite direction, but I feel it's too risky. I won't do anything to draw unwanted attention and risk the pairs or risk the knowledge of shifters. That's assuming every other shifter out there has also kept their double life a secret."

"So, you're waiting for them to give up a search for extraordinary wolves that saved a woman by attacking her assailant with a single bite?"

"Yes. They will. There's nothing else of interest here. It will get boring and other things will need their attention."

Asher could almost see the frustration crawl up Zachary's neck, like a creature with tiny claws that never stopped climbing. One hand rubbed the back of his neck and his other held his head.

"It's hard being separated." He looked up at Asher. "Why don't you feel it?"

"I do. It's been a tough week. I'm just okay at the moment. How did you get separated in the first place? It scares me to think of them separated from us now. Smoke was unhinged when he attacked the pack."

"It's my fault."

"What is?" Gwen spoke softly. Her wish to comfort was warm through him.

"It doesn't matter. It only matters that I find him."

"Have you found other shifters before?" Asher needed to know if he was the only one who happily lived his life under a rock.

"I think I've smelled a few when I was younger, but I was still learning then. I couldn't pinpoint who the scents came from or what they were. You?"

"I know of a bear shifter here in town, but that's only a recent discovery, and he doesn't seem to give a shit about finding others. He said he's spotted, or smelled, a few before."

"You interested in finding others?" Zachary sat and leaned back, crossing his arms.

"I am now. I'll tell my tale if you tell yours." Zachary chuckled and Asher grinned. It was the first moment with zero tension.

"Before you two start down memory lane, I have some questions." Both men looked at Gwen. "How did you know to come find me?"

"I was in the same restaurant as you when you were in Hull Creek. You smelled like a shifter, but I quickly figured out you weren't one. You smell like him." He nodded to Asher. "A lot like him. And I also smelled Smoke. I followed you back to your hotel."

"That's what I thought. You were the one watching me when I left?"

"Yes. I did some digging to find your name and where you were from."

"Digging?" Gwen raised her brows. He didn't answer.

Asher offered drinks then listened to a story similar to his own, only it featured a grey wind and a grey wolf pup. Gwen tried to stay awake, but she was falling over beside him.

"Go to bed."

"Mmm." Asher kissed her until her body responded, giving her energy enough to make her own way upstairs. "Night," she said lazily. "Goodnight, Zachary."

"Goodnight." Zachary's lips twitched in some form of a smile. When they heard the bedroom door shut, he asked, "What are you two? Why does she smell like a shifter?"

"I didn't realize she did. Her scent is overwhelming to me, at least it used to be. Now, it's a distinction I recognize. It took me a few days to figure it out after I first met her. She's my mate."

"Mate?"

"The bond is still growing, I think. It's strong, other-worldly, physical. Once we were together, I could hear a call to mark her, to mark my mate." Asher shrugged, having difficulty explaining further to someone who was still a stranger. "Did you ever tell your parents?" Asher changed the subject.

They spent hours asking each other questions. He welcomed the comfort at finding someone who experienced some of the same things Asher had. Their own personal terminology differed for some things. They laughed through the night at some of their stories.

Asher sighed. "You're welcome to spend the night, and more, if you want. Until we can go find the pairs, or wolf brothers." Asher added Zachary's title for Smoke.

"Thanks." He nodded.

Asher showed him the spare room, then entered his own to wrap himself around Gwen. He hoped what he could build with Zachary was a friendship. Even a partnership. Asher believed it was time for shifters to find each other.

CHAPTER 15

Gwen spent a significant amount of her morning trying to convince her parents that everything was fine, and that Zachary was a *friend* and that Asher wasn't involved in anything nefarious. Things had gone well last night until Zachary knocked on the door.

Tension still held itself between the two wolves, but Asher told her they talked through some things and learned from each other. The lack of Kai and Smoke put them on edge. Asher pushed it down, but his worries bubbled back to the surface. As his emotions increased, so did Gwen's. And so did her senses. The more upset they were, the more her senses kicked into the defensive.

By the time she hung up the phone and went to the kitchen to get another cup of coffee, the two men were sitting at the table scowling and twitching. One tapped their fingers and the other bounced a leg. She poured her coffee and leaned against the counter. She wrapped her hands around the mug and eyed them, taking in each shifter in turn. Zachary rolled his neck and shoulders. Asher straightened, stretching his back.

Gwen tilted her head. She heard something. It didn't come from anything outside. It came from within the two shifters.

"Do you two hear that?" Like an echo off the mountain rolling toward them all.

"Hear what?" They both snapped. Asher shook his head and looked at her apologetically, but Zachary looked at her like she might be a little bit crazy. Obviously, they weren't hearing the same calling she was, but it wasn't a calling for her. Their emotions balancing on the edge clouded their minds. It reminded her of Smoke shortly after they found him. A little unhinged and unpredictable. It was the separation.

"When was the last time either of you shifted?"

"Since the attack." That she knew of Asher, but she was making a point.

"It's been a while. I shifted to search for Smoke for a while, but when I couldn't find him," Zachary trailed off.

"Let's go." Gwen drank down a few gulps of coffee and set her mug down on the counter with a thud.

"Where?"

"Anywhere that's safe for you two to shift. Doesn't matter if we have to drive for a while."

"Gwen, I don't dare. Someone could be watching me."

"Don't you trust your own instincts to tell you if someone is following or watching?" Zachary leaned on the table.

"Not when so much is riding on not being discovered. I can't afford to make a mistake. We can't afford to make a mistake."

"Or your life has just been too easy and you haven't practiced the skills you should have." Zachary's upper lip curled.

Asher snarled and braced himself to stand. Gwen took a

step closer, questioning her own wisdom of stepping between two wolves. But she hadn't backed down last night, she wouldn't back away now. She knew she grounded Asher, and Zachary didn't seem keen on hurting her.

"Easy, boys."

"Yeah, I've been lucky, but I've spent a lot of time with the wolves. I've learned more from them than you can imagine."

Gwen didn't yet know Zachary's past. He told Asher at least some of it last night, but neither shared with her.

"You're so sure of yourself." Zachary sneered, an unfriendly taunt. "But you've never been up against more than your equal, your pair. Even you said yourself it took both you and Kai to handle Smoke. You're sheltered."

Anger and embarrassment flooded Asher and hit Gwen. Zachary poked a sore spot in him that Gwen hadn't known was there. Asher's eyes flared and a wolf's growl emanated from his core. This had the potential to become more than Gwen could handle. She looked over at Zachary. He was the one prodding at Asher, but he was in the same state. His eyes flashed a brightened charcoal grey and his teeth showed between his lips.

"Asher. Zachary." She spoke low and calm, slowly stepping closer. Her own senses and instincts overrode her body, much like they did in Hull Creek. "If we can't go somewhere safe, then you two need to separate." She waited to see if they listened. "Now!" Her tone turned low. She snapped the word like a whip that cracked bonds echoed off of each wolf. They shook and their attention turned toward her. Their eyes didn't return to normal, but their glow dimmed.

"Your mate's right. We need to get out of here or I need to go back to Hull Creek. And I'm not ready to go back to Hull Creek without Smoke."

"Fine."

Gwen finally breathed once she was in the truck with Zachary following behind on his bike. Every muscle and point in Asher's body pulled taut, but he wasn't on the verge of shifting uncontrollably.

They drove north for an hour before Asher felt it was safe enough to pull over.

"Gwen, you're still hurt. You should stay in the truck."

"No way. Not with the way you two were staring each other down at the house."

"That's precisely why. I don't want you getting caught in the middle of anything." She laid her hand on his arm and tilted her head to look directly at him with a sideways smile.

"No," she said flatly. She opened her own door and got out of the truck. Zachary pulled up on her side, a similar calm rolled from him, but his wolf was ready to get out.

Gwen followed them into the trees. They stood still for a few moments. Their nostrils flaring and their eyes narrowing, checking in with their surroundings. Both men stripped.

She greedily took in the sight of Asher baring his skin, the lines and dips of defined muscles. Why she would look away, she didn't know. Similarly sculpted muscles on Zachary brought a blush to her skin. His skin was darker from a deeper tan. He was larger than Asher, although not by much.

He caught her looking and flashed a salacious grin, one that, had she not been bonded to Asher, might have curled her toes. Asher's growl vibrated against her back before he spun her around.

"Sorry," she murmured with embarrassment. Sharp teeth nipped her nose. Asher stepped back and shifted. She held her breath until he passed the moment of pain and saw the magic take over, the white wind swirling out and around him. She looked back at Zachary, too curious not to watch him shift. Slightly painful body changes moved him in place and a similar magic moved through him. A smoky grey wind entwined itself around him.

Gwen looked down at the ground and sighed. "It's a good thing I didn't stay in the truck or you two would have left piles of clothes for someone to find." She gathered their clothes and found some dead branches to hide them.

The wolves darted forward, then changed trajectories to slam into each other. Paws and jaws swung and snapped. Their fur stood on end one minute and the next their tails were swinging back and forth. They needed this to burn off the tension.

Seeing them put an ache in Gwen's chest. She missed Kai and Smoke and needed to know they were all right just as much as Asher and Zachary.

Gwen started a slow hike after the wolves, even though they ran far ahead. But only minutes passed before they turned their *fight* around and brought it back in her direction. They repeated the process, fighting and running, then coming back to check on her. Gwen enjoyed watching them and if she were honest, she needed this time to think and release tension as much as they did.

It had only been a week and she needed more time to heal, but she was eager to learn. She was eager to discover where she belonged in this world. The real one, and this secret magical one. Gwen needed to remind herself that took time. But time could be so uncertain.

Gwen had been right. They'd needed to shift. While it didn't take away all of his worries and pain from being parted from Kai, shifting grounded him. It allowed the animal some freedom and let his instincts reign. Fighting and playing with Zachary helped blow off steam. And they fought. They were both pissed off with their own personal problems and issues. It felt good to take it out on each other.

Zachary was strong. Admittedly, stronger than Asher. It wasn't impossible for Asher to beat him, but he had to work hard for it. He hated that being called sheltered got to him. The truth of it hit hard. Asher happily lived in his bubble. Until recently. Things were changing, and so were Asher's priorities. But for now, all Asher could do was wait for time to pass.

When they tired of each other, they trotted back to Gwen. Her brows were furrowed, and she watched the ground in front of her. She was experiencing her own form of limbo.

He stopped in front of her and nuzzled her belly. She giggled and ran her hands through his fur. Asher shame-lessly soaked in the attention before turning and crouching beside her. She slowly put herself on his back and settled onto her belly. Once she had a firm grip, Asher trotted along.

Zachary watched them, seemingly confused. How were either of them supposed to know what relationships were meant to be like? What is normal between a shifter and his mate?

Let's keep going for a while. Asher called back to Zachary, who caught up with them a moment later.

You let her ride you often?

There's been a few times. We've only been together a few

weeks. That's when it struck him. Their time together had been short, but it's beyond significant.

They stopped at a brook to get a drink and Gwen took a break, sitting on the bank. Asher shifted so he could check in with her.

"How are you feeling?" Asher sat beside her, thankful for the soft grass on his naked body.

"I'm good." She leaned her head on his shoulder.

"I mean your wound."

"Oh, it's okay. I might be a little sore later, but I needed this time out as much as you did. It'll be fine." She sighed. Asher felt a moment of contentment, but it only blanketed their discord.

"If you need me to slow down on the way back, pull my fur." Gwen tilted her head back against his shoulder. Her lips tilted up on one side.

"If you go any slower, then I might as well walk. Really, I'm fine. You feeling any better?"

"I am. You were right. Shifting reconnected me." Reconnection to his other self, to nature, to the magic that created him, and even though they were apart, it felt like a reconnection to his pair.

"Good. I couldn't take your stress much longer."

"I'm sorry." He kissed her hair and breathed in her scent. Florals, coconut, and something wild surrounded her. Maybe it was being outside running through the woods with them, or maybe it was the scent Zachary referred to when he said she smelled like a shifter. A new essence created by his mark.

Zachary came back and stopped in front of them. He shifted and Asher saw for the first time what it looked like. Body parts moved out of place then a grey wind emerged from him.

Gwen turned her head against his shoulder when he finished shifting. He stood as naked as Asher. Asher might have snapped with jealousy earlier when his emotions had been all over the place, but he was calm and grounded now.

"It's okay, Gwen. It's not like we have much choice. I shouldn't have reacted the way I did."

"I'm going for a hunt. It's been too long and I'm feeling something." His jaw tensed and his shoulders straightened. Asher knew the feeling.

"I understand. We'll be here."

Zachary shifted and loped off.

Asher lifted Gwen and settled her in front of him between his legs. He wanted to wrap himself around her, to protect her, to possess her. Their bond grew by the day, reaching overwhelming proportions. Her injury stopped him this past week, too scared of hurting her. He ran his nose along her neck. His cock hardened, and she arched her back against the pressure.

"Asher?"

"Gwen, things are changing between us."

"I know. I can feel it too."

"There's something I haven't told you yet." She turned in his arms. "I love you."

"Asher?"

"It's coming from me, not just the mate bond. You're brave, kind, and stubborn. Fate didn't need to intervene for me to find you and keep you."

"Oh, Asher. I love you too." Her voice cracked. Asher claimed her mouth. He knew his eyes flashed to wolf beneath his lids. The surrounding wilderness guarded his senses to anything but Gwen. It filled him with a distinct energy, a different purpose.

Mate. Mark. Seal.

He turned her back around so her back was against his chest again and ran his hands up her sides. He pulled off her sweater. One hand ran up her centre and over each breast. Her nipples hardened to tight peaks against his palm. Her chest filled with air and pushed them against his hand. He kept moving upward until his hand circled around her neck. Fingers put pressure on her jaw and he tilted her head to the side so he had access to the smooth column.

Asher kissed, licked, and nipped from her shoulder to behind her ear. His lips firmed, turning rough, as his other hand unbuttoned her jeans and delved beneath. The only movement Gwen made under his control was the up and down wave of shallow panting. Her fingers dug into his thighs. Asher found her clit and instantly applied pressure. Her hips pushed outward to meet his fingers. Her arousal increased, the sweet scent reaching his nose.

"On your knees." He helped her up. "I need to be inside of you. I hope you're ready." He pulled her jeans and panties down as far as he could get them. With a firm grip on her hips, he guided her back, not stopping to give her time to adjust. He forced her down onto his cock. Gwen cried out, the sound ending with a moan. She tightened her grip on his thighs. Asher moved her up and down, pleased she followed his motions.

His cock swelled further. It wasn't enough. It would never be enough. Asher growled, the sound reverberating off the trees and hitting him in the chest.

GWEN FELT CONSUMED. Not just by Asher, but by what was happening between them. The intensity that flowed from him took root in her core. She felt it through his palms, through his fingers. He was frantic until suddenly he lifted her off of him. An odd calm blanketed him.

Asher set her in front of him and slowly stood. She felt empty and shuddered from the breeze against her bare skin. He came back to the ground in front of her. There was something different in his eyes. That same intensity she felt, but there was determination, love, and his wolf. He leaned forward and helped her down to the ground. She gasped at the feel of the cool grass against her back. At least it was soft. The forest floor wasn't meant to be neat and tidy. But here on the bank beside the water, lush greenery coated her back.

He reached for her legs and finished undressing her.

"I've had a lot of thoughts going through my mind lately."

"Oh?" she asked, her voice huskier than she thought it should be.

"A lot of worry for Kai, for life as a shifter, for our life together going forward." Her eyes softened, and she felt the worry he talked about. She'd always felt it, but it was stronger coming out of him with words. "But I've also been thinking what the mate bond means for us."

He grabbed her ankles, one in each hand, and firmly pulled them apart and upward to bend her knees. His eyes landed directly between her legs. Watching him stare at her pussy made it throb. Her breath shook and her core clenched, attempting to tighten around something that wasn't there.

"It means we're permanently connected." He kissed one of her knees. "Bound by more." He kissed her other knee. "By more than what the rest of the population realizes is even possible." He trailed kisses up each thigh, stopping when she only started to feel his breath on her folds. His mouth scalded her skin and the wet heat with sharp teeth grazed the sensitive part of her inner thighs. Her legs quaked when he reached the centre for a third time, and she whimpered when he pulled away to do it all over again.

Asher grinned against her leg and she realized he was enjoying this. How did he go from being utterly frantic to in control? They rarely had control with each other when they came together. No matter how much they tried, sex was always wild and urgent. Now, he was being as assiduous as he was with the rest of his life. He applied that calm dominance of an alpha to her.

"The bond makes both of us stronger." He finally closed his lips around her clitoris and she gasped at the sudden pleasure. He created an intricate pattern with his tongue before sucking and nipping. One hand traced up her side until he reached her breast. He ran his thumb along the underside, gradually moving upward. His pattern matched the one from his mouth and his touch burned in all the right places. His hands were slow and sensuous, and his lips were firm. Her body was on a different plain.

He finally reached her nipple and her back arched, begging him to do more, to give her more. The pressure was building, but he wasn't allowing it to reach the top. He squeezed her nipple, twisting and pulling gently, the sensations shooting down to her core to join the delicious current his mouth was creating.

She felt him adjust, then his fingers probed at her entrance.

"Asher, please," she begged.

"Oh, you will. I want to taste it when you do." His words made her pussy clamp around what little of his fingers were inside her. Asher froze, his mouth, his hands. Gwen lifted her head and looked down. His eyes brightened, and he thrust his fingers deep, curling them instantly. Gwen let out a low moan and her head fell back to the ground, disturbing the scent of the grass around her. His tongue worked hard over her clit and his fingers rubbed over her sweet spot.

It was only seconds before she came, electricity firing throughout her body all centred from the points of contact between her legs. She cried out, the sound echoing. It was carried off with the breeze. The same breeze that soothed her overheated skin. Asher worked on her until her tremors slowed, then he moved lower, his tongue lapping at her juices. She whimpered as her pussy clenched, needing more from him.

"Delicious." His husky voice was a low purr.

Asher moved up over her body and grabbed her wrists. He locked them in place above her head. His cock stretching her comforted the ache of emptiness. He touched his forehead to hers. His movements were measured and hard. Their breaths mingled between them. Warmth spread through her and movement to her side caught her attention.

They both looked. White wind danced beside them. She'd seen what it looked like when the wolves shifted. The wind was a part of them. But she looked on in amazement at what she saw now. It was different. It was the physical wind in the air. It rushed toward them. Gwen felt its embrace.

Her body became hyper aware, feeling so much of Asher as he picked up his pace and pounded into her. Their eyes locked, ignoring the white air around them.

Something changed in Asher's eyes. One hand released her wrist and wrapped around her neck. He didn't squeeze, but she felt the power in him. Words echoed in her mind as Asher spoke.

"Bound by Fate. Blessed by the wind. Forever you are mine."

Her response whispered from Gwen's lips almost involuntarily. She didn't fight it. "Bound by Fate. Blessed by the wind. Forever I am yours."

Asher claimed her mouth, his tongue moved in and over hers, exploring her as if it was their first kiss. There was no way to know where one began and the other ended. They were fused. As was their pleasure. She could feel his rise to the peak just as she could feel her own.

His fingers tightened around her throat and he ground himself down over her mound. Finally, they went over the crest together. Her walls squeezed his cock as his fluid jetted inside her. Her mind whirled. Her body floated. Her skin tingled. They frantically chased the peak for as long as it lasted.

Gwen had no idea how long that was, but she was drained and so was Asher. His hands loosened and he collapsed on top of her. He was still hard inside her, swollen and unmovable.

Tears streamed down Gwen's cheeks, her body and mind so overwhelmed and sensitive. Eventually, Asher slowly lifted, taking his own weight. His features were soft, and he thumbed away her tears.

"What just happened, Asher?"

"You felt everything I did. Don't you understand?" He shifted his weight and dried her other cheek.

"I think I do." She felt it in her soul.

"Our bond is sealed."

The words they spoke to each other drifted through her mind. *Bound by Fate. Blessed by the wind.* Fate created them as mates, but it was up to the wind that was a part of Asher to bless them and bind them. Forever theirs.

CHAPTER 16

T he sun was low in the sky when Asher helped Gwen dress, and Zachary still hadn't returned. He heard her stomach groan with hunger.

"Time for something to eat. Think you can gather some stuff to start a fire?"

"I'll try," she said with skepticism. Asher shifted. It would be easier to catch food as a wolf, and it was much warmer covered in fur. He went down to the water in search of fish. He waded in carefully and focused his eyes beneath the surface.

He dunked his nose and missed, his teeth grazing the back fin. Lifting his head from the water, his eyes followed the current. Two more tries and he caught one, his teeth sinking into the meaty flesh. He swung it behind him toward the bank. The fish flopped on the grass, its gills gasping. Turning back to the water, Asher focused and caught three more fish, throwing them each back to the bank.

Once out of the water, he shook, droplets flying from the fur on his head, legs, and belly. He piled the fish, then one by one, with minimal struggle, cut them open with a tooth.

If the meal was for himself alone, he'd eat them as they were, but he needed to feed Gwen too. Once they were all gutted and cleaned again in the water, he gathered them in one bite. Further up the bank, Gwen had made a pile of sticks, branches, leaves and moss. She created a pyramid of sticks with a bed of moss and sat there staring at it. Asher set the fish down and tilted his head to look at her.

"What? I got this far." She threw her hand out toward her structure. "I should have a pack to bring with us when we go on runs."

Asher shifted. His eyes connected to Gwen's. She watched him in awe, leaving him feeling exposed. She got to see the most vulnerable part of him. His deepest secret. And now she was bound to him.

"That might be a good idea. I can get it started. You did good." He kissed her forehead, then bent next to her pile. He got the fire started and built it to a solid flame and shifted back to a wolf, leaving Gwen to tend it.

He brought the fish closer and sat. His tail wagged and he gave her a smug canine grin. Gwen looked at the fish then back up at him.

"So that's all the help I get, huh?" Asher moved forward and nuzzled his wet nose into her neck. "That tickles. And it's cold!" She pushed him away and he laid down by the fire while Gwen figured her own way around how to cook a fish over an open fire in the wilderness with no tools. He almost felt bad, but he enjoyed watching her. She was smart. Her instincts ran true. Pride welled within him.

Asher grabbed a branch in his jaw and laid it on the fire. He panted to feed air and help it build enough that she could cook the fish.

Asher's ears pricked and his nose caught a scent on the breeze. He lifted his eyes and he saw Zachary return with a few small animals hanging from his jaws. He approached and dropped the animals near their impromptu camp site. Zachary tensed then he leapt back, his eyes darting between Asher and Gwen. Asher stood.

What the fuck happened between you two? Asher didn't realize that the mate bond would be outwardly obvious, any more than it already was.

What do you mean?

I don't know. You're stronger. I can sense that. But something else is different with Gwen. With you. Zachary still wouldn't come closer.

We sealed the mate bond.

Zachary shook as if to push off whatever aura Asher and Gwen created. Slowly, he picked up the animals and brought them closer.

Gwen eyed the critters. "I'm not touching those." Zachary barked once and pawed the animals.

Gwen cooked two of the fish and left the other two raw for him. Zachary ate his own catch. By the time they all finished, the wolves long before Gwen, the sun had set. The fire was going strong and twilight sparkled above them. It hadn't been Asher's intentions to spend the night, especially with Gwen out here too, but it seemed that was what they would do.

Asher gripped her sweater between his teeth and pulled until she understood and laid down with him. Even with him as a wolf, she was small against him. She curled her back and they laid in the shape of a crescent moon.

Gwen only took a few moments to fall asleep. He watched the fire. Zachary did too, stacking it with more wood. They didn't need the fire, but Gwen did.

That bond is strong. Any shifter will sense it off of Gwen instantly. Unless they know what it is, it will confuse them.

Thanks for the warning. I feel it between us, not coming from her.

I wonder if it's the same for all of us. Zachary looked back at the fire, his head hung low.

I'd put my money on that. If all shifters had similar experiences as to how they were created, then the rules Fate decided for them were likely the same. She decided and controlled mating.

She's cold. Zachary looked at Gwen the same time Asher felt her body shiver, disturbing his fur. Zachary added the last of the wood to the fire and sauntered toward them. *No snapping.*

Asher huffed and laid his head down along Gwen's. Zachary laid down on the other side of her and curled in the same shape. They sandwiched her between them, their fur keeping her just as warm as it did them.

Asher wondered why he was so comfortable with Zachary. He was thinking of asking him to stay in Alder Ridge, at least until they could track down their pairs. He wanted to ask them to stay longer. But he barely knew the man. How could he trust him?

It must be because he learned to trust Smoke. For the brief time he'd known Zachary, it was apparent his and Smoke's personalities aligned. As did Asher's and Kai's. If you could trust the pair, you could trust the shifter. Gwen's thoughts on keeping a record of what they learn was sounding like a much better idea than Asher expected.

GWEN WOKE AGAINST SOMETHING SOFT, but beneath her was hard. Not Asher's bed, the ground. They'd slept in the woods. She blinked and saw grey fur in front of her. She turned her head and found Asher's white fur behind her. Warmth settled and Gwen smiled to herself. The two wolves had worked together to keep her warm through the night.

Tentatively, she reached out and spread her fingers through Zachary's fur. He tensed and lifted his head, watching her from narrowed eyes. Gwen didn't pull back. After a minute, he rested again with a grunt and allowed her to pet him.

Asher whimpered behind her and she laughed. Gingerly, she turned herself onto her stomach, resting her weight with her forearm so she didn't strain her abdomen. She ran her fingers through his fur and around his neck.

"Thank you, both." She pushed herself up and both wolves braced her with their heads in front of her. If she lost her balance, they would catch her. She winced and rolled her shoulders, rocked her hips, and tried to stretch her limbs. "Sleeping on the ground wasn't the best idea for me."

Asher crouched beside her for her to climb on his back.

They trotted back through the woods, abandoning their makeshift camp. The crisp morning air cleared her system and cleared her mind. She never would have done any of that before she met Asher and she surprisingly enjoyed roughing it with the wolves. Gwen was proud of herself. She hadn't balked at attempting a fire. The gathering of materials and the attempt was more than she'd ever done. And she had cooked freshly caught fish. She hadn't curled her nose or asked if they could go home for the night. She was content as long as she was with Asher.

Asher. What happened between them last night was strange. Beautiful. Scary. Magical. Gwen believed that it was magic. Something started this, brought shifters to life, just over twenty years ago. Maybe they already existed, or they existed a long time ago. There was a power that brought them here. The words they spoke when they sealed their bond told them more than they ever knew. Fate and the winds shifters followed were the higher powers of their race. And now hers too, she supposed.

Gwen knew the importance of their sealed bond, but the problem was, they hadn't grown up following those traditions, the traditions that came with Fate and the winds. Even Asher hadn't. This was the equivalent to marriage, but society, and their families, wouldn't understand. She didn't want to hide their relationship, even part of it. With their bond sealed and not able to introduce him as her husband bothered her.

It was a long way back, and by the time they reached the edge of the woods, she'd given herself a headache. She'd ruined her happiness with society's expectations. And she hadn't even consulted society yet. Her parents already had reservations about their relationship. If she announced their engagement, or that they decided to move in together, or that they were already married, they'd try to talk her out of it. They were accepting of a lot of things and had even been willing to accept her relationship with Asher until Zachary showed up at their house. But marrying a man after only a few weeks was absurd. If she wasn't living it, even she would think it was crazy.

Asher crouched to let her off. She waited while the two wolves shifted and retrieved their clothes.

"Everything all right?" Asher stood in front of her, his hands on her arms. "You're scowling."

"I'm just thinking." She tried to reassure him, but her forehead still wrinkled. Asher searched her face, his gaze direct and firm, but then he sighed.

"Let's go home." He wrapped his arm around her, and they met Zachary by the truck. "I'd like it if you stayed with us until it's safe to find Smoke and Kai. I mean, you're welcome if you'd like to stay."

"Thanks. I have some things to do back in Hull Creek. Knowing he's being taken care of and safe for now has helped. I owe that to you two and your pair. I'll be back."

"Are you leaving now?" Gwen asked. Zachary nodded.

"In that case, can you come back next week?" Asher looked to Zachary. He stood tense beside her.

"Most likely. Why?"

"I want to bring shifters together. We're a race that knows nothing of each other. I believe that should change. My problem is, I don't know many shifters. It will take time, but I want to start with what I have."

Zachary sighed. "I don't know. Yeah. Maybe." Gwen knew his noncommittal opinion bothered Asher, but he didn't show it.

"We'll see you next week." Asher spoke with confidence that Zachary would make the right decision and join him on his quest. Zachary held out his hand and Asher shook it. He held it out to Gwen. She reached out to grasp his, but he turned it and kissed the back of her hand.

"Congratulations. And thank you." Gwen had a moment of incredulity. Zachary was rough around the edges, much like Smoke. His gesture belied his personality.

"You're welcome. See you soon." If Asher could be confident about his plans, then she would stand strong beside him.

◢

"It's time to tell me what's bothering you." Asher stopped Gwen in the living room before she settled on the couch. He crossed his arms and stood in front of her. She'd been frowning since she woke up, and he felt the turmoil in her mind.

"Since when did you get so demanding?"

Asher's lips twitched, betraying his intimidating stance. "It's a new trait."

"It suits you." Gwen smiled, soft and sexy while nipping her bottom lip. She tilted her head and her eyes locked onto his.

"You're evading my question."

"You didn't ask a question," she said with a touch of sweetness.

"Gwen," he sobered from their banter, "we can't hide from each other. Seems we never could."

She sighed and plopped herself down on the couch, wincing when she bounced. Her hand covered her wound for a moment before she fidgeted with her fingers in her lap. "What would you say last night meant?"

Asher took his familiar seat in front of her. "We're permanently bound together." He spoke slowly, cautiously, uncertain if her feelings had changed since last night. He didn't believe so, but there was something not right.

"Which would be the equivalent of...?" She dragged out her question, leaving him to fill in the blank. The light came on his head and he relaxed.

"Ah. Married."

"Yes." She straightened and her hands slapped her knees. "We don't even live together. We haven't known each other long. How are we going to explain to our families we're married without having an engagement or inviting them to the wedding? And oh my, I would not have wanted them at that wedding."

There was no stopping himself. Asher laughed, hard. When he didn't stop right away, Gwen started laughing too.

Having a fit of laughter with the woman he loved filled him with joy. It cemented his sense of rightness. When they calmed, they were both leaning forward, their foreheads touching and their lips still smiling.

"Last night was beautiful and I wouldn't have changed our union for anything." Asher kissed her, holding her hostage while he nipped and played. She sighed against him. Asher reached forward and pulled on her hips, bringing her to the edge of the couch. He released her mouth, pushed her hair away from her face, and cupped her jaw. "Move in with me." There was no question. They were past that. "Officially."

"Yeah, I will."

He ran his thumb over her plump lips, eager to taste them again. "Marry me." He paused, drawing in a breath. "There's time to learn what happens with shifters and to learn or create those traditions. We can start now. Our families won't understand the rush, but they'll get over it. They'll see we're happy and accept it. We'll have a ceremony that celebrates our binding. Marry me."

"How do you do that?" She shook her head slowly.

"Do what?"

"You fix my concerns in a matter of minutes. Every time."

"You're overthinking things. Nothing has to be that complicated." Asher was used to keeping things simple.

"I think you're going to eat those words some day." She raised a brow and had a sagacious lift to her lips.

"Gwen, will you marry me? In whatever form of a celebration we choose."

"Yes, Asher. I will. But I don't think a traditional wedding is right."

"Neither do I. We'll figure it out."

Asher captured her again, kissing her, this time pulling her from the couch and onto his lap. He slowly drank her in, running his hands up and down her body, taking the time to follow each curve. When he reached below her ass, he lifted and carried her upstairs to the shower. He didn't leave an inch of her untouched, teasing and stroking every sensitive spot of her skin until she whimpered in his arms. When she tried to reach for him, he grabbed her wrists and held them behind her back until she promised to keep them there.

With only his fingers, he slowly brought her to climax and held her against him as she shuddered. The water turned cold. He cranked the heat long enough to rinse them comfortably, then pulled her from the shower. After drying her thoroughly himself, he laid her in bed and pulled the covers up.

"Rest. Your body is still tired."

Gwen grabbed the back of his neck and pulled him down to kiss him herself. She took charge of him for a change. Her teeth caught his upper lip and tugged lightly as he straightened. "Night." Her eyes drifted closed, sleep carrying her away. He watched her for a moment, then finally turned.

Asher went downstairs and sat outside on the front porch in one of his Adirondack chairs. He looked toward the trees, wishing Kai was bounding out of them. Time and patience. And patience was getting harder to hold on to.

He had a lot to think about. He wasn't sure what he would do or how he would go about it. He wanted shifters to come together, to work together, and create a society of their own. But he would need to convince any shifters he came across to meet with him. He only knew two. That was where he would start. One by one. Step by step.

Asher allowed his mind to quiet, and he heard footsteps

travelling up the lane. He recognized his father's strong gait. Asher needed to talk with him and there was no better time than the present, despite his nerves over their conversation ahead. He watched him saunter across the lawn. The blond hair Asher inherited, darker and not all blond anymore, still covered his head in a thick mop.

"Care for some company?"

"Always, Dad." His dad took the few steps up and sat in the other chair. Asher knew at this point he didn't have to beat around the bush, and neither of them would like that kind of conversation between them. "How long have you known?"

"Oh, I think you were twelve or thirteen. Your mother had been convinced something was going on with you, but didn't know what. She asked me to talk to you. I went in late one night and saw you missing from your bed. I heard the front door and watched out your bedroom window. I could still see you and the wolf inside the trees. What a sight." His dad tilted his head and clucked his tongue.

"Why didn't you say anything?

"Took me a while, but I remembered your tale about changing to a wolf when you were little and felt guilty we never believed you. I hoped one day you'd try again and come to us."

"I'm sorry. I should have." He reached over and squeezed his dad's hand.

"What's done is done. But you owe me. I covered for your ass so many times with your mother."

Asher laughed. "I was wondering how I never got caught."

"I'm glad I wasn't wrong when I stuck my hand in that cage last week." His dad laughed to himself, then sobered a moment later. "How did it happen, Asher? The first time."

"How about a beer first? Still have your favourite stocked in the fridge. It's not a short story and there have been a lot more stories since then."

"You still have that left? Figured you would have drank that up by now."

"No point." Asher shrugged. "Beer does nothing to me."

"Really?" Asher smirked at the surprise on his father's face.

"Really." Asher fetched a few beer and returned, ready to tell his dad the story he wished they'd believed as a child.

CHAPTER 17

They had told their parents, friends, and families their good news at the end of that week, who all had taken the news as they'd expected. Poorly, except for Asher's father. Not because of the person they were marrying, but because of the rush. His sister, who he had to remind himself he loved, had asked if Gwen was pregnant. Specifically, she'd accused Asher of being an irresponsible asshole.

Gwen's wound was healing well, a little faster than normal. Another thing of which to note. She was picking up her mother to shop for the ceremony. He wished her luck when he left for work that morning. Asher had a meeting of his own. He'd tracked down Nathan Marks and invited him for a morning coffee.

Asher sat on a bench in the park and waited. The wind brought the scent of a bear from behind him. His muscles relaxed. Nathan sat down beside him.

"Thanks for coming." Asher passed him a coffee with the *Woods Bistro* logo on the cup.

"Yeah." He took the coffee and sipped.

"I get the impression you don't really care to make

friends. But I would like to connect with other shifters. I don't believe we're meant to be lone beings." Asher had struggled with how to start this conversation. "I have met another wolf shifter recently."

"Good for you."

"Look, we don't have to do this or get to know each other, but I'd like to make connections within my own species."

Nathan turned to face him, confusion mottling his features. "Species? You see us as a different species?"

"We are a different species," Asher replied firmly.

"I can concede to that." He nodded. "So, what do you want?"

"Just to talk. Listen to each other's stories. Learn from each other." Asher waited, but Nathan didn't respond. "And extend the same to other shifters we meet along the way. You said you've discovered some before."

"I don't talk to any of them and I'd rather not start."

"Then why did you say yes to me?"

"I don't know. Free coffee."

"Uh huh. Well, the other wolf shifter, Zachary, doesn't live in Alder Ridge. He's coming back Friday night. I'd like to hold a meeting of sorts. Here's my address." Asher had convinced Fish and Wildlife to give up on the wolves. They would probably watch closely, but all the cameras were gone. Planning a backyard wedding worked well for an excuse for privacy.

Nathan frowned at the card. "Why does this look familiar?" Asher pursed his lips, waiting for Nathan to make the connection. "Oh yeah. I heard about the wolf attack that saved a woman at the residence of a local veterinarian. Don't you think that was a little risky? Why not kill the fucker? Probably less attention to abnormal animals."

"There's more to it than that. Unfortunately, it wasn't

that simple. That was the safest option. And I will explain anything you want to know Friday night. I wouldn't be having this meeting if my property wasn't safe."

"I'll think about it." Nathan stood.

"That's all I ask." He started to walk away, but Asher called out. "Bring your pair if you want. If you can."

"My pair?"

"The bear you were matched with when you first shifted."

"Uh, yeah." Nathan gave a single shouldered shrug and continued to walk away. Asher hoped he had Kai back by then. He needed him by his side for this.

◢

"GWEN, please think about this. There's no need to rush. You two can slow down. You should at least keep your apartment for a while longer." Her mother hadn't stopped trying to convince Gwen to change her mind since she picked her up to go shopping for her *wedding*.

"Mom," Gwen stopped just inside the door of the store and turned, grabbing her mother's elbows, "you need to trust me."

"You love him."

"I do. Very much."

"Then okay. But your dad and I are here if you need us." She kissed Gwen's cheek. "So, what kind of dress are you looking for?"

"Not traditional."

Gwen searched the racks to find anything that didn't look exactly like a wedding dress. One thing she and Asher agreed on was to keep everything away from traditional features. She looked for off-white and vintage. She looked at bridesmaid dresses, prom dresses, anything that might have a hidden gem.

Discouragement was pulling her toward the door when her eye caught onto something green and blush in the corner. She pulled it out from between the dresses and gasped. It was a blush coloured, lace, strapless dress. Small vines with wildflowers decorated the bodice and dispersed down the skirt. It was perfect. It suited their relationship, their life to be, and the essence of their union.

Gwen's mind drifted to the wilderness in which they sealed their bond. She felt her lips lift, because everything fell into place as she looked at a dress that wouldn't have suited her only a few weeks ago. But she was looking at a new life. One that fulfilled her before it barely started.

"This is it."

"It's so charming. Are you sure?" Her mother's distaste didn't bother her. Asher's words echoed in her heart. Her mother would accept her decisions, eventually.

"I'm absolutely sure."

Gwen went home with a beautiful vision in her mind of their ceremony. First, she needed to plan a dinner to introduce their parents. That was something she needed Asher's help with.

Asher wasn't there when she got home, so she started something for dinner. She heard his truck drive up a few minutes later. She followed his footsteps into the house until he was behind her, and smiled with content as his arms slipped around her waist.

"That smells good, but not as good as you." His lips grazed up and down her neck. Gwen tilted her head to give him access. "How did shopping with your mom go?"

"Great, once she gave up trying to convince me to reconsider." Gwen turned in his arms and clasped her hands on his shoulders, corded muscles tightened beneath them. "I found my dress, and I had the perfect idea for a ceremony. I hope you like it because I even started buying decorations and ordered cake and food, the date pending, of course."

"I can't wait to hear it." He let go of her and pulled down a couple wine glasses and the bottle of wine from the rack he had hanging on the wall. He looked at her expectantly while he poured.

"A handfasting. A permanent one, not the one-year trial kind from ages ago. We can structure the ceremony how we want and have an officiant to make it all official." She waved her hand side to side in the air. "The backyard will be perfect for something like that. Simple foods, a simple cake. All we need to focus on is the vows we make."

"I say we use a version of the ones we made in the woods." He passed her one of the glasses.

"You like the idea?" A gush of excitement poured from Gwen.

"I think it's perfect."

Gwen set the glass down and reached up, standing on her tiptoes. She pulled on his neck and he leaned forward. Gwen kissed him, mimicking motions he used on her. She ran her tongue along the seam of his lips and smiled against them when he opened and let her in.

The smell of something burning tore her away from him. "Shit."

"It's still salvageable, don't worry." He helped her pull the pots from the burners. She sighed when she had every-thing stirred and cooking properly again.

"How was your day?"

"I met with another shifter."

"You did? The bear shifter you talked about before?"

"Yeah. I invited him here for Friday night. I hope to go find Kai before then."

"So, we're about to have our first shifter meeting." Gwen almost felt self-conscious saying *we*, but Asher had already made it clear that she would always be by his side.

"We are."

"There's another meeting we need to have."

"Oh?" His brows raised.

"Our parents. They need to meet each other." Gwen grimaced.

"Right. Saturday night. We'll take them all out to dinner." While Gwen was nervous, Asher once again seemed utterly calm and helped her see the simplicity of it.

"That sounds nice."

ZACHARY WALKED into Asher's house Wednesday night. "You ready? If you aren't, I'm going without you."

"Yeah, I'm ready." Asher just finished convincing Gwen to stay home. They both would rather her by his side, but he didn't know how far away the wolves went or how long they'd be gone. They also needed to cover more territory quicker. Even with her riding on his back, they would lose time, needing to slow or stop for breaks. He turned toward Gwen, waiting behind him. "Keep the door locked any time you're here. Go to my parents if you need anything. Or even stay with your parents until we get back."

"I'll be fine, I promise."

He kissed her long and hard, imprinting her on him. "Be careful."

"You too."

He stripped and so did Zachary. They left their clothes

in the house this time. Despite the cameras being gone, he didn't put it past Fish and Wildlife to do a search from time to time. The last thing Asher wanted them to find was clothing stashed in bushes. They left from the back of the house to stay closer to the trees to cross the yard.

First, Asher led them to the pack's old territory. The territory had been long lived in with lots of evidence they'd been there scattering the area, but no scent remained after two weeks on any travelled path leading away from their territory. They stood in the centre where Asher often played with the pups.

Which way would Kai go? Zachary asked.

Asher ambled around Kai's home and tried to imagine what Kai would have done first, where he would deem safe. It was hard for him to decide. It had been just as hard for Kai to leave as it had been for Asher to see him go. Then he saw a log in the distance. It wasn't their usual marker, but the resemblance was enough to catch Asher's eye. The single log looked out of place and he didn't remember one that big sitting there the last time he'd been here.

This way. That log. Kai and I use a three log marker to signal to the other caution is needed. That log is out of place.

But there aren't three of them. Zachary pointed out. Asher questioned himself, but not for long.

No, but it's not right either. It wasn't there last time. Kai must have thought it unsafe to use our usual marker. He's being cautious and trying to leave a trail. Asher hoped that was the case.

Let's go.

Asher prayed to whatever magic brought him the white wind and created him that Kai, Smoke, and the rest of the pack were safe.

Tracking was a slow progress. There were very few traces

left of their trail. Asher and Zachary moved slowly so they didn't miss anything. It was good they did. They discovered the pack changed directions a few times. Asher couldn't make sense of it. Was someone following them or was Kai only being cautious? He hoped it was the latter.

Twilight fell upon them, and even with their superior night vision, the trail was becoming difficult to track. However, they caught the faint scent of wolves. At least knew they were on the right track.

We have to stop for the night, said Asher.

We're so fucking close. I know it. Asher could relate to his frustration.

I know we are, but it's best to get some rest and get an early start when the pack is active. He knew it was the rationale decision, despite feeling the same eagerness to reconnect with his pair.

Fine.

They found a dugout created by a fallen tree. They settled and attempted sleep, but it was difficult coming.

There will be a bear shifter coming Friday night. Asher hoped changing the subject would take their focus off Kai and Smoke. Zachary lifted his head.

A bear?

Yeah. I intend for the night to be a meeting of sorts. A chance to get to know our own people, Asher explained.

Shifters Anonymous. Zachary joked.

What happens in Shifter Club stays in Shifter Club. Zachary's tail thumped a couple times before he settled his head back down.

Asher was eager for the meeting Friday night. Eager wasn't the best description of his feelings. Nervous and restless. The meeting could go well or it could be a disaster. It could be the start of something new, or it could be a failure before it began.

Asher shifted on the ground to get comfortable. There wasn't anything he could do other than wait and see how it turned out. He only hoped he had Kai by his side.

ASHER AND ZACHARY WERE AWAKE, alert, and on their feet in an instant, the instant before two wolves jumped down from the top of their dugout. Suddenly they were looking at mirror images of themselves. Asher and Kai charged for each other and ended in a playful heap, tongues lolling and tails wagging. They halted and leaned against each other.

It's good to have you back, Asher said to Kai. He looked back and saw Smoke and Zachary breathing heavily, staring each other down. The torrents of emotions that came from each of them were almost painful. Zachary took the first step, but Smoke growled, a quick warning to stay back.

Where did you go?

I'm so sorry. I came back for you as soon as I could. I didn't stop searching.

Smoke lowered his head and fell to the ground, exhaustion radiating from him. Zachary moved closer and dropped in front of him. They both lifted their heads to touch the other's.

I'm so glad you're safe, Smoke. I've been so worried.

So have I.

They all sat still, each with their pairs, to take the time to reconnect. Zachary and Smoke needed more time, but Asher didn't mind waiting. They both had it rough being separated. He didn't want to see any shifter or pair go through that.

Finally, the two grey wolves stood, neither fully cured, but Asher could feel strength in each of them that wasn't there before. It was something Asher should have noticed. They were stronger together, in so many ways.

Where's the pack? Asher looked at Kai.

This way. Kai led them past the fallen tree. He started into a run. Half an hour more, they reached a ridge that looked as if it ended off a cliff before hills ran up the other side toward the mountain. But they stepped closer and Kai climbed down. The ridge hid a small valley with plenty of rocks, grass, and bush. New dens were dug into the side. When they reached the bottom, Kai turned toward Asher and straightened his stance, lifting his head. *I want the pack to stay here.*

Asher realized he was making an announcement he thought Asher would refuse. *Of course.* He watched Kai visibly relax.

It's well hidden and safe. It's large enough to accommodate a growing pack. Kai still defended his decision, despite Asher's acceptance.

And not too far away. Asher finished his defense for him. He would never stand in the way of Kai's duty to see to the pack. *Will you come back with us for a few days?*

Of course. Kai echoed Asher's answer just before the pups, including a fully healed and happy Cinder, came barrelling out of somewhere and directly toward Asher. He was home again.

CHAPTER 18

Gwen wanted to go with Asher and Zachary, but part of her was happy she didn't. She had her own projects to start. She worked on wedding plans with her mother, told her parents about Saturday night dinner, visited Asher's parents and told them about the dinner, and picked up an extra shift at the bistro. But that wasn't all she worked on.

She put together her own hiking pack. She didn't intend to be left behind during runs or any other need to travel through the wilderness. Gwen went to the library and picked out books to study to learn the things that one might have learned in a scouts program growing up. Her cheeks heated when she checked out the books, and there was no reason for it. It wasn't a topic to be embarrassed about. She only wanted to learn.

It was Friday afternoon. Asher should be back soon as he planned a meeting for tonight. Gwen finished putting away groceries and looked down at the last project she wanted to start. Information and schedules for self-defence classes. She was looking for more martial arts, but she felt this was the best place to start. She had a bit more healing to do, then she could begin.

Gwen heard the crunching sound of tires on gravel slowly coming toward the house. She cautiously peaked out the window, squinting from the late afternoon sun. Her parents' blue car parked behind hers. She met them on the front deck while they circled, taking in Asher's house and property, and walking toward her.

"Hey. What are you guys doing out here?" She asked cheerfully, not wanting them to think they were unwelcome. If she wasn't waiting for Asher and Zachary to walk into the house buck naked, she would be happy to see them. She also battled anxiety, hoping and praying they were safe.

"Sorry for not calling first. We were already out and wanted to come see the site for the ceremony. I was hoping we could increase the guest list." Her mother clasped her hands in front of her and looked around the yard. It was difficult to get the guest list right when her parents knew so many people. They felt that everyone her father did business with deserved an invitation, whether or not Gwen had ever met any of them.

"Sure. This is it." Gwen waved her arm forward and stepped off the deck. "The back of the house is a lot closer to the tree line, so we'll have it out here in the front." She got caught up in plans with her parents, making final decisions on decorations, planning out parking and seating.

"Where is Asher?" Her father looked back at the house. Asher's truck sat in the driveway and Gwen suddenly panicked realizing she didn't have a suitable explanation for his absence, so she attempted the truth.

"He's out of town with a couple friends. He's supposed to be back tonight." Her dad raised a brow and pointed to his truck. "They all left in one vehicle." Gwen inwardly sighed when her father accepted her lie.

Her mother continued discussing seating arrangements and numbers, but Gwen didn't listen. Her senses suddenly flared. The breeze picked up, or it felt like it did, and she smelled Asher. They were back. She looked toward the trees and saw four sets of eyes flash quickly, two blue and two grey. The glowing eyes disappeared before her parents saw them.

They'd found their pairs. So much relief and joy settled in her chest, and she felt relaxed for the first time since they'd left.

She tried to finish up with her parents so the men could shift and get dressed, but her mother started in on flowers and Gwen couldn't resist. She imagined the entire yard covered in wildflowers. So much colour and so much greenery. Most of Gwen's choices surprised her mother, even Gwen sometimes, but her tastes had changed quickly. And Gwen was happy with the direction her life was taking.

Gwen was deeply focused on planning with her mother, both with excitement and an eagerness to finish quickly, that she didn't notice the truck pull up and park behind Asher's. The driver's door shutting snapped her head around. That must be the bear shifter Asher invited.

Shaggy brown hair moved with the wind. He had short facial hair over a hard face. His size rivaled Asher's and Zachary's, possibly bigger. Gwen swallowed, a trace of nerves being forced down to her gut. She breathed deep and had to remind herself that Asher invited him and that the wolves were close. It wouldn't be in this shifter's best interests to be hostile toward humans. She pulled up the same bravado she used on Zachary.

He stopped several feet away and glared at Gwen. His nose curled and he took a step back before catching himself.

"Are you looking for Asher?" Gwen broke his concentration and covered for his odd reaction.

"Yeah."

"He's not home yet." Gwen attempted a subtle look into the woods, hoping he caught Asher's scent. "But he should be back soon."

His eyes darted to his right toward the wolves and he nodded. He stood there and waited.

"Right," her mother said slowly and turned back to Gwen, but her father was eying the shifter. "Have you asked Reverend Tom if he can officiate?"

Gwen winced. "No, we've been looking for alternative officiants." Her father turned back toward her, and both her parents advanced.

"Why would you be looking for alternative officiants?" Her dad demanded. Gwen watched behind them as the shifter quietly walked into the woods, unnoticed by her parents.

"We've been considering a handfasting type of ceremony." Her parents stared blankly at her. "Nothing is official right now. We still have some time."

"Gwen, I just don't understand why all of this is so different and why there is such a rush. Let us all get to know Asher before you marry him."

"I love you guys." She stepped forward and kissed each of their cheeks. "But this is just how it is. Are you guys looking forward to tomorrow night?"

"It will be a comfort to meet his family," said her mom.

"You'll love them."

"Well, we won't keep you." Her dad turned. "Where did he go?"

Gwen shrugged. "Must be just walking around while he waits."

"Who is he?"

"I don't know his name. Asher hasn't introduced us yet."

"Be careful."

"Always, Dad."

Gwen watched while her parents got in their car and drove away. She felt guilty not being able to invite them in. Once their car was out of sight, Gwen retrieved the men's clothes from the house and started into the woods. They weren't close anymore. Gwen had to close her eyes and really listen. She heard low voices and followed them.

ASHER WATCHED Nathan pull up and eye Gwen. Just as Zachary had warned him, Gwen, and what she was, confused Nathan. Once Gwen distracted her parents and Nathan slipped into the woods, Asher met up with him and led him further in where the rest of wolves were heading. He hadn't intended to have this meeting as soon as he arrived home and also standing naked, but there wasn't anything he could do about it now.

They walked in on three wolves and a grizzly bear all growling at each other. Animal instincts flaring with their proximity.

"Relax." Nathan called to the bear.

They're one of us. Calm down. Asher stood beside Kai and shifted. Zachary followed suit.

"I apologize for our current state. I didn't know I wouldn't be able to get back into my house when we got back." Nakedness became natural for him long ago. Even now, with a couple practical strangers, he didn't have shame or a need to cover himself.

"What is she?" Nathan tilted his head toward the direction of the house.

"She's his mate." Zachary leaned against a tree with his arms crossed, clearing not giving a shit about being naked any more than Asher. "It's some intense shit."

"Is she a shifter?"

"No," answered Asher. "She's human."

Nathan frowned and thought for a moment, then shook his head. "So, what do you want to talk about?"

"I believe shifters should know each other, look out for each other, and learn together. We all seem to be on our own, and I can only assume that it's a similar situation for most others out there."

"I still don't understand what you're looking for." Nathan's pair sidled up next to him, further from the wolves.

"Sorry, man, neither do I." Zachary shrugged.

"I guess it would become a society of sorts." It all had to begin with baby steps.

"You're inviting us to join your club?" Nathan's lips twisted as he mocked Asher. His joke mirroring Zachary's.

"Pretty much." Asher stared him down. "Look, we all have our own stories and none of us knows more than our own. We are a different species and we know nothing about ourselves other than our own experiences. I also believe it's important we protect the existence of shifters."

A twig snapped and they all looked to see Gwen walking toward them carrying clothes. She passed Asher his. Love and strength flashed over her face and it hit him in the chest, calming his rising frustration. He pulled on his jeans while Gwen walked over to Zachary. Asher saw him wink and he aimed a growl in his direction. Zachary held up his hands in surrender.

"Seriously intense shit," he said to Nathan who looked at Gwen, perplexed.

"Her scent is unique. Substantially strong, energetic."

"If I hadn't already known what she was before they were bound, it would have confused me too." Zachary fastened his belt and pulled his black t-shirt over his head.

"Bound?" Nathan's glare wouldn't leave Gwen. Asher felt her shiver beside him.

"This is what I'm talking about. We all have knowledge that others don't." Asher tried to hold back the urge to growl at Nathan for staring at his mate. That wasn't how he wanted this interaction to go, but he couldn't do it. "Stop staring at her." The words were low and spoken through gritted teeth. His muscles tensed and his canines lengthened. Nathan's brown eyes flashed at Asher and he growled back.

"Stop it!" Gwen stepped in front of Asher with her back to the side, not giving it to either shifter. Nathan closed his eyes and looked away. Asher sighed and looked at his mate.

"You need to stop getting in between shifters. I'm starting to think tempers can easily run high when we're together."

"That's why I do it." She spoke sweetly and allowed a soft smile to lift her lips. Zachary snorted.

"What's in it for me?" Nathan had a hefty dose of disinterest and skepticism in his voice.

"Knowledge and friends. That's all this is for now."

"I'm creating a log of everything we learn and of everyone's stories. I'd appreciate your permission to add yours." Asher barely heard the quake to Gwen's voice.

"I'm fine living as I am, and my story is my own. Found a

bear and shifted. There's nothing else. So, I'll pass on the club membership, thanks."

"If you change your mind, you know where to find me. And I'd like to invite you to our wedding."

"You're fucking kidding me, right?"

"No."

Nathan shook his head and turned toward his pair, who stood vigilant beside him.

"Can I ask you one question before you go?" Gwen took two steps forward. It was hard for Asher not to haul her back. Nathan eyed her expectantly. "How often do you see the wind? Your wind, the one you followed when you first changed."

"Twice since then. Once when I needed to save this one from a fight with a larger bear when we were young," he pointed his thumb at the giant grizzly beside him, "and then a few weeks ago over his head." He looked at Asher.

"Did you know it comes out of you when you shift?" asked Gwen.

Nathan's eyes widened for only a second, then his jaw tightened, and he eyed each of them carefully. After a quick shake of his head, he then nodded at Asher, not saying any more. He walked away with his pair before they separated, the bear going into the woods and Nathan walking back to his truck.

Zachary sauntered over. "That went well."

"You didn't give your opinion."

He shrugged. "I'll keep in touch. And maybe I'll strike up a conversation or two with other shifters if I ever come across them."

"You're coming to the wedding?"

"Sure." He cocked a grin and nodded.

It wasn't the outcome Asher hoped for, but he could deal

with it, for now. He'd taken the first baby step and he would keep trying. In the meantime, he had a mate to take care of.

"KAI WANTS the pack to stay where they are." They sat on Asher's front porch waiting for the sun to finish sinking in the sky. Zachary had left, heading back to Hull Creek and Smoke had returned with Kai to the pack. Gwen worried about the tension between them. Even she felt it during the meeting. They were reunited, and that was what they both needed, but now they needed to heal. Gwen vowed to help. She didn't know what happened or why, making it difficult to support them.

"Are you upset by that?" Gwen reached over and placed her hand on top of his, resting on the arm of the wooden chair.

"No. I understand why he wants it. The place is beautiful and well hidden. I would make the same choice if I were in his shoes. But," he paused. Gwen felt a calm sadness spread through them. "I'll miss having him so close, always ready to run. I'll miss the rest of the pack too, especially the pups. It will be hard not to see him every day."

"We'll go often. I'm ready to wander into the wilderness with you."

With his head still leaning against the wood, he turned it to face her. His lips lifted. "Oh you are, are you?"

"I am." She nodded decisively. "While you were gone, I did some things of my own. I have a pack ready to take whenever we leave. I've been doing some research and still have more to do. I've also signed up for self-defence classes. I want more than basic self-defence, but I'll work myself up to that." She turned her head to look at him. "I intend to be worthy of being a mate to a wolf as magnificent as you."

Asher moved so quickly that Gwen barely had time to blink. He lifted and leaned over the space between the chairs. His hand grasped the back of her neck and pulled her forward. "Never question your worth," he growled. "There is a reason Fate chose you as my mate. Probably many reasons. But whatever they are, it is because you were already worthy to fill that role."

"Okay." It was all she could say as she choked back happy tears.

"Maybe I need to show you exactly how worthy you are." He stood and pulled her up with him.

"I don't think you'll hear any complaints from me." Her body heated in reaction to his. Sometimes, their connection overwhelmed her, and she already knew there would be many times they would get on each other's nerves because of it. But their love and their bond would never dim. Of that, Gwen had no doubt.

THE SCENE WAS BETTER than either of them could have imagined. Two months after the meeting, Asher and Gwen held their ceremony in Asher's yard. Vines of wildflowers decorated the trees, posts on the deck, the shed and all the chairs. Reverend Tom stood at the end of the aisle with Asher. He'd agreed to include their handfasting ceremony in place of their vows. In the end, they didn't care what deity resided over them as long as the one they knew brought them together was represented as well.

Gwen's face brightened to that of the blushing bride she was, and Asher's eyes flashed a brilliant blue as she started her walk from the front steps of the house. He closed them quickly, breathing deep through his nose before opening them again.

Their parents had gotten over most of their reservations after about a month, but her mom still tried to ask Gwen to explain the rush from time to time. Her only response was to kiss her mother's cheek and remind her to trust her. Gwen walked down the aisle without a single doubt. She agreed with Asher. She believed they would have chosen each other without the help of Fate.

They barely heard Reverend Tom while he spoke. Their eyes never left the other's. They felt the rope being wrapped around their hands. Warmth connected them and their bond flamed as they spoke together.

"Bound by Fate. Blessed. Yours." A hum of murmured awes washed over the audience. Asher leaned forward and kissed her, lingering while he gently supped at her lips. Their foreheads touched while the small crowd of close family and friends cheered.

"My mate," Asher whispered for her ears only. They turned to the crowd and even looked to the woods where Kai and Smoke were watching. Two pairs of brown eyes flashed lightly. Nathan and his pair had come, just not as a guest.

They took one step forward and froze. White and grey winds rushed up the aisle. An auburn one came from the trees. They were fainter than usual, ghosts of themselves. The crowd didn't seem to notice them. Zachary stood in the second row, the barest of frowns curving his forehead, still clapping his hands to match the people around him. The winds passed through them and to a spot near the house. Asher looked down at Gwen. She saw them too.

They turned. The transparent figure of a woman stood

smiling. Her hair was long over one shoulder and her dress looked cotton and reached the ground. She held out her hands to the winds that danced around her as if they were happy to see her. She laughed and twirled her hands in the air and the colours followed her motions.

Asher caught Zachary's eyes, then looked toward the trees. Nathan stepped from them, his eyes focused on the winds and the woman.

Asher and Gwen turned back to face each other, holding smiles on their faces for appearances in front of the crowd, but they watched from their peripheral vision.

The woman's lips moved, and her words whispered back through the air like an echo.

"The winds are healed and happy now that they have their purpose again. Live well and follow so I may rest in peace." She faded away and shortly after, the winds did too.

Asher and Gwen continued back down the aisle to finish their celebration. But their minds drifted to the woman's words. Something about them seemed final, but they raised more questions about their origins. He also knew that the winds' purpose wasn't complete. Asher truly believed he was on the right path. She said to live well and follow. He'd followed the wind whenever it showed up, without a doubt. There was more to come. Asher would never doubt the magic within him. He would follow, live, and build.

His mate, his pair, and the wind by his side.

They yard was empty except for the shifters. Nathan emerged from the trees and met Asher and Zachary.

"Congratulations." Nathan didn't feel as begrudged as he sounded. He nodded firmly and stuck his hands in his pockets.

"Congratulations, man." Zachary echoed Nathan, but he stuck his hand out and shook Asher's hand.

"Thanks." Asher said, looking like he'd just won the lottery. Everything was right in his world. Good for him. He'd had an easy life. It was just the cards he'd been dealt. Nathan's life wasn't much to look at. A mate, fated or not, didn't deserve him. He wouldn't be looking for one of his own.

"You both saw her too." Zachary wasn't asking. They all looked at each other after following the winds and seeing the woman.

"Who was she?" By the looks on their faces when they saw her, they didn't know any more than Nathan. He didn't like it, but he saw the reasoning behind Asher's plans to bring shifters together.

"I don't know. But the winds did. They ran to her like puppies." Asher turned and looked at the spot by his house where the woman had appeared. If the winds hadn't flown to her, Nathan might have thought he imagined her. He wasn't really one to believe in ghosts. That coming from a bear shifter.

"What do we do?" asked Zachary.

"I don't think there's anything to do. She came, she spoke, she left. We can try and decipher what she meant, but there's nothing else we can do except to keep moving forward."

"I wonder why we haven't seen her before." Nathan spoke low, wondering more to himself than to the others.

"I think she was waiting for something." Asher glanced back at the house.

"The first mate?" Zachary followed his gaze.

"Maybe. Maybe not." That was Nathan's two cents worth. He didn't want to be here to begin with and now the mystery was pulling him in. He needed to step back. "I'm heading out. You two enjoy your honeymoon."

"Thanks for coming. I'm glad you did."

"I didn't really have a choice." He paused, but didn't explain further. Nathan nodded and turned back to the woods where Bear waited. Bear stood when he came back through the trees. "Time to go home."

Nathan stripped, folding his clothes in an easy to grab pile, and shifted. Bones popped and an ache flowed. Nathan stretched, felling more comfortable covered in fur than bare skin. He picked up his clothes and lumbered through woods with Bear by his side.

He really hadn't had a choice about coming to the wedding.

The damned wind.

It had circled, poked, nudged, and even slapped, a harsh rush against his cheek, to get him moving. When he'd stayed stubborn and wouldn't move, the wind had pushed at his back, forcing him through the woods. He'd stripped and barely had time to grab his clothes from the ground as the wind kept pushing. Once he'd begun to run, meeting up with Bear by the lake, the wind had stopped pushing him, but followed behind.

At the wedding, he'd stayed in the tress with the pairs. Pair being the term Asher used for a shifter's matched animal twin. To Nathan, he was just Bear.

He trotted home with more on his mind than he wanted. He was fine on his own. He didn't need a damn shifter club where he could make friends. He attended the wedding for the same reason he met with Asher for coffee for the first time. The wind made him. There was something here that Fate or the wind, assuming they were different entities, wanted him to have.

Nathan didn't want it.

Once they got around the town and reached the lake, he and Bear slowed to a walk. They sauntered to Nathan's cabin. His childhood was spent in these woods. As soon as he was capable, he built his cabin. He started young and built it slowly over time. He was left alone out here, just as he liked it.

Fate was trying to pull him away from that.

WOUNDED WINDS SERIES

White Bonds

Auburn Ties

Silver Chains

And More...

Join my newsletter to receive special content, the most up to date information on releases, and special promotions.
https://sendfox.com/authorsarahurquhart

Also, visit my website at...
http://www.authorsarahurquhart.com
... to see my full book list.

Keep reading for an excerpt from **Auburn Ties, Wounded Winds Book Two**. Available now.

She's drawn to the wild and full of independence, but all that is threatened by the moves of a higher power.
Confused by her overprotective friends, Shaye evades their attention and follows the things she loved to do with her father. The wilderness called to her. So much so, that she follows with a demanding grizzly bear leads her to a lone cabin in the woods near the lake. A man steps out the front door, changing everything she's ever believed in.
He refuses to find is mate and pushes his past away.
No one deserves to be stuck with a man with Nathan's past. That's why he fought against Fate and Her plans. He holds onto the memory of one person only, the rest he's buried.
Nathan is better off alone.
But he learns fighting Fate only causes pain.
Their pasts are tied together. But danger lies there.
While revealing the events of days long gone, they discover a dangerous man. One that when he lays eyes on Shaye, he decides he has plans for her. To keep her safe, Nathan is forced to make an impossible decision. And there's only one choice if he wants to save his mate and put his past to rest.

AUBURN TIES
CHAPTER 1

Nathan rolled his eyes at the name flashing on the screen of his phone vibrating in his hand. He didn't have a problem with the guy, or his intentions, but Nathan couldn't decide if he wanted to be a part of Asher's plans or not.

"Hi, Asher," he said as he put his phone up to his ear, keeping his irritation inside his chest and out of his voice. Nathan got in his truck to head home from work and put the phone on speaker. The lumber mill wasn't a terrible place to work. It was a job, and that's all he cared about. If it didn't work out, he'd find another. But he had been there for almost ten years.

"Hey. Just wondering if you're coming tonight," asked Asher. Nathan heard Gwen, Asher's mate, in the background talking to someone else. The benefits of exceptional shifter hearing.

"Hadn't planned on it." His answer sounded as tired as his weighted body from a day's work.

"I have some news. Nothing urgent, but it's something I'd like to extend to you." Nathan got the impression there was more than the usual going on.

He sighed. "All right. What time?"

Asher told him and said he'd see him tonight and hung up. He hadn't been the first wolf shifter Nathan discovered, but Asher was the first to talk to him. Nathan never made the initiative to talk to another shifter, or anyone. He didn't care and he didn't want to care. His life was what it was, and Nathan had planned to leave it at that until the wind, his wind, dragged him to Asher's wedding.

At the end of the ceremony, the three winds had danced around a transparent woman off in the distance. White, silver, and auburn swirls had twirled around her like long lost pets who'd found their home. Nathan didn't want to care, but he couldn't stop thinking about the woman's words. The winds were happy and had a purpose to fulfill. It seemed shifters were that purpose.

So, he put up with Asher's phone calls and Gwen's questions, not that he answered many of them. He allowed them to make the connections with him, but didn't put any effort of his own into nurturing those connections. They were good people. He just didn't have a need for people in his life.

And if he were honest, the bond between Asher and Gwen scared the living shit out of him. The strangest scent rushed over him any time he saw Gwen. Everything about her screamed wolf, but she wasn't. She was no longer fully human either. She was some odd mix of magic. Powerful magic that pulled the two of them together in an unbreakable bond.

If that's what it was like for all shifters, he didn't want any part of it. No one deserved to be forced to endure him. And they would be forced. That's what that mating bond did. Asher and Gwen were lucky. They were a good match, but they didn't have a choice. Nathan didn't want that for himself, and he didn't want that for an innocent woman who didn't deserve a strange life. Now he knew that bond existed, he avoided women altogether. Might not be the smartest choice he'd made, but he was sticking to it. For now.

Nathan didn't live in the same shack he had growing up, the one he'd lived in with his mother. Although he'd lived there longer than he should have. Alone. He'd had that roof over his head when he needed it and grew up in the wilderness with no reason to live in town or move to a different one. He'd worked hard and eventually built himself a cabin in the woods. Nathan stayed where he was comfortable.

Bear sauntered out from around the back of the house as Nathan got out of his truck. A four-year-old who'd recently lived through trauma didn't have the best imagination for naming animals. So, he just called him Bear. He never called Bear's mother Mama, despite how she took care of him. He called her Auntie. Nathan had never had one of those.

He shook himself from his thoughts and ran his hand through Bear's fur, feeling the connection of his brother.

"We're meeting at Asher's tonight. Can you get there?" Bear nodded his head then lay down beside the deck. Nathan went inside to shower off the sawdust that covered his skin and left an itch.

He made himself something to eat and threw Bear a fish from his fridge before he left. Sometimes living as a human made his skin crawl, but he knew it was necessary. He had to function in both worlds, and that meant he'd had to catch up to learn as a kid. And he did that on his own. Once he finally shifted back to human, a child. No one had ever found him after his mother disappeared. They thought she disappeared. Nathan knew the truth. But they had also been looking for a little boy.

Pulling up behind Asher's truck, Nathan saw the motorcycle parked beside it. Zachary, another wolf shifter, was also here. He couldn't figure out Zachary's reasons for meeting with Asher anymore than he could figure out his own. Nathan didn't think he held onto a similar vision as Asher's future for shifters. A society for their own species. The only reason of which Nathan was certain was Zachary's need to be close to his pair. Pair being the term Asher used for their matched animals. Nathan didn't bother calling his anything but his bear. Maybe brother on occasion.

Zachary and his wolf had been separated for a couple years. That was all Nathan knew and all he cared to know.

He walked toward the trees and met up with Bear not far in before hiking to their usual meeting spot. He smelled the four wolves and Gwen, pinpointing their positions long before they reached them.

"Hi, Nathan," Gwen's cheerful tone rose as he got closer. She was a sweet girl who tried her best to be worthy of her mate. She took on the role as mate to a wolf shifter with pride and determination. Yeah, Asher got lucky.

Nathan waved back, but kept quiet. He rarely said much at these *meetings*. Asher called them meetings, but once they had all told their stories and the things they'd learned over the years, there was nothing else to discuss. They only gathered to shoot the shit. Although, Nathan still hadn't told them about his past. He wasn't sure if he ever would. It was none of their damn business.

"Glad you could make it." Asher stood beside his wife, his mate. It became natural for them to interchange the two. Even Nathan referred to her as a mate, despite her not being his. Asher had a point when he referred to them as a different species. They had instincts they didn't realize existed. Callings and whispers from within.

Nathan nodded, then nodded at Zachary who stood off to the side.

"I'm building a cabin," Asher announced and nodded toward the white wolf standing near. "Deeper in the woods. Close to Kai's pack, although the space and terrain around the area has many places for wildlife. I want it to be a safe house, or a headquarters, for us and other shifters we meet. A place that will always be stocked with non-perishables and clothes. I want you both to feel welcome to use it."

"When will it be finished?" asked Zachary.

"A few months, most likely more. It'll take a little longer as we can't use big equipment to build it. I won't destroy the forest to build a haven inside it."

"Need help?"

"Probably." Asher nodded. They all looked at Nathan. Well, hell. He didn't want to be dragged further into their shifter club, but here he stood anyway.

"Yeah, let me know if there's anything I can do," he said, the words pulling themselves out of his throat.

"You work at a lumber yard." Zachary pointed out.

"I work there. I don't own it. I can't do more than tell you the cost and who to talk to about the purchase."

"Thank you," said Asher, as if that's all he was looking for.

"A place like that could be useful." Zachary agreed with the idea from a distance. Nathan noticed Zachary's wolf near him, stiff with tension still holding pain coiled inside. Each of the shifters felt it. Whatever happened between the two of them still needed resolving. No one knew why Zachary had abandoned his wolf. Smoke stayed with Kai and his pack, and Zachary was trying to reconnect with Smoke.

Nathan couldn't imagine any scenario that would keep

him from Bear. But he grew up differently than either of the wolves.

"I need to call it a night. See you next time."

"You sure you have to go so soon?" It surprised Nathan to hear Zachary ask. It was usually Asher that tried to encourage Nathan to stay.

"Yeah." He waved and nodded to Bear before heading back to his truck. The others enjoyed these meetings, making plans for the future with an independence they thought they'd never have. That was great for them, but Nathan still didn't want to be part of it more than he already was. And if it hadn't been for that damn wind and the woman at the wedding, he wouldn't be.

Shaye threw the last bag in the back of her truck. Now, she waited for Jerry, Jenna, and Chase. The only friends that had been by her side since they were teenagers and the only friends she made time for. She pulled down the tailgate and used her palms to jump up. This was their first camping trip of the year. Excitement hummed through Shaye. As the assistant to the top realtor in Alder Ridge, she had to always be ready to move at the drop of a hat and never have a detail out of place, always busy.

She craved the peace of the lake. She kept one of her old cell phones to use for camping. No smartphones allowed for her, and while camping it was only for emergencies. She wouldn't be stupid and go into the wilderness without some form of contact. But she safely tucked away her smartphone in her nightstand. Taking away all temptation and contact with work. Camping was the most vacation she got between work and her friends, and she was fine with that. As far as she was concerned, there wasn't anything better.

But relaxing didn't describe her life. It was the office life for her. Except the times like these when she chose otherwise.

Shaye's lips lifted with anticipation to breathe in the air off the lake. They didn't travel far for their camping trips. They didn't need to. Alder Ridge had beautiful landscapes and wilderness surrounding it and beyond. Thanks to the town's proximity to the mountains.

Her love of camping and all things wild came from her dad. He had done great at the single parent thing. They'd bonded as best friends. Shaye's fingers turned over the locket around her neck and she allowed only a moment of sadness. She sent up a quick prayer, then started swinging her legs in the air while she watched the road for her friends. Some things didn't need to be thought about at a time like this. No matter how much she missed her father, she wouldn't let it sadden her camping trip. Not when it had been the most shared activity between them.

Finally, a blue Jeep pulled up and her three friends barrelled out with whoops and hollers. Shaye hopped off the tailgate and closed it.

"Throw your bags in the back. I'm ready to go."

"Always in such a rush, Shaye." Jerry nudged her shoulder as he passed carrying two bags.

"Until she gets in the woods, then she's all mellow," said Jenna, extending the last of her words and swaying her shoulders side to side. Shaye shrugged off the teasing of her friends.

Chase touched Shaye's elbow before she could climb into the driver's seat. "Why don't you let me drive?"

Shaye reared back and raised an unbelieving brow. "You

are not driving my truck." The rest of the group laughed, and she threw a smug expression at her friend's envy. His old beater had finally given out last week. Shaye swung back around and hopped in with a bounce. She'd worked hard for this truck. It was her baby. She wouldn't let just anyone drive it, no matter how close a friend they were.

She started the truck and waited for everyone to pile in. Chase sat in the front and Jenna and Jerry sat in the back, Jerry's arm pulling her tight against him.

"And we're off." Shaye cranked the radio and sped off.

The drive out to the lake only took half an hour. It wasn't a regular campground, but it wasn't uncommon for locals to rough it by the lake. Shaye preferred to rough it. It didn't feel like camping to her if there were amenities, roads, trails, and playgrounds. Her friends didn't like it much, preferring to find a glorified space with the brick fire pit, firewood already stacked, and full showers. But they knew she wouldn't camp with them if they went anywhere else.

She set up her small one-person tent, then helped her struggling friends with their larger one. Chase sidled up to Shaye when they finished.

"Please don't make me share a tent with Jerry and Jenna. They're insufferable." He lowered his head and his voice. Shaye shrugged.

"I told you to bring your own tent. Mine isn't big enough." Shaye walked off to finish setting up, enjoying the pout on the man's face. She should be sympathetic, but she didn't like to share her dad's tent.

She organized the coolers and settled them in the truck's cab so the food wouldn't attract bears and other wildlife. Once finished, she set up a fire pit and built the fire. That's all she cared about. Sitting by a fire, fishing, and swimming in the lake, an escape and reset for her mind and body. She might live and work in town, but this was where she belonged.

"How do you always make this look so easy?" Jenna unfolded her chair and plopped down beside Shaye, having finished setting up their tent and throwing their bags inside.

"Because it is easy." Shaye passed her a beer.

"Jenna, she's been doing this since she was two. It's not easy. She just knows what the fuck she's doing." Jerry looked at Jenna as if she asked a stupid question. Their camping trips always started with this same conversation. Shaye let it roll over her every time. Once they got it out of their systems, they all moved on and everyone had a great time.

Shaye let the wilderness settle in while they finished their banter. Once the conversation lulled, she stood. "I'm going fishing."

She saw Chase pull a ten-dollar bill from his pocket and hand it over to Jerry.

"Told you, man," said Jerry.

"Told him what?" Shaye's eyes darted between the two guys.

"That you would go fishing as soon as we all sat down." Jerry lifted his hip and tucked the bill in his back pocket.

"I don't do that every time." She looked at each of her friends.

"Yes, you do," they all said in unison.

"We know you do it so you can be alone. It's okay, Shaye." Jenna reached out and touched her hand. Sympathy echoed in her quiet voice.

Shaye huffed and walked to her truck to get her gear. Did she do this every time just so she could be alone? She didn't do it intentionally. But she also wouldn't deny she enjoyed the quiet by the water. Her friends would come fish with her once or twice on their trip, but Shaye knew that was only to spend time with her. They'd rather swim, then get drunk by the fire.

Shaye let it go. These trips were for clearing her head, not dwelling on her habits. She cherished this time away. Nothing would ruin it.

ABOUT THE AUTHOR

Looking at a crossroads, Sarah chose to write. With a deep love of anything romance, it was natural that romance stories flowed into her journal. From the East Coast and living in Alberta, Canada, she enjoys life with her family and the beauty of the province around her. She gets hilariously excited when new stories and characters pop in her head and can't wait to write them out whether in the sub-genres of romantic suspense or paranormal romance. She hopes her readers enjoy her stories as much as she enjoys writing them.

You can find Sarah on Facebook and Instagram @authorsarahu, in her reader group *Sarah's Suite*, and on BookBub.

www.ingramcontent.com/pod-product-compliance
Lightning Source LLC
Chambersburg PA
CBHW021308190726
48288CB00003B/753